The
Second
Inheritance

MELVYN BRAGG

SCEPTRE

Copyright © 1966 by Melvyn Bragg

First published in 1966 by Martin Secker and Warburg Ltd.
Sceptre editions 1990, 1996
A Sceptre Paperback

The right of Melvyn Bragg to be identified as the Author of
the Work has been asserted by him in accordance with the
Copyright, Designs and Patents Act 1988.

10 9 8 7 6 5 4 3

A CIP catalogue record for this book is
available from the British Library

ISBN 0 340 51113 3

Typeset by Palimpsest Book Production Limited,
Polmont, Stirlingshire
Printed and bound in Great Britain by
Cox and Wyman Ltd, Reading, Berkshire

Hodder and Stoughton
A division of Hodder Headline PLC
338 Euston Road
London NW1 3BH

To my mother and father

ONE

Nelson pushed out his jaw and drew the long cut-throat razor down his hard cheek. The skin was calloused by weather and carelessness. The stiff cream unrolled a patter of blood pricks, each welling instantly, the blood following the razor down his face. In the snapped-off mirror, he saw the gargoyle reflection of an enormous white chin, black eyes high above the tilted snout glaring down, mouth open with an effort. The harmless sunny Sunday afternoon stayed outside the bright white-washed walls of the kitchen. Not really a kitchen; the place where the boots and brushes were kept, with a wash-basin jammed in one corner so that the hired men need not always wash in the outhouse next to the byres. Nelson did not look beyond the mirror to the small window's outside scene. He finished shaving and wiped the razor with his thumb and forefinger.

He scrubbed his face and neck in a fresh bowl of cold water until his skin smarted. Then he took his suit out of its brown paper, put it on, polished, yet again, his glistening shoes, put a cloth in one pocket to wipe them again at the other end and, faster now, took a clean handkerchief – a proper one, not a flour-bag – scraped at his hair with a steel comb, remembered at the last minute to scratch out the dirt from underneath his nails – he did this with his teeth – and – without a word to anyone – went out and set off, fearing only rain, because he had never wasted money on a mackintosh.

Nelson walked the few miles to the town, soothing his irritation at the expedition with the knowledge that the visit had to be made some time – and he had succeeded in fitting it in appropriately – this being his free afternoon anyway. He could even persuade himself that he was not worried at the lost opportunity of doing a few hours' work for someone else and so earning extra money. It would be worth it.

The tea had been laid out by Elizabeth. Mr Webb, her father, sat in a large, grand, horsehair-stuffed fireside chair which, he said, he had made himself.

'I've made everything in this house myself' he added. 'Everything that's any good.'

Nelson looked around with respect. He had been hired by one or two farmers who had been rich like this, but this was nearer to him, belonging to Elizabeth's father. The entire wall and ceiling area was bastioned by dark, thickly brown paper, and every foot of floor-space supported proof of Mr Webb's trade of carpentry – just as every inch of flat surface on the drawers and sideboards and dressers and small tables supported the ornaments and embroidery of the late Mrs Webb. Elizabeth would get half of all this.

'Lizzie!' Mr Webb shouted. 'Mash the tea.'

Nelson hated the sound of 'Lizzie'. All his sisters were known by their shortest, easiest possible names. He prided himself on saying 'Elizabeth'.

'Sit over there,' the old man said. 'Lizzie – you can sit here. I'll sit here.'

He sat between them at the four-square table. Opposite him, his wife's chair was neatly tucked under the table.

'Now then. What do you want to eat?'

'I'll start with bread,' said Nelson.

'You might finish with it for all you know. These cakes are just for show!'

Mr Webb's face twitched, grimly, and Nelson controlled his reaction by reaching, smilingly, for a thin, round slice of brown bread. The old man, white haired, white moustached, with a clipped white collar and a stiff black waistcoat – the gold chain looping across it like a link with a secret society – ate without saying much. Nelson waited. Elizabeth faded away completely; she had met him in the no-man's-land where they could be alone, she knew that she wanted to marry him – did not care that he was a farm labourer – and had, with tears, brought about this first invitation. Now she was out of it.

Mr Webb sank a cup of tea, his face buried in the cup for a long time. The stiff cuffs slipped back and showed sparrow-wrists; he was living in imitation of his former force.

'They tell me you're at Freddie Wilson's,' he said, eventually.

'Yes.' Nelson was pre-armed, prepared for this cross-examination.

'Tell me.'

'Yes.'

Mr Webb looked at him distrustfully for breaking the gun.

'Tell me,' he repeated, slowly, 'does he still have a squiff in his hair?'

Nelson looked at Elizabeth. She was staring at her plate.

'Yes,' he replied, for the third time.

'Always did have!' The old man grunted, with disapproval.

Tea was cleared away and, with it, Elizabeth. The two men sat down in facing arm-chairs.

'Now then,' said Mr Webb. when they were settled. 'Maybe you can tell me something else.'

He paused, as if to show that he had scrupulously considered whether or not to trust this question to so young and unknown a man and, after much thought, had finally decided that he might just chance it.

'That farm,' he went on, 'that farm this side of Brownrigg – sold about five days ago – what did it fetch?'

'You mean Freeman's?'

'Yes.'

'Two thousand, eight hundred and fifty pounds.'

'All in?'

'All in.'

'Hmm.'

Elizabeth came back, shaking a large medicine bottle, making its contents flurry like a snowstorm. With it, she brought a dessert spoon, both of which her father took from her with a glare at Nelson to still any presumptuous inquiries. There being none, he said:

'I take this after every meal. Four times a day. Doctor's orders.'

And he swallowed two exactly filled spoonfuls while his daughter stood, head bent, beside him. As he lifted the spoon to his mouth with his left hand, so, with his right thumb and forefinger, he lifted his nose, thereby taking his moustache out of danger. Throughout that silent operation there was not the beginnings of a smile on the face of anyone.

'I suppose you want to see the business side of things?'

Nelson nodded and jumped up: he was too fed up to answer. While the old man looked for his spectacles Nelson turned to stare at a photograph; the four Webbs, posing as for their Last Stand.

'Ready?'

He spun around and sent a blue-and-red shepherdess toppling, smashing on to the floor. Mr Webb put on his spectacles and looked at the fragments.

'Lizzie!' he bellowed. She was ready. 'Sweep it up!' Then, turning away slightly – 'some folk appreciate nothing.'

Then Nelson knew finally that there was no chance. His dialect, despite painful straining, was as thick as moss, he said 'what?', scattered his limbs in a chair like any dirty farm labourer, had no family beyond a gaggle of quickly estranged associates with the same name, no power, no land. No right to be in the house of Mr Webb. He was viciously envious of the old man's assurance and manner. It would be his, some day. He would take it.

'Well?' said Mr Webb. 'Have you nothing to say for yourself?'

A violent blush smoothed the asperous surface of the young man's skin.

'I'm sorry.'

Elizabeth, released by the apology, scuttled to Nelson's feet with a brush and pan, and tidied everything up.

'Hmm! Come on – come on! We haven't all day.'

They went to the workshop across the narrow street. Slipped through the sun like bats through a streak of moonlight.

Nelson needed nothing explained to him in the matter of lathes, vices, chisels, saws, T-squares, protractors, plumblines – and the old man did not expand on any of the secrets or successes of his trade.

'Raymond helps me, you know.'

Nelson did know. Raymond was Elizabeth's brother. But he

withheld the knowledge hoping that, perhaps through this, the old man would get to the point.

'He's away bicycling today – with the club,' said Mr Webb, reluctantly.

'Is he?'

'Yes. At Whitley Bay. They go there and back in one day . . .'

'Yes.'

'. . . easily. Do you have a bicycle?'

'No.'

'You should get one. Join a club. They enjoy themselves at these clubs.'

'I know, I've seen them.'

'Raymond likes it anyway.' Mr Webb had finished.

'Does he do it a lot?' Nelson wanted to hit the old bastard – and leave him.

'He does it when he has time,' Mr Webb snapped. 'He doesn't like wasting time. You can miss your life that way.'

Silence.

Mr Webb tidied an already tidy bench, adjusted the position of a perfectly stacked plank of wood, wandered down the workshop and back up again and finally –

'Seen all you want to see?' he asked.

'Yes.'

'Hmm.'

By the time Nelson had reached the farm he had decided what to do.

Two nights later, Elizabeth met him at their usual spot.

'What did he say?' Nelson demanded – already knowing the answer.

Elizabeth began to cry.

'He doesn't like me – my type?' Nelson said. 'Doesn't like me job and me face don't fit? That it?' He watched her crying – let her. 'Didn't you tell him I saved?' he shouted. 'Didn't you tell him aah got more bloody munny than any man my age in my position? Didn't you tell him aah'll have my own farm sum day?' He paused. 'Bastard!'

He took her by the shoulders. She did not know whether he was going to throw her away, or embrace her. Fiercely, slowly, he pushed her on to the ground. While she continued to cry, he undid her blouse; then he lifted her skirt and drew off her pants. Still she cried, hopelessly: he had never taken her.

Even when he had finished, she was still sobbing.

He jumped up and – for the first time – looked around. In the wide, yellow field, protected by high hedges and trees, all quiet so that only the summer soughing of insects could be heard – a quiet deeper for the silent country afternoon which stretched for miles around them – there was no one to disturb, no one to know.

She was still lying as he had left her. He felt a quick desire to take her again. Standing directly above her, he let himself fall, fall straight towards her face, only to catch himself on the two props of his arms.

Their faces were almost touching. He laughed.

'Lizzie,' he whispered. Then, again. 'Lizzie. Lizzie! Lizzie!'

Arthur heard the procession long before he saw it. He was in the summerhouse, hiding from Pat. She thought that it was part of the game – but he had chosen his place thoughtfully – to be away from her. He heard the horses, the wheels of the carts, shouts, whips. He ran out.

'I see you!' shouted Pat. 'I see you! I see you!'

She was two years younger than he was, and wore jodhpurs. The prep school – to which he was to return in a few days – excluded women except in History, and then they wore dresses.

'I'm going to look,' he said and, thrusting his hands into his pockets, he marched past her. She followed.

There. On the small road outside.

'Come and play,' said Pat. Arthur ignored her.

There on the small road which led a quarter of a mile to the village. Arthur looked for a moment, still, then he scrambled up the wall and on to one of the pillars which held the large gates opening to the drive of their house. He counted.

'Fourteen!' he shouted to Pat. 'Fourteen!'

Fourteen carts – each drawn by enormous carthorses. The mighty horses, with shaggy-haired legs knuckling to the rhythm of the hooves, heads heavily mastered in strips of leather, long manes lifting at each step – pulling along their loads, and the men on top of them.

And in the front cart – Nelson. Behind him, Lizzie, sitting on one of the horsehair chairs that had come with her father's death. She watched her daughter, Shirley, two years old now, old enough to climb around the moving furniture without slipping. She would be glad when it was over: she was pregnant again.

Nelson turned, cap at the back of his head.

'Just beyond that place!' he shouted. 'No more than another five minutes!'

The men behind him cheered. They had brought all Nelson's things with them for twelve miles, brought them because he was young and had somehow – from nothing – got enough together to take the lease of this new place and he needed all the help he could be given. Most of the men were labourers, as he had been, let off for the day with a horse and haycart because the harvest was in, the farmer could afford it – and was 'glad to help' a young fellow who was helping himself. Helping himself to her money some of them said – but that didn't matter. He had earned it by saving so hard himself. They appreciated the risk he was taking. For Mr Webb's money, passed on quickly by Raymond like some stolen haul, though it had helped Nelson to a position in which he could buy some of the stock he needed for a farm did not in any way provide courage. And it was this that the older farmers saw in his decision to tenant a farm immediately. One bad winter in these bad times for farming and Nelson would fall into the vicious downward spiral of debt, sale, loss, debt, out. Their help was the recognition of a dare which they themselves would not have tried.

Now, as the long procession came near its arrival point, everyone opened up. The land was looked at critically and compared with that they had left, the road was praised because it was fair – but they waited for the track to the farm. The cows and sheep at the end of the line jostled forward as the boy who was driving them walked faster. The pigs and hens squealed and cackled and the big pile of furniture swayed as it had done at the brisk beginning of the journey. The boys on top of the carts stacked high with hay and corn to keep them steady, stood up, and shouted out the features of the new place. The men leading the horses felt in their pockets for the cigarettes and tobacco that could wait just a minute longer until they got there. And the big horses, feeling the quickening, snorted puffs of grey breath from the cold nostrils and shook their hooves higher as they went.

'What's that over there?' someone shouted. 'Over there!'

Nelson turned back.

'A wall!' he said. 'A hundred bloody miles across! A wall!'

Never had he been like this. He flicked out the long lash of the whip and his horse opened to a small trot. A table, which Shirley had been mounting, slid across the cart and banged into Lizzie's outstretched hands.

'Whoa!' Nelson bellowed, and he pulled on the reins.

But he could not wait. He was impatient with the pace. There, beyond the big house, at the top of the small hill, there was his farm. Soon, he would be his own boss. The horses behind him could not snort heavily enough to express his own great roar of satisfaction.

'On you go, boy!'

Arthur could bear it no longer. The procession was almost on him. Jumping down from the pillar, landing on his hands and knees, he ran into the road, wanting to be part of the show, the noise.

'Out of the way!'

The boy skipped to one side. Then he began to trot beside the cart.

'Who're you?' Nelson shouted.

'Arthur Langley,' the boy replied. 'My father's Major Langley: he owns . . .'

'I know your father.'

The boy kept up with Nelson exactly: never gaining or losing a foot.

'Are you Mr Foster?'

Nelson grinned.

'That's right!'

'Are you tenanting Wall-End Farm?'

'Right again!'

'Can I come up beside you?'

Without breaking the horse's movement, Nelson leaned down and scooped Arthur into the back of the cart. Then, an afterthought, he did the same with Pat who glared at him firmly throughout her flight and readjusted her jodhpurs as soon as she was safely landed. She neither introduced herself; nor was she introduced by Arthur.

Now, the line of carts turned from the road on to the track which led to the farm buildings. It was late autumn; bad weather for moving in, and although the road had been all right, the track was gutted. Slowly, the horses pulled the loads towards their goal. Nelson could hardly bear to go so slowly. The long line on the hill with the Wall beyond was like a train of ancient pilgrims.

Arthur went into the kitchen with Lizzie – 'Mrs Foster', he called her. Some of their things had been delivered the previous day and with two other women who had come to help her, she set about making dinner for all the men. Hams were ready, bread and scones and cakes had been made. She got out some of her jams, her cheese and butter. Potatoes were there, cleaned for peeling at about three in the morning before going for two hours' sleep; carrots, turnips, eggs. Arthur circled in the trails of the women around the kitchen, bewildered but completely absorbed in the smells which reeked through the room. Men barged in carrying wardrobes and beds. A boy – not much bigger than Arthur – brought in paper and sticks and started a leaping fire in the large grate, which he fed constantly, running in every minute with lumps of coal in his hands. Pat stood beside a wall, ignoring everyone except Arthur, who ignored her persistent demands to be taken home. Beside her, Shirley bobbed and gurgled in a large cot – but neither noticed the other.

'Away you go!' said Mrs Foster cheerfully. 'Away you go! You can't stand there and do nothing.' And she shooed him out into the yard.

The yard was crammed with horses and carts. Pigs squalling and kicking as they were rushed or carried to the sties. Hens fluttering on to the carts, on to the granary steps, on to the window sills, the horse-trough. Cows drearily moving in a bending line to their stalls. And the loud barking of dogs, hampered by no action, howling out their choruses of help. Arthur saw Mr Foster carrying a sack under each arm.

For Nelson nothing could be done fast enough. He wanted everything settled, everything tidied, everything ready – now! – then he could start on his own. He shouted his instructions – heard even above that packed well of noise – and as well as doing almost twice as much as anyone else, he constantly tested the strength of the walls, the soundness of the roofs, the state of his stock, his eyes measuring all things.

A saucepan banged against the flagstone outside the door and the men went into the farmhouse.

Arthur was left with the yard empty of all men and boys but himself.

'We'll be very late for lunch,' said Pat.

He looked to see where she was.

'Up here!'

She had scrambled on to the low roof of one of the outhouses.

'I'm going to stay,' Arthur said.

Pat slid down the roof and, gingerly, swung herself on to the ground.

'These people are horrible,' she said.

'I might be able to help,' Arthur replied.

'I saw Ted coming up the road.'

'Well?'

'He must be looking for us.'

'Well?'

'Come on!' she took his arm.

Arthur looked at the kitchen door. It was closed. A dog scratched against it unheard. He envied the noise and warmth which he knew to be inside.

'Come on.'

He waited. They would come out and invite him in – ask him to help. The dogs began to bark – short, aggrieved barks.

'All right,' he said.

They met Ted on the cart track. The boy could not stop himself from turning to look at the farm again on his way down to the big house. They needed help.

* * *

The blizzard had long stopped, but the drifts were so bad that this was the first time Nelson had been able to get to his top field. Now, the sleet came down and the deep snow was beginning to melt. Loose holes, giant thumb-prints in endless white candy floss showed where it lay lightest. There, Nelson and Dickie could get through. Dickie was one of Nelson's brothers who had come from Aldeby, three miles away, to help.

'They'll be nowt left in this,' said Dickie.

'Aah'm three missin',' Nelson replied.

'Rawlinson lost eighteen,' Dickie said. 'Stiff as steeples. All in the one pen.'

'At least he had a pen. I haven't even got a bloody decent pen for them.'

'One of them was frozen with its feet against, wall. Tryin' to jump.'

They were looking for sheep. Both the men had shovels though Nelson did most of the work, digging out a little trail from the farm. The snow, white-banked on each side of him.

'Couldn't they cuddle up agen that Wall?' Dickie asked.

'It's nowt but rubbish this side. And t'other side –' He struck into the slack wall of snow with his shovel. On the other side of the Wall was a straight hundred-foot drop.

Nelson was so concerned to get to the fold that he said nothing more. He forced the passage; Dickie patted the path down behind him.

Never such a winter. The farm, previously tenanted by two brothers and their sister – all furrowed through decades standing still, clinging to what had worked when they had been strong, leaving all that demanded new effort undone. Staying on until their seventies, when first one died, then another – leaving the sister refusing to leave, still cooking meals for three, four times a day. Nelson on his own, with the occasional help of Dickie, trying to start everything – and then the snow.

His shovel struck at the soft back of the drift. The snow was dirty, stained with brown and black. Nelson refused to wear gloves – and his hands were bright red at the end of tatty sleeves, the veins of his left hand swelling out like thickening rope as they always did in the cold. The sleet stopped.

The sheep-fold was beside the Wall. A drift, like the angled sweep of covered cathedral steps, ran from one side of the fold almost to the other; separated there from the locked stack of uncemented stones by a narrow strip of bare grass which gleamed its lush colour back to the sun, now sifting through the loosening clouds and helping to curl the edges of the snow to a wet brown.

Nelson drove for the middle of the drift. He had not yet lost a sheep. He could not afford to lose one. Dickie stood back to let him get on with it, amused at the soft effects of such hard work; the snow, lifted in large heaps, slung to one side, floated gently, silently; baby-play.

'They're not here.'

The fold was now seen; a poor, badly kept thing, with the walls low and broken.

'Must have jumped out.'

'Can't blame them.'

'Maybe they're over there.'

Nelson went the few yards to the Roman Wall. The ground was almost bare. The blizzard had come from the North and hit the steep front of the Wall; this part, immediately behind it, was untouched; the next fall had landed crushingly on his fold.

He was on the Wall. At this point, it was no more than a wide band of stones as if some prehistoric shudder had crumbled a perfectly planed, endless cube. To left and right – where the Wall swung down and on – there could be seen places where some of the lower part of the Wall was still intact; the husk of a turret or even a mile-castle. Here were only fragments and a sheer drop.

Nelson walked over to the edge. Almost immediately below him, the top of a drift which must have been about eighty feet deep.

'That's that,' said Dickie. He took out a cigarette.

Nelson did not reply. He could not afford to lose them; could afford nothing. He gazed at the spread of glittering snow for any signs. Then he left Dickie and went to look further.

He found only one – and that stretched stiff, ice matting its wool; birds had pecked out its eyes.

He came back and looked at the fold; a poor farmer's fold.

'Let's build it up while we *are* here,' he said.

'With what?' Dickie demanded. He had had enough.

'These.' Nelson kicked at the stones on the Wall.

'Private property.' Dickie replied.

Nelson spat out and haunched down to collect and pick up a massive pile of large stones. He carried them over to the fold.

'We can fix one side, anyway!'

Dickie waited until the burn on the cigarette had been pulled down to his lips. Nelson, in that time, made two more journeys.

'It's useless now,' Dickie said. 'Everything's dead anyway.'

The point was to do something solid; the point was to go back to the farmhouse knowing that the farm was better; the point was to work.

'Bugger off if you want to,' Nelson replied. 'I'm putting this wall right.'

As they worked, another quick shift in the kaleidoscope of breaking weather drew the clouds thickly across the sun, and their heavy bellies pressed down touching the snow on the near skyline.

'Halloo!'

Nelson jerked up his head.

'You – over there!'

He found the voice. It was Major Langley – over on that part of the Wall which bordered his property. Nelson cupped his raw hands around his jaws.

'Yes?' he bellowed.

The Major was flanked by men with broad road shovels over their shoulders.

'Those – stones – are – not – your – property!'

'Bugger him,' said Dickie.

Nelson needed the stones. Still, with his face clustered by red hands – he bawled out his case.

'. . . And – I've – got – to – mend – it – now – so – that – it'll stand-up – when – t'snow melts!' he concluded.

He waited. Slowly, like a tolerant forefinger wagging at the nose of a stupid child, the Major's head swung from side to side.

'Sorry!' he shouted. 'Those – stones – have – to – be – left – where – they – are.'

Nelson stared at him.

'Tell him to push off,' Dickie whispered.

Tell him to leave him alone; to go; to realise that he had wasted an afternoon looking for three dead sheep. And that he could not afford it, could afford nothing.

'Sorry!' The Major bellowed. This was followed by an elaborate hitch at the shoulders of the massive greatcoat; which, at that distance, was to pass for an apologetic shrug.

But he did not leave. He stayed to watch the dismemberment of the new wall; the cowed, bitter transfer of the stones to their original rubble-heap.

'Sorry!' Again, when they had finished. Then, he left.

Nelson went straight back to the farmhouse, without attending to the eye-pecked sheep. Dickie left immediately after tea.

Lizzie was busy from tea until supper. Shirley had a bad cold but her sad mother-trotting, her small snivelling which cut to its quick the tight silence of the cold kitchen – these had to be ignored. If time had to be spared, then it was to be given to John, two months old, deeply blanketed in the large old cot near the iron-grated fire. But Lizzie did not like to stop; to do that was to think about the work she had to do, and then its pressure would make her dizzy.

She was afraid to ask him. Yet she always had to ask him. He never gave her money without imposing that unpitied humiliation on her. After supper, she took out the large cardboard box full of collars to be turned, cuffs stitched, tails re-made, breeches patched, socks, her dress. She looked through the silence – balanced, now she was sitting down, by her own hopeless emptiness – waiting for the scales to tilt in favour of a question.

Nelson was crab-gathered around the papers in front of him. The kitchen came right off him; gaunt, rough, moaning for the chance to be new. The furniture was as it had been dumped that first day – no time to re-set it; and no one had come to see them since then; too far. The room was cold – cold despite the fire which gurgled its rich flames around the rooted logs, and kept them there, not bothering to invade the corners of such an unwelcoming place. There was no clock to tick, no outside sounds to bring percolated memories through the thick walls, no noise save the lapping glow of the paraffin light against its fine-waisted glass.

Nothing was said – and would not be said until he decided to go to sleep. She had to begin.

'I've got to go into Aldeby tomorrow,' she said.

He looked up: startled to see her so close to him.

'Why?'

'Well, I could get it at the village,' she countered. The village was no more than a quarter of a mile away; Aldeby, three; either would be gone to on foot; the village would save time.

'If they have it,' she added.

'Money!' he said. 'That's what you want, is it?'

'It's been nearly three weeks you haven't given me any,' she replied.

He jumped up and banged the bundle of papers on to the fender. His open neck and head slid into a shadow the lamp threw – and the fire licked ruddy the red of his skin.

'Well, why the bloody hell didn't you say so?' he demanded.

'Sorry.' Immediately she regretted saying that word.

'You're sorry! I'm sorry! Everybody's bloody sorry!' he shouted. 'You're sorry all the damned time.' She looked at him to stop. He went on. 'You're sorry you ever met me – I bet. Sorry your old man left you t'money for us to be able to take this place.'

'No.'

'Oh, yes! Well I'm not sorry. I'm not sorry I came – and I wasn't sorry when t'old bugger died. He didn't give twopence for me.'

Confused by the diverging lines of his outburst, he straightened himself by going to the dresser, taking out his cash-box, and bringing back two stiff ten-shilling notes to his wife. He thrust them on to the table.

'That enough?'

'Yes, thank you.'

'Don't thank me. You're richer than me. All this – all this is your money. Ha!'

The last word was a mad yell which stopped all talk; the silence rushed around them again.

Lizzie let the notes lie where they had been put. She waited for the baby to cry – and left the kitchen with relief when it did.

Nelson went to the door. He picked up the torch and let its beam play around the farmyard. Nothing had gone right for him. He was worse off than when he had started. He had no more money to pay for feed for his animals. No more.

With its dirty stacks of snow and sad walls, the farmyard looked beaten. His hand still smarted from the pain of the swollen veins.

Before she began, Lizzie looked around her like a comic, gangster; she knew herself to be doing so – and laughed gently at first – and then louder. She was as happy as that.

It was summer 1947. The farm – way behind her – had been abandoned for the afternoon while Nelson went to the auction – and the field in which she was sitting swept up to the three slender birch-trees which guarded that farm, flourished up a great splendour of yellow hay whose smells and hidden flowers poured over her the wonderful fallen scent of slyly taken pleasure. To spend whole afternoons with her children – this was an instinct which had grown to a romance in her mind. Now – for the first time in the way in which she had envisaged it – it was happening. Nelson was away and would be away for hours. The complication of necessary chores had been pushed aside, a picnic prepared, her dress brought out and put on, the children washed – the long, sweet-weary walk down the sloping field to the tiny river – hardly a river, a beck – which cut under the bushy hawthorn privacy of the neighbouring Langleys – and the last, happy thought, spinning out on top of all her other happiness, a book brought down – from which she would read to all of them.

Three. Shirley, now twelve, flat on her belly with her nose rubbing against the dry shafts of the stalks, her fat legs plumping into the air with a lazy swish; John, two years younger, nestled beside his mother, his eyes fixed on the book in her hands, his arms and legs agitating with the heat and throb of summer which every moment threatened to up-end him in delight; Avril, born a year later than John, cross-legged and calm, daintily looping a buttercup chain to add to the daisy chain already around her neck.

It was a fine book. One which had come from her father's shelves, large and respected with gilded binding and inside, clear steel-engravings.

'It's about Norway,' she told them.

She began to read at the beginning. Unused to reading aloud, she listened to her own voice – but not to catch its quality – rather to employ both her ears and her eyes to catch the full impress of what was being deliberately, happily, stored for long memory. As she read, she neither remembered what had happened to her previously, nor cared what might occur in the future. The present wiped the past and put the future in its shade. There, with her three children on an endless blue summer afternoon. No time to waste on pity or selfishness or wistfulness. There.

When Avril moved away to look for more flowers, and Shirley, startled by a field-mouse, transferred her fright to its cause by chasing it – Lizzie did not mind. Nor would she have minded John's moving away – though she was glad that he stayed.

He got up, eventually, and she stopped. But it was only to look to see the pages. She turned to one of the plates. It was an engraving of a forest of silver birches.

'Like ours,' said John.

'Yes. Lovely, like ours.'

'But not as big.'

'How can you tell from a picture?'

He screwed up his face at the trees. Then he shook his head.

'Not half as big.'

Someone laughed.

It was Arthur Langley. He was in uniform, a second-lieutenant. Lizzie had seen him and his sister so rarely since the day of their move that large areas of his growing-up were completely unknown to her. But she recognised him – and from the gentleness of his laugh did not resent the intrusion.

'I'm sorry,' said Arthur. 'I've only been here for a moment.'

He looked at John, who, suddenly released by the laugh and excited by a stranger, leapt into a tumble of somersaults which rolled him along the edges of the hay, flattening the brittle stems as he rolled over them.

Arthur was standing in a hidden slit in the hedge but John's action brought him out on to the narrow bank of the tiny beck, and Lizzie's pleased laughter brought out his own. He stepped over the ditch and stood, awkwardly, in front of her.

They talked in a friendly question and answer fashion. He asked the ages of the children and she, outside all her shyness in the freedom of her afternoon and Arthur's easy pleasantness, asked him how long he had been in the army: eighteen months, signed on for twelve years. She guessed his age – at twenty, maybe even younger. Mr Foster looked as though he could be sure of a fine crop of hay; yes; and he had heard that electricity had been put in throughout the farm; yes; they had their own engine to make it. Was it Patricia – that was his sister's name, wasn't it? – she saw riding on that lovely grey mare? Was that man who worked for them really Polish?

And then, mutually reassured and each of them – perhaps because of the accident of the meeting – unusually relaxed, they touched, lightly enough, but explicitly, on what was important to them. His father, Colonel Langley, had been badly injured in Burma – internal injuries – been in hospital for two years, retiring, coming home for the first time for seven years. Her husband, Mr Foster – and the pride grew with the strength of the titled name – was going to try to build up a pedigree herd; starting from nothing. Did he want his own farm some day? Yes. But that would come – that would take a long time: he could build up the herd meanwhile. The young man was so kind.

'Arthur! Is that you?'

'Excuse me, Mrs Foster.'

Arthur turned to the hedge.

'Yes!' he shouted.

'Where the hell are you?'

He put one foot across the ditch and peered into the hedge.

'Here,' he replied.

Lizzie looked down at the book.

Pat came through and joined Arthur in the field. He introduced her to Lizzie and although they had seen each other at various distances for the past ten years, they felt little embarrassment at acknowledging each other as strangers. Pat was even more beautiful than Lizzie's quick glimpses had hinted she might be, but there was in her – as Lizzie was to say later to Mrs Trott (her one friend) something odd, something – she could not describe it.

'I thought we were going for a swim.' Pat spoke loudly. Arthur looked at Mrs Foster in apology; once more, she turned away.

'I was coming along,' he said.

'The water starts to cool down after lunch.'

'Not true,' he corrected her, and still he did not budge. An overwhelming impulse to redeem any offence which might have been taken by Lizzie, prevented him from an abrupt departure; but it was impossible to do anything about it.

'Well?' Pat demanded. 'Are we or are we not going?'

'We are.' He coughed. Lizzie looked at him. 'Good-bye, Mrs Foster.'

'Good-bye,' she echoed, carefully.

She watched them go along the bottom of the field; watched them – who had everything – whisper and accuse each other until, finally, Arthur slipped an arm around his sister's shoulders, and they went out of sight.

John, Shirley and Avril were scattered out around her. She did not call them. Her feelings had been too set to be disturbed by the interruption, and she was quite content to sit and watch her children play as if nothing had happened.

When they got back to the house, Nelson was waiting for them. He said nothing, and in the moist coolness of the large kitchen she hurried to get him his tea. They began to eat.

'Where were you?' he asked.

'The bottom of the field.'

'Ay, but where?'

'Just at the bottom.'

'I didn't see you.'

'We were there.'

'Nowhere else?' he demanded.

'No. Just there.'

With a slice of bread in his hand, he got up from the table and went to the window. Outside was the garden – shortened to a mat-patch by the extension of the top field – and on its boundary – the three tall birch-trees. Nelson looked out and shook his head.

'Beats me,' he said. 'Upstairs, downstairs, *their* bedroom, *our* bedroom, back, front – every damned window there is in the place, and I still couldn't see you.' He laughed.

'It would be from that window,' said Lizzie. 'Or the one upstairs.'

'It's them trees,' he replied. 'You can't see that bit for them three trees.'

Two days later, when he chopped them down, she felt hit by every strike of the axe. The soft silver bark flaked off gently where the blade struck.

'Your grandfather could do that easily at your age.'

John looked at the sack. Nearly eighteen stones of wheat packed, crushed in the coarse tub-toughness of matted coarse fibres.

'Go on,' said Nelson. 'Try it.'

John did not move. Brought out after his tea – still in his new school blazer – wanting to do his homework quickly so that he could read the book he had taken from the library, he resented his father's test.

'Scared?'

The granary steps were in the corner of the yard. Deep blocks of stone. The sack of wheat had to be carried, on the boy's back, right up the steps and dumped in the loft. Eighteen stones, carried without a pause.

'Did it when he was twelve,' continued Nelson. 'Could fight any man about when he was still at school.'

He baited his son without being moved either to amusement or satisfaction at what he was doing.

John went over to the sack. His body was buttoned stiff in the thick blazer striped with biros and pencils and compasses. His school cap, quartered blue and navy blue with the Stag crest and Latin motto, was set squarely on his head. He pulled up his long, grey stockings so that they almost met the fat-wadded hem of his short grey trousers. He did not look at his father.

'If I do it, can I go back in?' he asked.

'To be with your mammy?'

John waited, then tried again.

'If I carry it up there without stopping?'

'You'll be a better man than your father was.'

But the boy was not going to budge without the promise.

'Then I can go back in?'

'What for?'

'Homework.'

'Don't you waste enough time at that bloody cissy school of yours as it is, without bringing it back here?'

Again, John did not reply. He could think of one need at a time. Everything else – shut out. He had to lock what he needed: tight.

Lizzie saw the whole thing from the kitchen. She feared it but could do nothing. Shirley brought in the dishes from the table, and, still looking through the small window, Lizzie turned on the tap, hitched her worn sleeves and, with no more than a rare glance at what she was doing, let instinct lead her dry scrawny arms and hands through the work in front of her while she watched.

'All right,' Nelson surrendered.

John tugged at the ears of the sack to test its weight. It rocked slightly. Then he turned his back to it and knelt down on one knee. He put his arms over his shoulders and pulled, firmly, so that the wheat leaned against his shoulders. Then he bent his head forward and tried to heave it high on to his shoulder blades. It seemed comfortable. He inhaled his breath deeply, and tightened his hands, tightened all the muscles in his legs.

'You'll never do it that way,' his father said.

The boy paused – then heaved. The sack barely budged. He set himself steady again, and again tried to hoist it up. This time, it lifted clear of the ground, and he pressed his feet hard on to the stones, straining to stand up. The weight pulled him back and he toppled on to the sack.

'Got you beat?'

Now, John bent down even lower so that the sack jutted out over his head. Before attempting to stand up he eased and shuffled himself right underneath it. But when he tried to press himself up, it slipped forward and slid over his shoulders and on to the ground.

'Hurry up! I can't waste all day watching you.' Then, 'If you want to give it up – just say.'

Taking the sack by the two twisted top-ends – their coarseness almost leathery smooth now from the sweat of his hands – the boy dragged it along the ground to the steps where, very slowly, he hauled it up the first two. Then, after manoeuvring it to the edge which fell down into the yard, he jumped down and found it ready at the exact height he wanted.

It dropped on to his back and he walked round to the bottom of the steps. He felt for the first move with his leg before beginning to climb. If he did it without swinging the weight ahead of him he would fall backwards.

'Get on with it, then!'

He had to pause on the fourth step. As he paused he was slowly squashed on to the stone. He wanted to unbutton his blazer. The sack slipped, and he felt its pull riving his shoulders.

The step in front of his was dappled with bird-droppings. It was not like his father to leave them like that. Shirley would have to wash them off.

His neck stretched so that his mouth opened stiffly as a beak. He kept his eyes on the corner join of the two stones and his foot clutched a grip.

Lizzie saw him fall. He lay face down; the sack still held in position. She banged on the window.

Without looking round, Nelson shouted:

'He's all right! Aren't you?'

A sudden jerk and John was on his feet; the next step was taken, the next – and then he stood, almost upright, his hands cramped around the tough sacking, the wheat hanging straight down his back.

It fell. John did not move.

'Never mind,' said Nelson. 'Damned sight better than I could have done.'

John would never move. His body was buckled with a stiffness which struck out all feeling, all pain. A wispy dance lilted in his mind but he had no responses to swoon with it. There was the loft-door, closed. He could never have opened it without letting the wheat fall.

Much later, when work had strengthened him, he could have run up the steps with the weight slung over his back: but he would never do it . . .

'I think he should stay on at school if he wants to.' It was Lizzie's first intrusion into the argument – an argument decently conducted by Nelson with his better self and propounded in front of John as though it were about some complete stranger.

John was sixteen, had passed his ordinary level exams with sufficient success for him to be accepted into the sixth-form – two years away from university entrance – and all done so calmly that only now, two months after his post-summer return to school, had Nelson realised that his son had the opportunity to leave.

'I just want him to know what sort of an opportunity he might be missin',' he went on. 'He should know!' Lizzie made no protest. 'Now, if he stops and does well and goes on and one thing and another – he might be all right: granted. He might not. He might find out that sittin' on his behind's only good for backache – but he might. Right. Now then: what's to keep him here? Not an easy life: no denying. Not big wage packets: true again. I know he likes to work – or if he doesn't he's never told *me* – but I won't let that harm what I'm saying.'

Then he turned, equitably, to John.

'But if he works with me – he can have what I have,' he said. 'Maybe not much: maybe not: now. But it could change. It's always got better and there's no reason for believin' it won't keep gettin' better. And it's all his: if he wants it enough to work for it.'

The reasoned cunning covered the despotic edge but only with the loose-cover of reticent prejudice. This, Nelson produced like the new tractor; something which would help him to get on with his one job. When the tractor had broken down at the end of only a week – during which time he had chased it through every heavy transport job that the farm could demand – broke down at the bottom of the field it was ploughing with the slap of glee still marked by a greasy handprint on the glossy mudguards – then Nelson had raged in vicious, childish fury and kicked, even scratched what had been the repository of his pride.

'Besides,' said Nelson, 'it'll make it a lot easier for me.'

It would make it a lot easier for Shirley and for John's mother. It was on them that Nelson forced all the jobs that one or even two men should have been hired to cope with; on them and, when he would come, on Dickie.

'You must admit, I haven't forced you to farm-work.'

But the only way to live with such intensity was to be part of it. Time away from his father's business was time outlawed.

'Let him make his own decision,' said Lizzie. John heard her, gratefully. Loved her.

Nelson glared at her as soon as she began the sentence – and it tailed to a whisper. She was scared of her husband. This made John's choice for him . . .

'Why don't you go out?' Lizzie asked him.

John shrugged, without taking his eyes away from what he was reading. He should have gone to his own bedroom where he could have been certain of peace and quiet. But everyone except his mother was out, and the kitchen was yellow-brown warm, inveigling.

'Are you sure you're not being worked too hard?' she persisted. And even though her husband was out her voice dropped to caution.

Again, John answered without saying anything.

'He thinks everybody can work like him, your father,' she went on. 'He won't see that it's too much for you if you don't tell him.'

'It's all right,' John replied, eyes still to the page, 'it doesn't bother me.'

Nor did it seem to from the way he looked. Lizzie saw him

suddenly spread outwards and upwards, reached into manhood with an attained strength which already seemed mature and powerful.

'What are you reading now?' she demanded. It was so rarely that they were alone. She wanted to resolve all her worries about him at once.

'Nothing much.'

'What?'

He could not bring the title to his tongue. Spoken, it would somehow appear feeble or ridiculous. Then, as his mother made as if to come over to him, he said:

'*The Moon and Sixpence* it's called.'

'What's it about?'

'I've just started.'

And he went back to it. He was too tired to appreciate the shy fingers of her anxiety.

'You're sure you don't want to go out?' she repeated.

'I'm all right,' he mumbled. He was nearly asleep . . .

'Eighteen today!' Dickie announced to the crammed bar. 'Drink that up.'

John took his fifth glass.

'Only eighteen, only eighteen,' Dickie chanted.

'She loved him so – o –

'He was too young

'To fall in love

'But he was old enough to know.'

The landlady winked at John.

'Come on, Dickie!'

'A song!'

Dickie was not to be taunted. Sing he would – he had a good voice, grant him that – but out of turn or because of an occasion. Not just like that. And with John on his first 'blind' this was enough of an occasion already. He shook his head which shook his hand and he bent to the pint to save it. He would stay with John; the boy would pay.

Later, sodden, John went to the bar.

''Nother two,' he whispered.

The landlady shook her head. His hands gripped the glasses tightly, did not let them rest on the counter.

'You've had enough,' she told him.

'It's my birthday today.'

She took the glasses from him, slowly. He was drunk – and looked stubborn.

'Now then,' she said. 'Happy birth-day – to – you. Happy – birth-day – tooo – youuu.'

His hands were empty.

'You've had enough.'

'I like your beer,' he muttered.

'Why don't you go to a dance, eh? Why don't you find yourself a nice girl? Eh?'

John shook his head. She saw the suppurating pallor.

'Outside!' she barked. 'No sick on my floor.'

He went. Afterwards he walked along the road on his own. Liked to be on his own. Better on his own.

TWO

They could work for twenty-four hours a day and it would still be no more than half, quarter, a hundredth done.

'That's the point,' said Oliver. 'There's always something more to do. If it were like other jobs and you could feel that an end of some sort had been reached – then it wouldn't be half as much fun!'

Arthur nodded, but he had not the energy to commit himself to verbal agreement. It had been Oliver's idea.

'One ought to try it out in one's own country first. God knows there's enough to be done! Besides, we might be deluding ourselves.'

Arthur had resigned his commission at the same time as Oliver. They had met each other at school, overlapped in the OTC, served together for a few months in the Middle East, and latterly found themselves once more in an identical situation, working at the War Office. Now they shared a flat.

'The situation, as I see it, is this,' Oliver had stated. 'We could stay where we are; sign on for another five or ten years. Or we could go to our respective hearthstones – you to play the country gent, myself to pretend to be a business man. Or we could do something useful.'

Arthur was not disturbed by the clipped precision of Oliver's alternatives. With him, explanations were given almost as an apology for his emotions. Arthur had never known anyone as constantly, straightforwardly good as his friend.

'And, after all,' Oliver added, 'if we don't like it, we can always throw in the towel.'

Oliver, Arthur knew, would never do that. His preoccupation with helping those who needed his help was too well, too long known. Its force was such that it had sustained all the attacks on its naïvety and utility in the often absurdly incongruous context of the army.

'Of course, you mustn't do it unless you want to.'

'I don't know whether I want to or not,' Arthur replied.

'No one does – really.'

'Yes they do. You do. But if I say – "Would I feel that I were really letting myself down if I didn't do it?" – then I'm not sure how I could reply. I'd like to – it's certainly the most attractive of your alternatives – but I don't know whether that's enough.'

'Why not?'

They had left the army in June and agreed to work through the summer helping a Dock Settlement Welfare Group in London.

'I'm afraid it will all seem rather small beer,' the vicar said. 'It's a question of doing two hundred tiny things so that you can attempt The Big Thing.' He grinned. 'I've been here three years now, and I've never managed to do a Big Thing yet!'

Arthur worked harder than he had ever worked in his life before. He would be up at six and in the church hall by half-past; Oliver went to early morning communion with the vicar and never more than five others. Arthur did not go to church, he was tentative about the sacramental impositions it would lay on his actions. By seven he would have helped with the breakfasts for the forty men who nightly used the doss-house which the church had set up next to the hall; this dumpy, broken-fronted terrace house – bought by the church and furnished with beds from an army surplus sale and sheets and blankets from a contact-convert in Petticoat Lane – this was too distressing to allow anyone to see by daylight; and so the men were brought out to the church hall for breakfast. Arthur had Mrs Echland to help him; and she had Dolly, a West Indian girl, to help her. The women worked in the kitchen, Arthur set up the trestle-tables, laid the oil-cloths and, on them, the plates, cutlery, cups; then he went around with packets of corn-flakes, filling the dishes, ready for the men to start on immediately they came in. The smell of bacon and fried bread, floating in large pools of hot lard, swept through the maggot-ridden hall like poison gas fumes. There was the milk to collect, the tea to make – his job – and, when the men came in, a waiter-service to run. They had tried the experiment of self-service but it had collapsed in forlorn disorder.

Most of the men were old, many were covered with sores, scabs, flaring cuts, debilities which came from another century. All were filthily dressed and unwashed for weeks, occasionally for months. Their smell, swirling against the stench from the kitchen, made Arthur feel so sick that he had to keep moving so as not to faint. Goitres, palsied shaking, matted hair – thick, visibly matted with grease like rotted toffee – loose mouths which swung against cups and sucked at the dribble spilt down unshaven chins. And eyes – empty, dead, dazed, hidden, frightened, lost, mad. Stunned sockets of eyes.

Oliver and the vicar came in to help him with the clearing up. After church, they went to the dock-gates with collecting boxes and pamphlets, taking the ancient Land-rover with them, which they piled with junk – old shirts, boots, chairs, crockery, curtains, lamps, stools, carpets, coats, tools, wood, books, tins, bust baskets, ruined sofas, useless souvenirs – everything – all this collected from certain long-arranged loading-stations – and then they would help Arthur to clear the hall.

This doss-house – three and six a night and less for some – this was the Welfare Group's main achievement. It demanded so much auxiliary effort, however, that the vicar with his voluntary helpers scattered through the area of eighty thousand bodies, scavenged daily to keep it going. And there were other things to be done besides.

So Arthur devoted himself to the doss-house. After the hall had been rearranged – and after he had taken a guilty cup of tea from a small pot kept really for Mrs Echland's private use and so fastidiously cleaned – this with three or four slices of bread taken from their package by Arthur himself and buttered by him – after this, he would go into the house and start.

Before he came Mrs Echland had swept out every day, Dolly had tidied up after her, Mrs Crawford, the part-time caretaker, had seen them at their work and then seen to her own invisible doings – and the sheets had been washed once a fortnight, if that. By persuasion, passion and a certain bribery, Arthur had

altered the system – and now he and Dolly washed the sheets
every morning. The blankets, they were forced to leave for a
week. On Saturdays, Oliver helped him to scrub the floors from
top to bottom. On other days, they were mopped by Mrs
Echland with a pungent solution of water and disinfectant.

Those sheets were the most disgusting things that Arthur
had ever seen in his life. They were always screwed into creased
knots, they stank of urine; there were traces of excrement,
saliva, blood, sometimes sperm; and they were black with dirt.
Forty pairs of sheets to be got through every morning; the spare
set put on by Mrs Echland, these dirty ones dried through the
afternoon to be ironed at night – occasionally by Mrs Crawford,
but more often by Arthur and Oliver – ready for the next day.
Washed in huge tubs with the water heated up in the urn that
was used for tea, and the sheets moved around by squelching
them up and down with a long wooden pommel. He knew that
it could take all day if he did them all properly. So, with three
tubs going at the same time, he gave each load a certain number
of minutes and that had to be that. They were washed, if not
cleaned. Dolly and he wrung them out in a long narrow back-yard
which was strung with drying lines like a sail-ship. A washing-
machine was his next ambition.

After two months of this, Arthur could not think of the army
as more than a pleasant peroration to a long adolescence. Only
a few strange incidents stood out – and they were not much
more than diminished flag days. The rest was evenly powdered,
levelled to the bottom of his mind.

Lunch was beer and sausage rolls in a pub. There was soup
in the church hall, but the vicar superintended that and Arthur
allowed himself a free half-hour. He bolted his meal in ten
minutes and then went – ran – to the river to breathe some air.

But there he could see only the same thing. The scum and
loose plants, tins, paper washing against the petrol-grimed walls.
Rusting metal, water reeking of sour glucose, ugly buildings,
dissonant noise, grinding, bleeping, dirt.

In the afternoons he joined with Oliver and went around the
area, visiting, organising, and doing hundreds of little jobs.
Oliver worked as if he started afresh every hour. He arranged

coach-trips for people who thought that they would perish before crossing their porches again, he visited people who had neither friend, relation, neighbour nor dependant, he sold tickets for raffles, consulted with local bodies on this and that possibility of co-ordination, bought food for the evening like a housewife, bought paint with money of his own and began to re-decorate the crumbled, scabby front of the doss-house, sorted old clothes that came in, encouraged the ladies who ran the small shop – the only place open in an otherwise condemned row of cottages – and sold what the Welfare Group could not themselves make use of. He had already decided that he was going abroad in September for an organisation which did refugee work in North Africa.

It was a blazing hot summer. By the middle of the afternoon, Arthur would be exhausted; by the end of it, he had dust clogging each pore of his breathing skin, the smell of hot tar in his nostrils, the sound of drill and saw, crane and engine in his ears – and in front of his eyes, all the crunched rehabilitation of an area living in the past and the future, the one to be eliminated, the other thrust up at any cost to anyone. They walked the area on foot; across building sites, up narrow alleyways made for boys with hoops, across little patches of newly born greenery made for design patterns, through junk jungles made for rats only, into one-roomed bed-sitters where tin served for cups, into municipal and corporation blocks where offices were made for other problems than theirs. By early evening, Arthur was dizzy and frightened.

Then there was the supper to be made. Served at eight o'clock. This he feared even more than the breakfast. The men came in from God knew where; slumped in and on to the benches beside the trestle tables – ready to eat the last scrap of anything. Mrs Echland, back from her afternoon off – Arthur wanted her to have the day, every day off, with her ankles swollen, three children, no husband, poor sight – back in the kitchen with black pans – cauldrons steaming potatoes and one or the other sort of stew.

In that cool hall, alone with the forty or so men each drawing a day's blank drama on to them with hopeless, helpless dejection,

Arthur moved almost frantically. Doing anything to keep himself a dynamo, not to pause, not to hesitate, not to join them. And beyond them, the hundreds of thousands, millions of others even worse off.

After the supper was the clearing, the ironing, the planning for the next day, paper-work, perhaps a scrubbing-out of the church hall; more work.

Home, with Oliver in his own room – probably still arranging something, and doing it in a way which could evoke only admiration and awe in his friend – Arthur lay in his bed – ashamed of its softness, the tasteful, sophisticated ease of the room – and held himself tight to stop shaking. He had not told his parents about this; he had wanted to keep it a secret until he was decided one way or the other.

His eyes were stare-wide open. Outside, the sound of the city curdled to droning sticky restlessness, beat against the small windows of his room. He would have to be up at six. He lay on his back, stiff, tensed. He wanted to sleep.

THREE

Planting his feet on the pretty little floor, as if to force his legs through it and touch the ground, John stretched his whole body into a tight, shuddering tremble; holding the thick-shivering judder of his body for as long as he could. His muscles curled to bunched tightness, and he quickened to their sweet pull against the skin. He lifted his hand from the bar-counter and slowly, tensely, watched his fingers extend to their full length. He was nineteen.

They had seen him coming in. They had said nothing. If he ignored them they might not cause trouble.

John had hated every day of his week at the holiday camp. The first holiday he had ever had. Promiscuity enforced by nubile men and women in white shorts and royal-blue blazers. 'Every-body-hap-py?' 'Yes! Yes! Yes!' They tore the hesitant tendrils of his willingness. It was his own fault; he had expected his isolation to meet its like – in some way – in the voluntary self-immolation of so many. Cold, plastic bars – all over the place. This one deserted save for that gang.

'Bloody virgin!'

They jackalled the challenge across the floor. John was glad it had come. He turned – and walked straight towards them.

'Look who's here.'

'Old silence-in-bed while the judge eats his chips.'

'John, John, the farmer's son –'

'Saw a maid and gave her a bun.'

He looked at them without allowing himself to register the insult in their remark. There were five of them.

'Make room for the man.'

'Next to me – please!' Shrill as a ginny old woman. 'John. Jo-ohnnie.' A cockatoo. 'Come and sit next to me.'

'No, now. No. Leave the lad alone – Johnnie's going to sit next to me – aren't you, John?' Donal lurched his face forward with spaniel sincerity – and reassured his friends as to which side he was really on by a brothy wink. 'John's a fine lad, a nice lad, aren't you, Johnnie? – and he knows his friends from those who don't love him and he knows I do –' He turned in mock reproof of a dirty gurgle of laughter – 'yes, I do – and you shouldn't laugh at a man you love. Now sit down here next to me.' He fussed out a chair, dusting its bright, skidding surface with his sleeve, pestering out his wild Irish act for all it was worth in these early stages.

John placed his drink on the table, and took up his position behind it. He was opposite Alec, the leader.

'We were just on V – maidens,' Donal continued, with over-weening blandness, bustling himself in his chair like a little budgie jiggering its tail after an excretion. 'And – just when you came in – we had arrived at the conclusion –'

'They should be blown up!'

'With a big stick,' shouted Keith. The others howled.

Donal turned on him; serious.

'Now then, Keith – don't be crude. Remember your company. John's a nice lad – and we don't want to hear your family secrets.'

Keith flushed furiously. Realising his mistake, Donal rushed on to cover it with as much equally filthy patter as possible.

'And we had come to the conclusion,' he gabbled, 'that with one notable exception,' a smile at Keith; he had not caught on; never mind, he would make up for it yet, 'they were the loveliest, the liveliest, the fastest and the tightest things on two legs.' Flat. Donal squinted at Keith and asked, lispingly, 'Hath anybody a thin thixpenth?'

Keith rose.

'You have to treat it first!'

'What with?'

'Whatever nature sends.'

'Nature doesn't need any encouragement from you!'

Keith grinned, flattered. With relief, Donal again turned to John.

'What do you say?'

John answered by pulling out a packet of cigarettes, using the action as a cover for his tremble of distaste, selecting one for himself with an obvious determination not to offer them around, waited.

Donal did not want to break the silence – but nor did he want to lose the centre. Not yet. He lifted his glass right up to his face and pressed his nose against it. Then he stuck out his tongue, and its pink flab smeared into the squashed nose and spread everywhere – flecked by the old yellow scrabblings of froth on the inside of the glass. His eyes lurched from side to side above the rim – from John to Alec. Alec, back to John. The action was sickeningly ugly.

'Don't you think he's right?' asked Alec.

'What about?'

'Women.'

'I wouldn't know.'

Alec snorted. John had not cracked. Donal kept on.

'Of course he doesn't know. Alec – I mean – how could you expect him to? Eh? About the sort we were talking about. I mean – you don't think John here bakes his own bread? Eh? He's for the real women – married, willing and able – aren't you, Johnny boy? Never miss a slice off a cut loaf – do they?'

'I don't know.'

The laughter was uneasy. They might as well give up. Alec cleared the matter for a quick finish.

'Why don't you know?'

'Because I mind my own business.'

'Watch it!'

'I will.'

'He does,' screamed Donal. 'All the time.'

'Shut – up!'

It was Alec's affair. He coaxed John.

'Is it right you've never had anything?'

John edged forward in his chair, hunching himself slightly, ready.

'You'd better answer,' said Donal.

'Bloody well shut your trap!' Alec spun around on Donal. It was his business alone now.

There were no bottles on the table. John held back the rush – the gorging anger that was stampeding into his body. Filth!

'What's wrong?' Alec persisted. 'Have you got no tongue either?' Then, 'Do you know what this means?' He made a v-sign.

Now, John was looking for his opening. Alec held John's face with his eyes; his right hand went across to his breast pocket. The squat fingers dipped into the tight slit and immediately found what they were looking for. He slapped them down on to the table.

'Do you know what these are for – eh? Did your mammy never tell you what your daddy does with these?'

'I hear you can handle yourself,' John said.

'What?'

'Look after yourself. Bit of a tough-guy.'

Alec looked around quickly as if for the person who had betrayed him. Donal stared at his empty glass. His turn was past.

'What of it?' he demanded.

John twisted his shoulders, put his right elbow on the table forearm straight up as a mast, hand open-clawed, ready for a grip.

'Try that,' he said.

Alec did not want a personal fight – especially not a clean one like this simple test of strength. He hesitated.

'Somebody told me you'd never been beaten,' said John. 'At this.'

Alec stated his conditions.

Donal squinted at John – no grinning now – ready to crow over the refusal.

'Fine by me.'

Quickly, excitedly, the Irishman pulled out two cigarettes and cut each of them in half. Then he lit and drew on the four butts – two at a time – until the tobacco burned, a tight, dull-red cone. Delicately they were placed upright on the table – two on each side of where the hands would clasp, exactly positioned so that the hand which was forced down would be pressed on to the burning ends.

Alec flexed his fingers, fluttering them into a fist and then out straight, doing this a ritualised number of times.

'Free hand can't hold the seat or the table. Must be down at the side,' Donal announced.

The two elbows nestled firmly against each other. Then the grip was taken.

'Now!'

John's energy was still. His shoulders were set on a half-pivot, and their only movement was the harder fastening of their original position to resist the immediate thrust.

The two hands trembled, in slow motion, hardly moved. The butts were already covered with a soft cushion of flaking ash.

Suddenly John pushed his shoulders forward and stretched his back to its full length. Alec kicked out under the table; his face was horribly riven with thick sweat; his free arm held steady till now, snapped from his side and sprang into the air – like a balance. The locked arm began to swing slowly down.

Now John could do as he liked. He pushed the arm down gradually. Now, he was in control of his anger – but that control was so fierce that the passion which it bred could be appeased only by destruction. He could stop whenever he cared to. Alec was beaten. But he did not think of Alec; only of the hand against his own. He was in the power of his own fury. An instrument.

He thrust the hand down and held, held it on the two burning cigarette ends – even pushing it farther down for a second – then he released his grip, jumped up, and backed away from the table.

Alec had neither moaned nor shouted out. He bent over his hand and sucked at the burns. The others waited for him to give them the signal.

John backed to the door. Then he turned to go through it.

'Hey!'

He almost leapt around. Alec looked up from gobbling his skin.

'See you soon,' he said. Then he pulled out a handkerchief, spat on it, and dabbed it on his burns.

John nodded and went out without answering.

'Thanks very much, John. I won't forget it.'

'It's all right.'

'No. Really. I won't forget it.'

John wanted him to go away; the whole business was long finished: but he knew that, if he were short with Edward, then he would immediately feel ashamed of himself.

'Honestly,' Edward went on. 'They would have got me if you hadn't stopped them.'

That was true. Edward was spindly, buck-toothed, gormless and he smelled. It was depressingly predictable that he would be butted as a fool. But he had not the fool's flexibility; he was too brittle to bear his treatment passively. John had just intervened in time when Edward, the previous evening, baited contemptuously, had been about to lose his weak-chested temper with one of Alec's gang.

Weak chested! John caught his own judgement and cursed its implication. He was the same as everyone else; people were judged by the number of women or the number of fights they had had.

'Good,' said John – to feed something to Edward's gape.

Edward moved forward – pushing his smell ahead of him. He could have done something about that, at least. Or perhaps a certain combination of disadvantages had no other power than to breed others. John stretched out his legs on the bed: that might prevent a conclave if not a confidence.

'I wish you'd mashed him up,' said Edward, simply. 'I would have liked to see him smashed up.'

One puff, and Edward would scud across the chalet like a brown paper bag; a kick in the jeer and he would go right through the bloody thing. John was held by the concern he felt for Edward's safety – even though he had known him for no more than the few days for which the holiday-camp's planners had made them co-inhabitants, with two others, of a paper-strong cardboard-box. But, he was finding it difficult to suppress the impatient cruelty which made him want to push Edward away.

Edward grinned all along his braced teeth. He wanted John to be Superman – just for him. Go away!

'Go away!'

Edward's neck triggered its head to one side – to face up to the words.

'Go away!' Mick repeated.

Edward looked down – Mick was on the lower bunk on the other side of the room – decided that Mick was harmless, at least until pushed very far, and he had learnt a little from the previous evening, grinned stupidly at John his shield, now the spectator of his own valiant deeds, and stuttered:

'Who do you think you are?'

'I'm trying to read.'

'Well, I was talking,' Edward replied, scoring heavily.

Mick hoisted himself up on to one elbow.

'Can't you read somewhere else?'

'No,' Mick explained, patiently. 'It's too late to read anywhere else.'

This could have gone on for hours – but John, put in a good mood by Edward's displayed persistence, opened the book he was reading. Edward turned to him in protest. Mick went back to his book, Edward turned back to him. Too late.

'You two going to read?' he demanded.

The day's official activities were over, most people were in their chalets – only Donal was missing from this one – but Edward wanted to verify, at least once, the story, later to be told, of 'staying up all night'. Half the night would do.

They kept on reading. No sense in it, they could read at home. He stood between them and considered carefully. If he went out – they would do something and he would miss it. On the other hand – he had seen people reading before: it could go on for hours.

He walked a clumping, constricted, half-circle – giving both of them the fullest opportunity to realise that conversation could be had for a cough. He even turned his back on them – spinning around after a few seconds as if playing 'Grandma's Footsteps'. But neither had moved. Finally he sat down on his own bed and, after watching them to make sure they were turning the pages, took down his pink-and-red striped 'Happy Camp lore' folder – and reviewed his opportunities for the next, the last, day.

John's arm was still aching, but he enjoyed the pain. He had enjoyed the whole scrap. He could easily have avoided it. But, it was at times – as then – the only defence for his solitude. This holiday camp week – urged, secretly, by his mother – and meeting with the tepid consent of someone who at last tries what is best for him if only to prove that it is not – this had been miserable. John knew that he was his own misery's cause but, even so, the bartering of experiences over housey-housey for the sake of an exchange of partners at the American Dance Night: in this, he could take no part. Nor, however, was he accustomed to the role of the interesting solitary – cosseted in the near end by all and all the more intimately because of his late coming. He was reading Guy de Maupassant's short stories. He had brought them in the town just near the camp. That was one of the new things he had enjoyed about his holiday. He had felt sufficiently confident to go in a bookshop and take his time. Usually, in Aldeby – or at sales where books went fifty for two-and-six – he was embarrassed; even at the library, he would sometimes wait outside for half an hour before going in. Here, he walked in to a display of paperbacks such as he had never seen in his life before. He had bought six. He liked to own the books he read.

'John-nie!' Donal, outside. John ignored it. A soft voice.

'Johnnnie!' Two voices. Still whispering.

'Jooohn-niee!' Four – five voices. Quiet.

John was glad he had kept his shoes on; he was lying on his bunk as he had flopped on to it when he arrived. He would stay inside. It would be more difficult for them to do anything if he stayed inside.

Edward had frozen on his bed. John realised that, if they came in, Edward would probably get the worst of it.

Someone scratched at the window. Another hand scratched at the window on the other side of the door. Soon the windows were crawling with drubbing fingers. Giggling, drunken faces peered through them. He saw Alec's bandaged hand.

There was nothing in the room which could be used as a weapon; the beds were some sort of iron – riveted to the floor; the wash-basin was fixed – no shelves – curtain rail – plastic. They would not do anything immediately outside the chalet. But behind this row – Row H – was the children's playground. They would try to get him there. He had looked at that playground: giant ducks, a massive shoe, helter-skelter, a toy castle, see-saws, swings. He could keep them happy there.

Donal opened the door. He was viciously plastered.

'You know what we've come for,' he said. 'If you don't come to us – we'll come to you.'

He left the door open. Outside, on the pretty lawn, with the rose-trellising behind them, they stood in an uncertain half-circle, neither clear nor silhouetted, grey shadows in the cinema half-lighting which protected the campers through the night.

'We could barricade the door and yell blue murder,' said Mick. But he spoke this as an emphatic hypothesis: it was none of his business.

'They'll kill me anyway,' said Edward.

John slid forward on his bed – stretched out his leg, and kicked the door shut. They were arguing among themselves. He indicated to the others to keep quiet. If he shouted, that would stop them for a second – all he needed. He was ready.

'Come on in then!' he yelled.

Then, instantly, he yanked open the door, turned, sharply, to his left, side-stepped them all, and belted down the path to the first turning which led to the playground.

They were after him.

It was useless to hide. He had to keep moving, and he had to get as many of them as he could singly. He ran to one of the swings and jumped on it hard. A few kicks, and the boards splintered. Then he realised a better idea and hung on to the bar while he unhooked the two chains which held it. They were half-way across the area. He went to his right, where the meeting of the tennis courts marked a border; there he started to pull the chains around his head like a hammer.

The first one to meet it – on the shoulder – fell. The others held back. He shortened his grip for a faster stroke. They were spreading out. Waving it in front of him, he charged to one side – before they were settled. The man dived out of the way. John threw the chain and boards down on him and raced across to the big shoe. One of them was suddenly right behind him. John ran faster – then stopped, sharply turned, and stuck out his two arms: the man bounced straight into them; he went down – but John knew that he had not hurt him. He was losing.

The castle. He went through the tiny door and up the little circle of wooden stairs. On top, he could kick anyone who tried to come up.

No one did.

He heard them talking.

The castle was about nine feet high. He jumped down. His ankle turned, slightly, and they were on him with a tremendous thud.

He lashed out with his feet and fists as long as they were free. Soon he could not feel his blows registering.

'Don't kill him! Keep him!'

His forehead knocked against the hard cement. Someone had screwed his right arm up his back.

'Keep him for me!' Alec.

They stopped. He could hardly hear them. Again they were arguing. Donal. He was dragged off. To the middle. Quieter. Virgin.

'This'll do.'

Then they set on him.

FOUR

There was nothing he could do to disguise it. There was a long cut over his right eyebrow which had been stitched and dressed by one of the doctors at the camp. That could have been an accident. But the thick bruises on his jaw and cheekbones could not be so easily accounted for.

Confession was out of the question; he would have to joke about it. As long as his mother did not see his body.

Shirley met him at the station with the van. Her expression flew to a sympathy which understood too much for him to enter into the role so sullenly prepared on the tittering train; he stated his position grimly.

'We were jumping about one night and then somebody turned nasty. Got out of hand. A joke, really.'

Nelson was delighted.

'So you met your match! Eh? By God, I wish I'd seen it! Oh, dear! What a face! What's t'other fellow like?'

'T'same.'

'Are you sure you've had it properly seen to?' Lizzie asked.

'Must have been a hell of a do!' Nelson smacked with satisfaction. 'One hell of a do,' he repeated.

'Do you want me to get Dr Barwise just to be certain?'

'Hooligans!' said Avril. 'You're just like a lot of hooligans! Babies.'

'There was this gang from Newcastle and this other gang from Glasgow,' John muttered.

'They nailed *you* anyway!' Nelson shouted. 'My boy, they sized *you* up soon enough.'

'What a lovely holiday you must have had,' said Avril. 'So civilised! Pathetic.'

'Here's some tea.'

Lizzie watched it being drunk as though waiting for the immediate effect of a magic potion.

'Did you have a nice time – apart from that?' she asked.

'Great!'

'Oh, marvellous,' said Avril. 'Just a few broken arms and legs. Stupid.'

'Well,' Nelson stated, suddenly sombre, 'it'll teach you. You needn't worry about that. It'll teach you right enough.'

Evading, refusing, being rude, misunderstanding, saying nothing, John avoided any real enquiry.

All he wanted was to be alone. Yet for the next few days with Nelson, as usual, driving him around like a private army, and when Nelson left him, Shirley, whose official position was that of Lizzie's help but who, in fact, worked on the land almost as much as Nelson and John – with his mother, it seemed, pursuing him to watch that he did not suddenly collapse, and then the working force suddenly expanded to four by the arrival of Dickie who came up from Aldeby for a few days, driven up by a poverty unusual even for him in its seriousness and presenting himself as the leal saviour of his brother and family, pitching into the meals with the energy others kept for their work – with all this, John went around in unsubsiding turbulence.

And when he did come to an equilibrium which allowed him to look back, he found the past no profit but painful explosions of untaken alternatives, unnecessary vanities, uselessness.

That autumn and winter, he kept close to the farm. Before his holiday he had begun to go out – with Dickie, sometimes with Alan, another farmer's son working, as he did, for his father about ten miles away; he had been to a few dances, even considered playing football for the village. Now he worked, stayed in, and read.

Nelson's plans could take all the energy John had. With such an easy landlord as Colonel Langley – never saw him, marvellous! – he had lined and refurbished the property until it was so well creased by his ambition that everything could slide into it. John had to fight to keep up with him.

'I don't mind him going on at me, but he should leave Shirley alone,' he said to his mother.

'I know.' Lizzie was nervous when he spoke against his father and yet she wanted to share in any confidence. 'He thinks everybody should work as hard as he does himself. He doesn't realise.'

'He should.'

'Why? What did he do?'

John shook his head. Nelson's injustices were more in the attitude than the action.

'Does he never think of anything else?'

'No. No, he doesn't.'

He caught the lift of pride in her voice; his father's consistency had grown into a rock and they were bound to that which gave them shade and solidity.

'Aren't you supposed to be draining that bottom field this afternoon?' she asked, timidly.

'I've decided not to.'

'Oh.'

'Gone on strike.'

Lizzie looked out of the window, ready, it seemed, for her husband to charge in and line them against the wall for squandering time.

'Oh,' she repeated. Then, 'Are you sure?'

He put his arm around her.

'The pipes didn't come,' he said. 'There was nothing more I could do without them.'

She smiled.

Only Avril had got out. She worked in the Midland Bank in Aldeby. A reluctantly tolerated release.

Little was tolerated. Since her marriage, Lizzie had seen her brother only twice; there was a nephew she knew of only by name and through the scrawled acknowledgements to her birthday and Christmas presents, secretly parcelled, regularly sent.

Yet, outside the rules, everything could be done – provided that Nelson did not see it and it did not interfere. Determination had cast a code which demanded absolute obedience; but it was not a total order.

The pains went from his body. But sometimes he thought that he could feel them, sharply again. The kicks. And what had been unconscious solitude became determined isolation.

Just before going to bed Nelson would come out for his final inspection. Sleep was a valueless intrusion and he let it interfere as little as possible by carrying his work right to its edge.

Sometimes John would accompany him on this last round. That was the way he would live. That was his inheritance.

Both of them knew the real reason for Pat's sudden visit to Aldeby. Neither would admit it; yet it had to be stated. It was almost three o'clock in the afternoon.

'Look, darling,' Mrs Langley was saying, as they walked across the dappled sunny yard to the van, 'you won't forget to buy the tomatoes at *Stevenson's*, will you?'

'No.'

'And do check that they're not squashy. He doesn't mind if you pick them up.'

'Is there no way of telling that they're squashy *before* I pick them up?' Pat asked.

'And the matches. Annie forgot them this morning.'

They had arrived at the van. Aware of the incongruity of her mother chaperoning her across such a safe area, Pat smiled at the thin solemnity which so uncertainly covered her mother's true purpose. Even as a girl, she had not been able to take her mother seriously, and as she had grown older – until now they faced each other, the one poised to enter the long period of slowly settling, little changing maturity, the other ready to leave it for the slope to old age – she felt again that irritated arrogance which often slipped to anger at her mother's mantled earnestness. During that long time since Pat's leaving school and being established now as an apparently permanent single woman at the house of her parents, Mrs Langley had never quite been able to discover the tone which appreciated her daughter's independent, adult existence. Just as she had never found the will to understand her husband's true condition.

'And if you *should* see your father,' she said, vaguely, desperately, as Pat got into the driving-seat, 'then perhaps you would remind him that the Terraines will be coming for dinner.'

'Doesn't he know?' Pat started the engine.

Her mother nodded. The engine revved up and the trailing coda was lost.

'So he's got to be back early?' Pat shouted.

Mrs Langley waved her hand. The message had been given. And Pat wanted to be on her own. She had taken what she needed; Arthur's letter was in her pocket.

She drew up to read it, once through the village. It was addressed to her mother, but as he had long since stopped writing to her personally, Pat regarded every letter as her own private property, obliquely dispatched, perhaps, but only truly comprehensible to herself.

'I have decided to stay in London to think things over,' it read. 'Oliver has gone abroad "to work with the poor", and I may join him, although, at present, I think not. I have made a few enquiries about jobs – the usual things – and none of them seem to be much more than straightforward sacrifices to a gradually increasing income and a perpetually decreasing interest in anything but the income. Fortunately, I have enough to see me through for the next few months. Perhaps something will turn up. I may come home for a while at the end of the summer.'

Since resigning his commission, he had been home only once, at Christmas. Pat dismissed the coolness of that visit as the inevitable preoccupation of someone undecided. But if he did not come at the end of summer, she would go to London to see him.

Colonel Langley was at the bus-stop. There was one single-decker bus which went around the bare, dilated area north of Aldeby every morning, and again in the middle of the afternoon. He preferred this method of travel to any other.

Although it was high summer, he was lashed into a long trench-coat, a thick tweed suit beneath it, heavy brogues. He came across to her, discovered that she would be about ten minutes doing the shopping, and said:

'See me outside Willie's.'

Willie Armstrong was one of the town's three bookmakers.

When not in the Crown, the Colonel could always be unearthed at Willie's.

Pat watched him march stiffly across the empty street. Although his habits were well-known in the town – although, in fact, his increasingly rabid and unconcerned self-indulgences had been observed by that street since 1947 when the internal wound had precipitated an unwilling retirement from active service, remarked on even more when he retired from the Territorial Army – yet no one smirked or even, it seemed, cared. This was not altogether due to a general forbearance – eccentricities could become merciless objects of uncovered sneers; nor was the Colonel's rank and past position a protection – all the more reason to get him now that he was down. It was the walk. At once rigid through a former grasp on authority, and fragile through a present regard for lost dignities. Inviolate.

She went about her pointless shopping half-heartedly. She did not like Aldeby and the town responded by recognising her with little acknowledgement, accepting her with little enrichment, almost as indifferent as she was herself. No one she knew had come in for afternoon shopping; most of them went to Hexham, Carlisle or even Newcastle. She was soon back with her father.

'No good,' he said, cheerfully, as he bent into the van. 'They don't run as fast as they used to, these days.' He laughed.

The short exposure to the sun had melted the tight shine of his brick face and now he was blotchily sweating. Whisky spread through the closed car redolently obtrusive as musk.

'You know that the Terraines are coming tonight,' said Pat.

'Who said so?'

'Mother.'

'Why?'

'For dinner, I suppose.'

Colonel Langley turned away from her in disgust. With an effort, he refrained from obviously tempting rudeness.

'In that case you can take me to Rosley,' he said.

She drove there without arguing. It was a tiny hamlet just above the Fosters, with a pub way outside the policeman's stamina and open almost all the time. Her father would often go there for long afternoons of whisky and cards.

'Shall I come and pick you up in about two hours?' Pat asked.

'No. I'll walk back.' He grunted. 'Do me good.'

She went a long way round to reach home. She knew that it would have been easy to have gulled him into coming home, simply by refraining from any mention of the Terraines. She had understood that before she had said it . . .

John set off right after lunch, telling his mother and no one else. It was laid down that he could take off one Saturday afternoon in three, but this was the first time that he had taken advantage of it for months.

He took his gun and then, at the gate, decided to ride Dan, the pony which Nelson had had for years and kept now because he was afraid that as soon as he sold or destroyed it, then he would need it. It earned its keep by doing small jobs around the fields.

There was a time when John had ridden the pony as often as possible. Then, he had established various routes which would take him an eremetic full-circle. The only people he would see would be one or two shepherds, a delivery van on a tiny road, sometimes the hunt, occasionally Pat out on her own.

Although they were neighbours, the Fosters and the Langleys scarcely met. Nelson paid his rent to Mr Williams, a solicitor in Aldeby; if he met Colonel Langley, then he would chat for two or three minutes with him; but apart from the few times when he had approached him about improvements to the farm, the longest time they had spent in each other's company remained that afternoon on which his original tenancy had been agreed. Nor did John find it unusual that there was no contact between Avril, Shirley and himself, and Pat and Arthur. The area in which they lived was so large, so rimlessly open, that the huddling to a fraternal precinct was no intrinsic part of the life there.

He set off to go over the Wall and right round on the north side. It was a warm summer afternoon. After riding for an hour or so, he regretted having brought the gun with him; he did not feel like shooting anything. The freedom of the ride was itself enough.

He came to Rosley at about seven, stopped for a drink, and

then moved on along the small pony track which led down to
the Wall and from there to the back end of both the Langley and
the Foster lands.

At first, he thought that Colonel Langley was sitting down to
rest. As he blocked most of the track, however, John nudged
Dan down into the steep field. The ground was dry and baked
into dangerous indentations. He got off and led the pony.

The old man was asleep, but his breathing, far from being
even, was caught, clutched and then gasped out in an irregular
succession of painful sighs. His face was white beneath fine
purple tracery on his cheeks. He was lying awkwardly. He must
have fallen.

John shook him gently by the shoulder. The old man moaned.
More firmly, John joggled him again, bringing him upright with
the strong grip.

'Are you all right?'

Colonel Langley opened his eyes, weakly. They were yellow
and bloodshot.

'Are you feeling all right?'

'What's the matter?' The words were barely comprehensible,
feebly coalescing.

'I wondered if you were well.'

The Colonel looked around him.

'You been sent?' he demanded, mumblingly.

John shook his head.

'Do you want a hand up?'

The old man dismissed the question and tried further to deny
it by scrambling his legs underneath him and pushing against the
ground with his hands. John went behind him, hooked him under
the shoulders and hoisted him upright.

'Many thanks.'

For a few moments Colonel Langley stood quite still,
using the time, it seemed, for a faint-hearted brushing of his
trench-coat. His face was now pinkly flushed and he was pant-
ing.

'I'm afraid you'll have to give me a hand,' he said after a pause.

John went to get Dan; when he came back, the old man was
once more on the ground.

'Help me on to your pony,' he muttered. 'I'm too heavy for you.'

It was pointless to argue; John did as he was bid. The effort of mounting caused the old man to gasp and snort as if he'd been in a fight. The noise he made was frightening in the quiet, figureless dimensions of the empty uplands.

Slowly, walking slightly behind the pony's head so that he could be ready to steady the rider if necessary, John set off. The gun was a nuisance.

He worked out the easiest and quickest way there. The path dropped away so steeply to stubbly fields at this point that it would be safer to take him all the way along the Wall and join up with the road above his father's farm.

'Too slow,' the old man muttered. 'Too slow. We must cut across.'

By going right down and through the gate at the bottom, they would reach a path which wound directly into the Langley's place.

'It's too steep,' said John.

The Colonel slouched forward on the pony's neck. John took the bridle very carefully, there was no alternative. He led it down the hill.

The old man seemed to have lost what little power he had had. John stopped the pony and went back to heave him on to the saddle, as he did so the Colonel's foot swung out and kicked him in the face.

'Too slow,' he repeated, and swung back up, swayed up as if hypnotised.

Again John went to the pony's head and began to lead it. Again, after about twenty yards, the old man fell forward and would have toppled off had he not rushed back to hold him.

He stopped. It was impossible to go any more quickly. The field was pitted with baked sockets of earth and made even more dangerous by scatterings of lumpy rocks. Dan, old, unused to such scrambling, hesitated before each step.

'We'll have to go back on to the path.'

No answer. He went to turn the pony round. It climbed painfully, the Colonel sagging heavily. John went back and held him and, again, as always when given help, the old man stiffened and gripped his seat. They were near the top and here the incline was so sharp that Dan stopped altogether. John slapped its haunches; at the same moment, Colonel Langley, started to help himself, banged his heels into the pony's flanks and tossed the reins. Jumping forward, Dan caught a foreleg in a hole, poised wildly for a second and then fell, the leg snapping like a dry stick. The Colonel fell the other way.

The pony's eyes were mad with fright. It slithered uselessly in its own area and then suddenly grew still.

'Shoot it.'

John stared and did nothing.

'Don't be stupid, man; put it out of its misery.'

The crash appeared to have revived the old man for the moment. He was standing beside John, both of them looking at the animal's eyes.

'Give it to me.'

Colonel Langley took hold of the gun and began to pull it from John's arm. His new strength was still trembling, and the action violent.

'No.'

'Don't be stupid.'

The old man pulled hard and then, before he realised what he was doing, John turned round and hit him right in the face. He dropped, immediately.

John looked from one to the other. He could not act.

After what seemed like minutes stretched out to fill hours, the old man groaned and came to. John went down to him.

'Sorry. Please. I'm sorry.'

'Shoot the thing!' he murmured.

Dan whinnied; its whole body was shuddering with panic. Holding himself tight, John went over, put the muzzle behind its ear, and fired. It took only the one cartridge.

Colonel Langley was still stretched out. Throwing away the gun, John picked him up and began to carry him, half hoist lift, down the field.

Andrei, the Pole who worked for the Langleys was in one of their boundary fields. Together, they took the Colonel down to the house. As they came to it, Ted, the groom and odd-job man, joined them. John saw that they could manage him and left.

He could not go in and phone from there; it was equally impossible to go home. He set off for the pub at Rosley and it was there that he called the vet.

As soon as the arrangements had been made, he went back across to the pony. His gun was still lying where he had thrown it and when he went to pick it up, he found it covered with dew. Then he sat down and waited for them to come and take Dan to the kennels . . .

The Terraines were most sensible about it all. But indeed, their reactions counted for next to nothing when Colonel Langley entered collapsed on two shoulders, and Andrei burst into the dining-room with the news. Pat flying out before her mother. Annie standing fascinated in one corner of the kitchen. He was carried to bed. Pat and her mother undressed him. When Pat did go downstairs, the Terraines were still there, but waiting only to see if they could be of use.

'Could you ring Dr Barwise?' Mrs Langley asked Pat.

FIVE

Arthur came out of the theatre with relief. It had been a pungently contemporary play which had driven him far along a barren line and then, triumphantly, left him there. He could find no way of appraising it. In the No 1 dressing-room he said.

'It was so disagreeable.'

'Meant to be!' the main character replied.

'But I could feel no sympathy for any of you.'

'Well, *you* wouldn't, would you?'

'Maybe not,' Arthur conceded, 'but I wasn't even interested.'

'I don't mind that!'

'I couldn't see any point in it; none at all.'

'Well, why did you come?'

He found it was impossible to stand still and consider what to do; people seemed to come out of the theatre with the same preconsidered purpose as that of children released from afternoon school.

He walked down towards Piccadilly. When he had first come to London, it had been enough to wander around in the evenings; the restaurants and lights, the calls and window-dressed music – this had been sufficient to sustain an hour or two. He had even gone, with Oliver, to Covent Garden, to the Caledonian Market at four or five on a Friday morning, ambled alongside the river, obtained a ticket for a late sitting in the House of Commons. Now the flavour was thin and soon digested, leaving him still anxious for something but ignorant both of its identity and of the means of discovering its identity.

He turned and went into Soho, stopping in front of a Strip-Tease club. Photographs of the girls – all doggedly naked – flashed their Technicolor lines at him as he stared.

'Fifteen bob. Continuous.'

Arthur shook his head. The man stepped out of the narrow doorway and nudged up to him.

'Twelve and six. Seven very original acts we've got in there.'

Arthur did not reply. There was something so horrible about the photographs, about the blandly swinging breasts; he shuddered.

'I'll wrap them up for you if you like,' the man announced, retreating to his strait gate.

Arthur glared at him.

'Yes,' the man went on. 'Wrap them up so you can take them away with you.'

He went swiftly up to Oxford Street. Someone he knew had a flat in a mews just behind Wigmore Street. Walking briskly, it was not until he had almost arrived there that he realised that it was impossible to call at such a late hour; nor did he want to see the man. His friends now acted only as reminders, yardsticks or, worst of all, fellow-sympathisers.

He was totally uncertain of where to go or what to do. He began to stroll up to Hyde Park. There was only one certainty, he did not wish to go back to the loneliness of his flat.

Oliver had gone.

'It's entirely up to you,' he had said, 'entirely up to you'.

Arthur felt that it was entirely up to him to accompany Oliver. Not to go would admit that he was up to nothing.

Oliver had spent a week with his parents and now, with most of his luggage crated and already shipped, he was finishing his packing.

'I really can't make up my mind,' Arthur replied. 'I know I should hate it. And what good would that do?'

'Entirely up to you.'

Oliver threw things into the suitcases with an extravagant impatience which suggested that he was giving someone the slip. Arthur wanted to calm this gusto, to turn Oliver to a more sympathetic consideration of what he was asking of him.

'Why do *you* think I ought to go?' he asked.

'Now then,' Oliver answered, bustling past his chair with a rumpled pile of shirts which flopped over the edges of the suitcase, 'you mustn't ask me that question. There's no necessity, you have no obligations, there is no duty. There.'

Arthur was unsure as to whether Oliver's 'there' was a conclusion to the sentence or a comment on his shirts.

'But I know,' he said, lifting his legs to allow Oliver to pick up the pile of books on which they had been resting. 'I know that there *is* a duty. I mean, whenever one thinks about it for a moment there's nothing to do but – go and try to help.'

'I wouldn't say that,' Oliver replied. 'Everyone can't just – rush off. Some of us have to stay behind and keep things going here. No,' he concluded, banging down the springing top of a suitcase. 'I wouldn't say that it was as simple as that.'

'And what use would I be?' Arthur was almost shouting. 'What use would I be if I went for no good reason.'

Oliver stopped his work, looked down kindly at Arthur's confused appeal, and answered:

'That's not for me to judge, Arthur. You know that.'

So now he was gone. As he remembered Oliver's actual departure, Arthur's step quickened, as if he were trying to catch him up.

And the flat was desolate.

At Marble Arch, the traffic glided in ordered convoys around the broad lanes. What had been a nesting-place, a focus, a part of London, was now a marooned monument.

He paused. He had no inclination to stop in his walk, but somehow the fear of meeting a tramp or someone obviously in need of help, a fear often with him since he had left the Dock Settlement, grew stronger as he faced that cavernous black park. He went into the Underground station and back to his flat.

He was nearly settled, he told himself. He just needed a little more time.

SIX

Nelson put on the farmyard light. He stepped out into the small cobbled square and was satisfied. The low rectangle of buildings flared with whitewash, looking almost pretty in contrast with the last black press of night. There was not one weed between the many, irregular stones on the ground, and no witness to sloppiness anywhere.

With a cup of tea behind him – his real breakfast came after the milking – he went about his work.

John was already in the bottom field with his dog, Ben. A mongrel of a sheep-dog, it patrolled quietly at his heels, not wasting energy in wild gambolling. John flicked on his torch.

'Bring them in, boy.'

And Ben streaked through the grass to move the cows. John controlled it with whistles: his father had once been hired on a fell-farm where the dogs had to be directed in this way. He had insisted on training each dog he had had to obey the signals he had learnt at that time, and insisted also on John's learning them.

John beamed his thin line of light around the field; it was no more than a slight intrusion into the darkness which concealed all the countryside. He whistled – one long call, two short ones, the last with a flicked, uplifted end cadence. Ben first stopped – having already moved the cows from the bottom left-hand area of the field – and then – quietly – swished through the grass to the right-hand area. Quietly, the beasts were gathered and brought to the gate. He went through the work steadily. He saw his mother at the kitchen window, Shirley and his father in the yard; it was too early to speak to anyone.

They champed through a breakfast which began with four

Weetabix, proceeded to three eggs on a carpet of bacon, moved to thick slices of bread and jam, and was attended by constant, tiny, cups of tea. Mrs Foster and Shirley ran a shuttle-service from kitchen to back-kitchen, pecking their food between journeys. Shirley had been up with her mother and the two men.

'What time is it?' Avril, brightly painted for the bank, a stick of rock in a pile of brown paper.

Her mother looked at her warningly. Avril looked at her father and repeated:

'Got the time, Dad?'

'Sit down and eat your breakfast and don't make so much bloody noise, half-past eight.'

'Plenty of time,' she said, and wriggling her neat bottom under its broad belt to its hard seat, she poured herself some tea.

'No toast?'

Her mother rose, the ever-light end of a see-saw, only to be clamped to ground by her husband's hand.

'Get it for yourself.'

Avril pouted.

'Now!' he shouted, and his free hand banged the table.

Avril, with the pause of an instant – the smallest expression of a dare, got up and went to the kitchen. Her mother, still bound, watched her.

'And you can mash some fresh tea!' he yelled. 'And' – he saw the bread plate half-empty – 'cut some more bread – and look bloody quick about it – earn your living for a change – do som'at that means work!'

He released his wife and she sat down. John noticed the chafed red mark on her wrist.

'It's all right, Avril,' he shouted through to his sister. 'I'll do that for you. You come and sit down and have your breakfast in peace.'

He went to the kitchen and after some scuffled whispers sent Avril back to the table. Then he did all that had been asked of her, and came back with the tea.

'Would you like some more tea, Mam?' he asked his mother. She nodded. He poured it out.

'Shirley?' Again, yes.

'Avril?' Again. Then he poured some for himself – and plonked the teapot down beside his father.

'You just watch out, my girl,' Nelson said to Avril. 'You just watch out. One of these days you'll go just that little bit too far – and you'll be out.'

John belched loudly. Then he got up and went to the door. 'Are we going to get some work done, then?' he asked his father, across the room.

Without waiting for a reply, he went out.

Later, they were working together. Nothing had been mentioned about Dan's death.

'I'm not worried about the pony,' Nelson began.

John winced, drew back his head, at the memory of the animal's fall. His father's tranquillity was unexpected.

'It was buggered, anyway,' said Nelson. Then, stopping his work with the deliberation which denoted at once sacrifice and seriousness, he went on:

'You see, it's the principle that bothers me. You don't give a damn – that's what bothers me. You act like any stupid hired man – like just anybody. You just wander off. I wouldn't care if you entertained yourself with some gang of lads. But – off you go. Never a word. All this – all I've done – Oh no! – that doesn't bother you one bit.'

'My free time's my own.'

'Ay! But what if I said that? I've worked for this land; your mother's worked. Done without. Said nothing. Borrowed nothing. What if I took time off?'

'For God's sake, stop whining.'

'Don't you swear at me, my lad.'

Nelson was upset. He had tried his best. He did not want this disagreement to end with the threat of blows.

'You just don't give a tinker's cuss for what I've done,' he said.

John ignored him.

'And don't pretend you're busy. You're only busy when it suits you.'

Nelson contemplated him. John worked, his back to his father.

'I needed help on Saturday,' said Nelson. 'Needed it.'

'Well bloodywell pay for it. You have money. Stop trying to run everything on hen-money – and pay somebody.'

'I shouldn't have to pay anybody to work on land that's my own.'

'You'll bury yourself. I know you will. Nobody'll be paid to dig your grave. No. You'll dig the damn thing yourself.'

'And what's wrong with that?' The voices had risen gradually. Now, Nelson was blistering out his words. 'Who can you trust to work for you but your own? Eh? Who? – I'm not mean – you can't call me mean – but what happens? I asked my own brother to come today. He knows I'll pay him. And he's my own brother. But does he come? Does he?'

'I wouldn't come either to work on a slave gang at half-price. Dickie has more sense.'

'Ay! He would have. Dickie would have more sense than your own father. Dickie hasn't a penny – not a half-penny – to him – but he has more sense than me. Oh, yes. He has more sense than I have.'

'At least he has the sense to laugh a bit now and then.'

'Oh yes. And that proves something, does it? So I should walk around pissing myself with laughing all the bloody time, should I? Maybe I should put a paper hat on, as well. Eh? Maybe I should dance a bloody Irish jig all morning and let your mother and you eat grass. Eh? That would be really sense. That would be clever.'

'Oh, shut up!'

'That's right. Shut up! he says – to his father. Let me tell you . . .'

'You've told me – six hundred times . . .'

'. . . Well this is the six hundred and first then, isn't it?'

John again turned away. He wanted relief from this baiting – ranting man. Nelson stepped around in front of him again.

'Oh, no! I'm going to tell you whether you want to hear it or not . . . If I'd spoken to my father the way you speak to me – you know what he'd have done?'

'Kissed your arse.'

Nelson stopped. Stiffened as it struck.

'All right. So you're clever. I know you're clever. You read books and then pretend you can't follow my meaning. That shows you're clever. I couldn't go to a grammar-school – I passed, but I couldn't go – I couldn't afford to go – but you go – and you stay long enough to make you clever enough to think I'm dirt. That's really clever. But – listen to what I say! – I don't care how brainy you might be – and I've known folk brainy who've never opened a newspaper, never mind a book, didn't have to – I don't care how much you know or how much you don't know – when you're working on my farm under me – you keep a clean mouth and you do what I say. And maybe you'll even learn something.'

'Then I'll be even more clever. Clever enough to leave you to your bloody ranting!'

Nelson turned sharply and walked off. John watched him go. Sorry. But let him go.

It was a large cattle-truck, but Nelson held the steering-wheel with one hand. His arm was crooked around the strong-spoked circle and his thick fingers spread out along it. He smoked and looked at the fields, driving fast, slowing only to lift slightly from his seat and peer at a new construction, some neat buildings, a man working.

He disliked going to Hawick to sell. It was always a waste of time to take off for most of the day and go to an auction. Carlisle was bad enough, but at least he knew one or two people there – and it was nearer. Now was not a good time to part with anything – but he needed capital.

Forcing himself to build, to improve and increase his stock, to bank any large sums he could for the farm he must, eventually, buy and own outright – often left him with little actual cash to get by on. The decision to sell two of his poorer heifers had been taken only when he had been made to realise that, without some money, he would not be able to supplement the winter feed in the way he wanted to.

The roads were deserted. He could drive twenty miles at a stretch without meeting anyone. The cattle-truck – hired for the day from Mr Langolm who farmed down from Wall-End, hired despite the fact that Langolm would have been prepared for Nelson to have borrowed it for nothing, said so in fact, stopped insisting when Nelson's reluctance became surly – held to the middle of the twig-thin passages. From his high cabin, Nelson could see across or through the clipped and autumn-shredded hedges which guided the public way through private land, and he hauled the truck around corners way over on the wrong side of the road.

He hated to be away from his work.

He was in Hawick by ten o'clock, and then the loitering began. He registered his beasts, put them in one of the side pens, and waited for his turn to go into the ring. If he could have trusted John to have done all in the morning on his own, he would have got away two hours sooner.

'Well, why the hell don't you go?' John had demanded.

'And leave you? Not bloody likely!' He reproved himself. 'You might take it into your head to harness a couple of steers to a chariot or summat.' Tried to make a joke of it. Newly afraid of John's fierce look.

'I can get it all cleared myself,' John insisted.

'Be quicker if we both go at it,' his father replied.

'Why don't you let me do it?'

'No reason. I mean – I might as well do *summat* useful today. Might as well do a bit now.'

He turned aside from his son's look. Yet he could not move off and begin the job. John was against him as he had been two days before. Nelson had wondered then – after their argument – why he had not hit him, forced him to concede. The chance had gone.

'But you know I could manage.'

No reply.

'Well?'

Nelson thought of the time already wasted. Still he could not move. John snapped something under his breath and went across to the byres. Nelson followed him.

Now he did not know what to do with himself while he waited for his sale. He was not interested in the exchanging patter which spilled into anecdote and reminiscence; he had neither talent for the former nor taste for the latter. There were one or two big farmers there of whom he would have liked to ask questions – but he did not know them personally; besides which, he was too wary of comment on his own scruffiness to attempt an introduction.

These men – the really big farmers, together with one or two of the more successful dealers, moved around the small auction area as princes. Their clothes were obviously made for the country but equally obviously, made in a big town. The auctioneer's clerks, the auction men, slaughter-men, men who worked for them or sold or bought from them – all edged into their cabal just waiting for a nod or a beckoning wave. Nelson did not want to know them. He did not even own the farm he worked. He was dressed in jacket, trousers and Wellingtons as tattered and patched as could be imagined. He pushed the nub of his cap up his forehead, drove his hands into his pockets, and wandered through the pens and alleyways – down to the pig-market, back to the ring to see how the bidding was going, into the dairy byres, back again, whistling and, occasionally, spitting into the gutter; branding what he felt to be already marked.

When his turn came, he decided to lead the animals round himself. Saved money. He stood in the tiny sawdust ring – sawdust spattered with thick turds and pocked by runnels of sprayed piss – and waited under the lofted auctioneer's box while details were barked out.

Then he started to take the beasts round. One at a time. It was always a loss to sell in pairs.

The ring was surrounded by steeply banked platforming. Its ceiling was a wide and complicated glass roof which had been stuck on to the thick walls as an incongruous helmet at the time the place was built, and not cleaned since that time.

Nelson walked around without looking at anyone. He was a broad man, strong, fine-boned, but as he led his beast, he drooped, trailed his feet a little like a boy, drew on to himself the shabbiness he most hated.

The auctioneer's voice was like a never-ending alarm. Walking-sticks poked across the rail which bordered the ring, digging into the animal's body and haunches. It was far from being a prize beast, but it was a good one. The bids went up steadily. He repeated the performance with the other beast. The price was not as high even though he himself considered this second one to be better. Both were bought by Alfred Wallace-Crawford, one of the big-estate men. Nelson was pleased that they had caught such a discerning eye and he passed them over to one of Crawford's men, cheerful that the ordeal was not worse than his pessimistic expectation.

Wallace-Crawford caught him up as he was making for the truck.

'Have a drink,' he stated, shortly.

Nelson wanted to be off.

'Thanks,' he answered.

The two men went back towards the auction and into the Bell and Anchor. Wallace-Crawford pushed open the door into the saloon bar and, short as he was, marched largely across the narrow strip of carpet in his burnished tweed suit, bristling with quick business and smacking projects.

'Scotch?' he demanded.

'Yes. Thanks.'

In the pretty room with its rubbed brass and tinkling small glasses, Nelson felt an oaf.

'Cheers!'

Wallace-Crawford threw the small golden drink into the top of his mouth and slapped his lips together.

'Another?'

Nelson had not even raised the glass from the counter.

'Two more, Jack.' He said this without looking at the landlord. Fresh drinks were brought. Wallace-Crawford picked up the one which was his, nodded to Nelson to do the same, stumped over to the small table beside the fire and threw himself down on to the seat. In doubt – not knowing whether it was his turn to buy or whether he could let Wallace-Crawford play host, Nelson followed.

'That's better,' Crawford announced, of nothing.

Nelson took off his cap. Then, undecided as to what he should do with it, he held it in his hand, waiting for an occasion to put it on again.

'Good beasts. Those of yours.'

Nelson sipped at the whisky.

'Not your best though. Been told about your herd. What's it like?'

He offered Nelson a cigarette and seemed to watch his taking it, lighting it and drawing on it as if he were conducting an experiment.

'So – so,' Nelson replied.

'Not what I've heard.' He slapped his knee. 'Saw them at the show. Huh!'

'It's startin' to build up.' Nelson was guarded; he did not like to be tricked.

'Use Frankman's bulls, don't you?'

'That's right.'

'Tell me you got a flying start with couple 'a heifers you picked up for nothing.'

'They cost enough.'

Wallace-Crawford grinned, with full-toothed understanding, thrusting the glass into the breach thus opened up in his crimson face.

'You've got the eye – Huh?'

He nudged his guest, heartily. Then, quite suddenly, as if a seizure of responsibility had requisitioned him for action, he dropped his smile, his voice, and his shoulders and discharged his message into Nelson's face.

'How'd you like me to come and look them over? Huh?'

Nelson did not move, but his mind curled back into itself, as if pricked by a sharp needle.

'Well?' Wallace-Crawford went on. 'Just a look-see.' His voice became even more muted until all the rasp went out of it and his breath blobbed puffily through blotting-paper. 'Maybe be something in it for you.'

'I'm not selling, if that's what you mean,' Nelson retorted.

Mr Alfred Wallace-Crawford recoiled as if slapped by a wet rag. That sentence ought to have been uttered, if at all, months later.

'You're rushing things,' he answered, eventually. 'I was merely about to propose that I come down and look your stock over.'

'You can do that and welcome,' said Nelson. 'But I won't part.'

His host stared at the two empty glasses on the small table. Nelson jumped up: it was his turn to treat. He replaced his cap.

'I'll be off then,' he said.

Wallace-Crawford nodded. Nelson almost scuttled out of the bar, accidentally slamming the door behind him, on to the wide street – down to his truck. He should eat – but he drove out of Hawick and stopped at a lorry-driver's café before turning into the side-roads which took him home.

He was proud of this approach, even pleased, in retrospect, at the way he had dealt with it. He must be some good if they were prepared to buy him out! He drove even more quickly than he had done on his way to the auctions. The sky was already slumping towards night and he wanted to look around before it grew too dark; he went right round the farm once each day, whatever happened.

'Where's John then?' he demanded, in the kitchen. He would take him around with him and tell him about it.

'Upstairs, I think,' Lizzie replied.

'What does he think he's doing there?'

'Well. He finished up early. And I think he's a bit worried about that old Colonel Langley.'

Nelson stared at her, totally uncomprehendingly.

'He saw him, you know,' she explained, 'just before he died.'

'Well?' Nelson demanded. 'What of it? Why isn't he out doing something instead of hiding upstairs?'

'We just heard about it after you'd gone. He was very upset.'

Again, Nelson failed to understand.

'I'm sure he'll come and help you if you ask him to.'

Nelson kicked against a chair.

'But he shouldn't need asking!' he shouted. 'He shouldn't have to be asked! He should know!'

He ought to have taught him a lesson in that argument. He had let him get away with it, he was getting soft.

'Come down!' he bellowed. He neither moved from the middle of the kitchen nor pointed his voice at the staircase. 'Come down here and get some bloody work done!'

He listened. Upstairs a door opened. Nelson nodded viciously and made to go out. Then the door slammed shut – loudly.

There was no sound. John was still in his room.

'So the poor old bugger's dead at last then is he?' Nelson disregarded John's disobedience for the moment. 'So the old bugger's dead.' He sat down to consider the new situation.

SEVEN

Arthur felt no pain, no sorrow.

'Death hath no dominion.'

The Reverend Craddock settled into his favourite sermon.

Arthur was unable to concentrate. His recall from London had relieved him from a dutiless vacillation, and his feelings, now freed, could settle nowhere but floated through the little mellow church, out into the empty quiet-bowling countryside around, powdering on to the absorbing peacefulness of indifferent and comforting autumn landscapes. He would not have believed there was so much peace to be found anywhere.

The Reverend Craddock articulated his sentences with particular clarity; partly because of the habit of his mouth which seemed, these days, to be determined so to fill with relish that every syllable spluttered out with over-lubricated enthusiasm; and partly because he held captive the almost unique haul of a congregation both large and – his conscience stumbled, but lamely, against the word – 'consequent'.

Arthur settled as comfortably as possible on to the T-squared rectitude of the dove-grey pew. It was a time to spin artificial generalisations. They relieved the precisions which had condemned him to inertia.

He observed that a man must do something very outrageous for his death to be much different from that for which his birth had fitted him. Colonel Langley was being buried with full county honours: honours which, in his last year or two – when he had finally decided that sudden death would be preferable to the cultivated feebleness of his blown-out body – he had tried far beyond their accepted limits.

The Territorial Army, in which the Colonel had held high office since his retirement, officers from his old regiment, members of The Hunt, of which – at one time – he had been MFH, officials from the local cricket and football clubs – he had been an indefatigable vice-president, although lately his duties had not much exceeded his subscriptions – they were there; so were the friends who had recently stopped coming to see him – usually, in fairness to them, because of a sudden and adamant announcement on his part that he would issue no more invitations to people with whom he came into contact for no better reason than proximity – and more friends, those who had travelled a long way for the service and were only now beginning to sense the mixed feelings behind the uniform expression of distressed forbearance. He was being buried in the village church – on his own orders – which, until recently, he had attended punctiliously.

Arthur wished that he had known his father better during the last two or three years. Meeting him then, he had been both impressed and amused at the way in which the old man had started to behave exactly as he wanted to behave. He had loved the rumours of his father's scandalous activities, and even though, in London, they could seem little more than the gentle balloon-pricking of a rumbustious second childhood – he knew that his father must have been enjoying himself enormously and this moved him in a way far more profound than the thought of anything else his father had done. But their encounters – when Arthur had come home on leave – had still been cold with inhibited formality although, if he tried hard and indulged his hope with imagination, he could remember a few glances, words, actions which seemed designed specifically for the especial secrecy of father and son; with reference to no one else and with the implied familiarity of an unformulated joke between two like friends. He ought to have come earlier during those last two months; even though his mother had never quite insisted that it was serious.

If the Reverend Craddock was precise, he was also merciful, and the sermon, though heavy, was short. Brevity was encouraged by the emphatic report of germ-free coughs which began like a ragged salute when he was no more than six minutes in and, from then on, continued steadily.

John was near the west door, in the back pew, barred from the rest of the congregation by three rows of empty pews immediately in front of him. He had not even bothered to undergo the indignation of argument with his father about coming to the funeral. Nelson would never allow himself to understand what he did not wish to know; for him, there were no explanations, only lapses. John had told his mother, dressed quickly, and left. During the service he had thought of nothing but his blow which, he was sure, had led to the old man's eventual death.

As the procession followed the coffin down the nave, John bowed his head. He saw Arthur and Patricia; they looked younger than Shirley, younger even than Avril. Yet they must be about ten years older than he was. He tried to work out their ages as the mourners filed past; he had to occupy himself with details.

The coffin was carried out and into the churchyard and then to the cemetery which lay around it. The graves were trimly kept, but now wrapt with russet, wine, old yellow leaves which curled, dead, on the fading hummocks of green. This was not the birthplace of a line of Langleys, yet there was some family tradition in that his wife's people had lived in the district for some time.

Arthur felt his mother weighted on his arm. He had found her stunned, suspended; the point had gone and left her in such a position of strain that she could move neither on nor back. She was desolate. As they crunched, gracelessly, along the short gravel path, he saw her face and looked away. She had not cried, yet the skin seemed stained with the abandoned scalds of unwept tears.

She had said nothing to him when he had got home. Pat had been with her, and he knew that he had come in at the end of an argument.

'He won't see her,' Pat announced.

Arthur winced at her blowsy abruptness.

'Is he in – the bedroom?'

'Dr Barwise is with him at the moment.'

'Will he have to go to hospital?'

'I don't think that they can do anything there that can't be
done here.'

His mother spoke up at last, ignoring Pat, directly to him.

'There is nothing at all that can be done for him,' she said,
and then, as if to gain momentum through some impasse – words
would do – she passed on to him a jumbled account of
Dr Barwise's diagnosis, trying to explain each term as she came
to it; monotonously going on, her gaze resting against Arthur's
face, seeing nothing.

Later in the evening, Arthur had gone up to his father's room.
Pat had opened the door to him and, without allowing him to
see inside, closed it behind her and joined him in the corridor.

'He doesn't want to see anyone but me,' she whispered.

He looked at her; he could not bear her exclusive excitement.

'Is he awake?'

'Yes.' Still she whispered. Arthur had spoken in a normal tone
and her whisper further irritated him by implying a reproach,
'but it upsets him if anyone goes in but me'.

'I'll wait until later, then'.

He left her. He wanted no details, no confessions.

He saw his father on the following morning. Pat had gone into
Aldeby with his mother. The old man was asleep. Arthur looked
at him and saw no one in the face. He glanced around the room
and saw nothing in the room. There were no reminders. He
looked at his father but could feel nothing. Guilty at this, he
tried to excuse himself by blaming his stupor on the last few
months; Oliver leaving, the long hangover of pressure of the
doss-house, his own indecision, fear. How could he respond
to his father's death? Yet – how could he not do so? He darted
out of the room when he heard the car sweep into the yard
below.

They were at the graveside. Freshly dug with the thick, rich
earth banking the sides, ready tossed for planting the most
delicate seeds. The Reverend Craddock was reading the burial
service. Arthur had been confused in the church. It did not seem
correct to have a sermon. It must have been his father's wish.

There was no established way for all those at the funeral to
stand around the grave and so, except for the family mourners,

those present crowded, tightly pressed together almost peeping at the long oak coffin.

Arthur looked at Pat. Her black coat and hat, the black hair which fell long beneath it, framed a face which contrast made appear marble. Her stillness added to its delicacy by showing off the wisp-brushed features with settled composure. Yet Arthur knew her face as quick, leaping from one mood to another, the cheeks a fine pink, touched brown with the weather, the eyes flicking with vivid feeling. She was very beautiful; he saw her standing beside her uncle, as straight as a boy, ready, somehow, to fly into another circumstance at a tinkle, yet withdrawn, even arrogant. She looked at him – steadily, almost probingly. He turned his eyes to the coffin. It would soon be over.

John left the black-coated clump behind him and went to the Elliotts for a drink. He drank a lot. There was no compelling reason to do so; but there was no compelling reason to do anything. There was no pattern which had been spoiled. Even in the church, in which, at this, one of its few essential moments, he had felt some impulses of a Sunday-school Pilgrim's Progress reach him – even then, he had been unable to relate his own life to a plan, a pattern and so to see the possibility, however remote, of pieces being reslotted, aims rediscovered. Christianity had been the spice in the growing forces which had channelled his paganism towards an acceptance of orderly humanity, but it did not comfort. There was no pattern.

Actions were taken depending on actions previously taken, and they fell away or intensified through the force of their original and accumulating interest; but that interest depended not on a whole, not on a code, but on the multi-fragments of motives which experience had driven into a rhythm.

It was the rhythm. The rhythm had been broken.

By two-thirty on the afternoon of the following Saturday, John was drunk.

'Cheer up, then!' said Dickie.

'It's my afternoon off,' John replied, soddenly.

'Well, cheer up then.'

'You would think I was pinchin' something.'

'Take no notice of him. He's always been a bastard. Always was. Still is,' Dickie answered unsteadily.

John prickled at this, but he was too drowsy in his drunkenness, and too inquisitive about anything said of his father, to want to stop Dickie. In a way, John's complaints were little more than words easy to find in the state in which he was, for the rankle against his father, though it had caused bitterness, was now too deeply a part of his life to bubble into such a facile lament. Nevertheless anything said about his father had to be pursued, and his curiosity lapped over his caution.

'Now then,' said John, even more torpidly than before, banging his glass on the table to emphasise his openness to confidence. 'Now then,' he repeated, waveringly, 'what makes you say that, eh? What – makes – you – say – that?'

Dickie felt sure of his ground.

'He's a miserable bastard, your father is. A mis-er-able bastard,' he explained.

'Now then,' John persisted. 'Granted,' he belched. 'Pardon.' His fist swung up to a mouth already closed, its job done.

'Granted,' said Dickie, primly.

'Yes,' John took up the point, 'but what I want to know is – why do you? What grounds have you for saying what you've just said? What grounds?'

'My grounds,' Dickie replied, 'is that I know the bugger.'

'Fair enough,' said John.

'Can't say better than that.'

'No. Can't say better than that.' John chewed his mouth around, as if sucking out a bit from between his front teeth, and considered his next move.

'Of course,' he began, 'you know him.'

'By Christ, that's true!'

'Always have.'

'By Christ, yes!'

'And he's always been the same?'

'No difference. Same when he was young, same when he started, same as he is now.' Then, calling up resources of fraternal and family remembrance. 'He's the only one of us who's ever been like that.'

'The only one.'

'Nobody else is miserable!'

'That's true, that.'

The Foster family spread throughout Cumberland like a scattering of sand; three sisters, two other brothers besides Dickie and Nelson – all rarely, if ever, in touch with each other since their childhood; all except Dickie and Nelson, modestly working as farm labourers, in small factories, the sisters married to men who did the same as their two more normal brothers. Dickie, if ever he met them, treated them rather grandly and gave long stories for drinks. Nelson was avoided by all of them.

'Why do you think that is, then,' John continued, 'that he's like he is?'

Dickie took a pull which emptied his glass, and only when its appeal had been patently noticed by John – noticed with a movement of the seat which promised expedition both to pocket and to bar – only then did he reply.

'Greedy,' he announced. 'Greedy as a bloody pig.'

John abandoned the subject and went for two more pints.

Outside, at quarter-past three, with the drink so solidly in him that he rocked on his heels like a doll with leaded ball-bearings under his feet, John stood with nothing to do. Dickie had popped around to the back.

On week-days there was the possibility that people were inside at work to explain the bareness of Aldeby's streets; on Saturdays, with no such possibility, and the streets seemingly barer than at any other time, the town was entirely withdrawn; not expectant, deserted. The houses were low-roofed and poor-looking; any exception – a large residence or a public building – seemed somehow impermanent, 'stagey', beside the seasoned dourness of the rows of cottages which opened straight on to the streets. The business and social centre for an area of scores of square miles was on this Saturday afternoon without sight of a policeman, a clergyman, a bustling solicitor's clerk, an assembled meeting or a function of any description.

'They're all playin' Pitch and Toss,' said Dickie.

'Where?'

'Over the railway. Coming?'

John followed him.

'It's a craze,' Dickie explained. 'They used to play it on Sundays just. Now it's whenever there's a minute.'

Down an alley between two rows of cottages, across a patch of allotments where one or two faces peeped up at them from the bare gardens and smoke from dead leaves laced lazy patterns from one to another, fusking the railed-off plots so that their owners, squinting up to look at the loud-footed passers, were as survivors on a rubbish dump. Under the half barrel, mossed and lichened, of a bridge slotted into the railway embankment like a toy drum. Up the narrow path which led on to the village where Avril's Tony lived. Off that, to the left, and they came to the clearing.

'You've got to be careful,' Dickie warned him. 'Police.' He looked serious. John nodded.

The ground was between two shoulders of green bank which looked like funeral mounds. The game was played between them as in an alley. At the farther end, where the peg was fixed, there was a copse which led to soggy, swampy ground – never deep enough even to paddle in, never dry enough to walk over – and the approach from the path was by a thin track which twisted considerably through high gorse bushes. A man sat on the top of one of the hillocks, keeping a look-out.

It was half-a-crown a game. The game lasted no more than ten minutes at the most. A lot of money could be lost in an afternoon. Sometimes the stakes were doubled, even quadrupled; once or twice, raised to a pound.

'You play,' Dickie advised, 'I'm too tired.'

The grey day, with slapping gusts of wind which lifted the skin, this filled John so that he floated across to the huddle of men. The game had been refined to crude simplicity; the coins were simply laid across the curved joint of the index finger and flicked into the air with the thumb; that nearest to the peg won.

John played four games without being in the first three, or even the first six; in the first, he flicked too weakly, and the coin fell no more than four yards in front of him; the second and third were little better, and on his last throw, he swung up his arm as he released his thumb-nail, and the dull half-crown flew way over the peg.

All the players were serious. Some crouched, others stood straight up; some stood sideways on, others four-square; from some fists, the coin lifted in a low trajectory, from others it swooped in a high arc. The game was played in silence which, it seemed, was only permissibly broken by the grunt of satisfaction or disgust allowed to the man who had just thrown.

One, more than any of the others, attracted John's attention; and sitting now, with the pints of heavy drink settling in his hunched stomach, his eyes took in less and less detail; he followed out the games by watching this man only.

He played nervelessly, each time jutting his body forward as he threw, scuttling up to the peg immediately to see his position. Standing rooted as he watched others come nearer to the mark than himself, slinking back to his dog, head buried in his knotted scarf as if in shame. This dog was a whippet, tied to a small log. Between games, the man would stroke its starved, shivering haunches, hand trailing across its razed coat without an eye to guide it; look riveted on the peg, the lob of half-crowns, the Winners.

It was obvious he had not much money; equally plain that he would not leave until he had lost what he did have. His face was cast in permanent thwarted determination. It was the face of an old grape, dried to grey slits but still somehow shiny from the seeping desertion of its last juice.

He tried and failed again. Three times John had seen him go to the heel-dragged brown line, toss his coin, and lose; the last time, he broke his walk back to the whippet and searched through his pockets for change to swop for half-a-crown. Some of those he approached tried to wave him off, to prevent him from losing more. He would say nothing, just turn his back and look for someone else.

John pushed himself to his feet. His legs were frailly attached to the tight lump of drink which lay inside his stomach, his hands were floating somewhere like the pole of a tight-rope walker, his mouth was strewn with the particles of a musty passage and his tongue touched numb lips tenderly.

'Here,' he said. Then he himself went over to the man.

'Here,' he repeated. 'I've a half-crown. Take it.'

The man picked it off the palm of John's hand and listed his trading pile of pennies and threepenny bits and two sixpences.

'Keep it,' John said. 'Have this one on me.'

'What for?'

'I want you to.'

The man looked at him, and, looking up, the wrinkles ran together so that his whole face was a pouch of knife-scrawled incisions – each moistened in its deep groove.

'What do you want to do that for?'

'I can't play myself,' John explained. 'Pissed. I want you to play for me.'

'What if I win?'

'Half and half.' He emphasised the deal by chopping his hands in front of his face.

'And I owe you nowt if I lose.'

'That's right.'

He regarded the heavy coin attentively. Then he nodded to John and took his place. John changed a ten-shilling note for four half-crowns, then he went to join him.

The first time, he lost.

'Have another go.'

'Still pissed?' the man asked, allowing the slightest touch of anxiety to characterise his face for the first time.

'As a newt,' John confirmed, belching to prove it.

The second time, he lost again.

'Another.' An order.

He took the coin and took his place. John was close to him. When his turn came, he began to give him encouragement and advice. But the man lost for the third time.

Again, John was ready with the coin.

'Just one more after this,' he warned. 'Throw it up a bit. Get your nail under it. Aim a bit the other side of the peg. And think about it, that's what you've got to do. Think about it. Pretend you've hit it before you start! Go on, now. Think about it!'

The other men were getting restless. John was speaking with the volume of the deaf. The man, willing to undergo anything for the chance to try again, listened and nodded and so encouraged him. John ignored the voices telling him to shut up. He saw Dickie waving to him or something, from far away; he shouted out to him to stop breaking his concentration.

The man came up to the line. John watched him, hopeless. He never got anywhere near it. But the man's face was so depressed, so burdened, crushed, exploited, abandoned, ignored – so painfully stamped by the boots of everything he had met – so much had hit him, so much more had missed him – that John yelled, this time, yelled him on like a one-man football crowd.

He flicked, and the coin plopped down, way out of reach.

'You've got to get it this time!' John bellowed. 'You've got to. I've got one more – and then that's it. Not going to change anything else! Come on! Think about it!'

'Shut up!'

'Be quiet for Christ's sake!'

'Give somebody else a chance, can't you?'

John took no notice of the remarks and kept on lecturing his legatee at the top of his voice. He stood beside him in the line, all the time encouraging him, showing how the action should be done.

'Not so noisy,' Dickie advised, cryptically. A butt stuck to his dry lip; John expected it to pop inside the mouth at an imminent whistle of danger.

'What?'

'They want to get on with their game in peace.'

'To hell with them!'

He turned to his partner. This time the man took terrific care. Looked at the coin, looked at the peg, back to the coin, up again to the peg, flexed his knees, jutted his chest forward, paused, and then:

'It's a beauty!' John thundered. 'A beauty! A winner!'

And dragging the pitcher along with him, he hurried up to the mark, treading on unsuccessful coins on his way there. 'You're right next to it. Eh?'

Someone tried to guide them away, to stop them crowding the target, but John pushed him off.

There were two more to throw. The first came close, but John's coin was still clearly in front. Its thrower stared at it, immovably, as if to look away would cause it to jump back. The last entrant came to his turn; he was the winner of the previous game. His coin spun into the air, seemed, at one stage, to be going far too high, then fell, smack on John's half-crown, sliding from it to rest in front of it, nearest the peg.

'A draw!' John shouted.

The man came up.

'To hell with that. I've won.'

The others joined him.

'That's what it looks like now,' John explained, 'but yours landed right on top of that one. So it's a draw. That's where it landed.' He pointed.

'It's not where it finished up.'

'That doesn't matter.'

'It does the way we play.'

'Well it shouldn't. You two should split it.'

The man who had thrown last was losing patience. So were the others around him.

'Look, lad,' he said. 'You've been making a nuisance ever since you came here. I won and that's all there is to it. Don't be so daft.'

He bent to pick up the coin. John jabbed out his foot to cover them.

'Half of this is his.'

One of the men who had been controlling the game stepped forward abruptly to end this.

'He won. He takes it. If you don't like our rules – go back to where you came from.'

John was ready for a fight. He widened his stance and glared at the interrupter.

'I say it's split.'

'What you say means nothing.'

John waited. The man crouched down to pick up the winnings.

'Leave it!'

He began to gather the coins.

'Put them down or I'll take them from you!'

Without looking up, he collected the money. Two or three others helped him. Soon the kitty was collected and the lot of them faced him. While they had been on the ground, John had stood, fists tightened, ready for – he did not know what.

The man he had helped had gone back to his whippet. John saw him undo the lead from the trunk and go away.

'I would go and sober up a bit if I was you.'

John nodded. Dickie motioned to him. They left together. 'Come to my place,' Dickie said. 'I'll see if I can find some tea.'

Once in Dickie's room, he fell asleep.

When he woke up, it was dark. The fire was out. Dickie had left. He dragged himself up from the springless sofa on which he had been lying and turned the light on. It was half-past eight. He went across to the chipped enamel sink and stripped to the waist before dowsing himself with cold water. The towel rubbing against his face shook his creaking head so that it ached. He tried not to think of his behaviour at the pitch and toss school. But an image of himself as he then had been persisted in his mind; bullying, stupid.

Dickie's room was so bare and shamelessly dirty that John was afraid of it. There was neither wallpaper nor carpets, the table was crammed with half-emptied tins and bottles, some having been used as ashtrays. What furniture there was was broken down and barren; the bed stank, the sheets were yellow. He was sick at the thought of Dickie's connection with this room – and with himself. If he could take – even take refuge in – the one, why not the other? It was foul.

He went out, down the street to the pub to collect his van. He was surprised to find it exactly where he had left it.

The streets were again empty, always empty, but at least, at night, there was some indication of a population – in the pubs. It was too early to go back.

Alan was inside, with his girlfriend. John brought them drinks, taking whisky for himself. He had not the strength to face the deep pints.

'Going to t' dance are you?' he demanded.

'No,' Alan replied.

'Thought you went every Saturday.'

'Not this. They're no good in this place now.'

His girlfriend nodded. She was shy yet brisk, with a jersey wool skirt which slipped slyly up over her knees, only to be caught every time before the stocking top, and tugged down to respectable length. John was fascinated by the smooth nylon burnish of calves, momentarily shown thigh, even the knees.

Alan caught his look.

'What are you doing here?' he asked.

John raised his glass.

'This.'

He swallowed the whisky in one.

'Another?'

Alan had a brown and bitter, his girl, a gin and orange.

'I've just started.'

The girl, in reply, sipped half her small drink away.

'You could do with another, then,' John said, sentimentally, 'let me get you another.'

She looked at Alan. He examined John, then laughed.

'If it means you can get yourself some more – bring them up!' he answered. 'And you can bring me one of them,' pointing to an empty whisky-glass, 'while you're about it'.

John nodded gratefully and went to the bar. The whisky had tickled his stomach – empty but for the flushings of beer – and he was extraordinarily quick and light. When he came back, it was obvious that Alan had been saying something about him – both of them were grinning at him with the expression which indicated that they were amused at his behaviour and did not mind if he knew it.

'What's the matter?'

'Nothing.'

'You'll be taken away one of these days . . . laughing for nothing.'

He sat down and pushed the drinks over to them. He had taken a double for Alan and himself. Alan poured his into the pint. They sat, silent.

'Come on then,' John demanded. 'Something went on.'

'I was just telling Jean that it wouldn't be long before you were having a go.'

'At what?'

Alan raised his glass and sucked hugely at it, sticking up his thumb and pointing to Jean while he did so.

'You never know,' John replied, steadily.

But he could not keep the uncertainty from his voice. One more quick, rather subdued drink, and he left.

As he drove he was as clear-minded as he had ever been. Only his mind seemed to be somewhere undiscoverable, a hard glint bedded in his slowly dipping body. Never been out with a girl. No reason he could think of. Just never been out with a girl. He slammed down on the accelerator and shifted the jeep to the middle of the road so that he would have more space for manoeuvre. Jean was all right though, Alan would be doing himself no harm there. He snorted at the veiled, enticing vision, rather dirty, which the thought called up. Doing no harm at all!

They were lying on the bank of the hedge. There was a wide grass verge, then a ditch, and beyond that a small margin of foothold which pushed up to a broad bank. Shirley was lying facing John's headlights. He could see through her coat, through the opened blouse, bare breasts. The man was half-straddled across her.

He pushed hard on the brakes; he had to reverse to come opposite them.

'Get in,' he snapped.

'Who do you think you are?'

'Hello, John.' She spoke as if they were meeting on a street.

'I'm her brother. That's who I am.'

'Pleased to meet you.' The man laughed.

'Get in then,' John repeated.

'We've got transport,' she replied. 'Thanks all the same.'

'Yes. We've got transport.'

John made the man out. He was broad, quite small, his face so smooth that it might have been treated with sandpaper. He wore a charcoal grey suit, almost new, pockets bulging, buttons tight fastened, an open-necked white shirt flapping out of the lapels.

'Have you been to the dance?' Shirley asked. He noticed that she had made no attempt to button herself up; her coat had been wrapped around her and she held it at the front with both hands.

'We went,' the man informed him. 'Good do, we're going back.'

John tried to steady himself, and in doing so, seemed to lever open an enormous capsule of whisky – the smell and taste from which rushed sickeningly into his mouth.

'I'm taking her home.'

'Are you sure you're feeling all right?' Shirley came right up to the van and poked her head into the open window-frame. 'You look awful,' she commented.

'You're coming back with me,' he mumbled. Then, feebly, 'Tart.'

'John!' She did not withdraw her head. If there was to be an argument it would be between the two of them. 'You've no right to say that.'

'Get in and shut up.'

'You've no right to call me that name.'

He looked at her. She was pleading, sulkily pushing back on to him the guilt which had not rested on her for more than an instant. John thrust his arm at her face, grabbed her hair and pulled her head towards him.

'You're coming with me. Now!'

She whimpered, and then, as his pulling grew firmer, she began to cry. The door on John's passenger side was yanked open and the man almost dived across the seat and snatched at John's wrist. For a few moments, he held on; then Shirley's boyfriend punched him in the stomach. He let her go. She jumped back from the car, coat wide open. He could see that her skirt had been swivelled around her hips so that the zip was at the front. That, too, was open.

The man punched him again.

'What did you do that for?' he demanded.

John did not reply. He thought he was going to be sick. Beside him the man quivered – daring a fight.

'Leave her alone,' John said eventually.

'What business is it of yours, eh? What has it to do with you? We were enjoying ourselves till you came. Eh? D'you want to make something of it?'

'If you don't get out of this van, I'll break your neck.'

'Try!' The man shuttled around on the seat so that his legs were half-drawn up underneath him and his shoulders were square on to John. 'Come on then. Try it!'

'No!' Shirley had run around to the other side. 'No!' she cried, 'I don't want you to fight. John! I don't want you to fight him. Please!'

'Go on!' the man repeated. 'Try it. Go on. Try it! Try it!'

John looked through the windscreen. He wanted nothing to do with either of them.

'Oh, go away and play your dirty games.'

'What do you mean by that?'

John turned the key and started up the car. Shirley opened the door and put her arm around her boyfriend's shoulders.

'Come on then,' he demanded. 'What d'you mean by saying that?'

He revved up the engine as loudly as he could.

'You want to mind your own bloody business, that's what you want to do,' the man shouted.

John jerked the car forward. Shirley started away from it. The man got out to join her. John slammed the door, and went off.

He made for the Wall, because it was a dead-end. No one was likely to trouble him there.

Walking the last hundred yards or so, he reached the edge. This was the sheer drop. A thick basket of blackness supporting nothing, concealing everything.

He had fumbled and dribbled through the day without either drugging himself or breaking the smothering inertia which had settled on him. Everything had been shabby.

He was on the very edge. One step forward. Over. He bent down and felt it. Here the Wall had been rebuilt, and was quite solid. Turning his back to the edge, he eased himself out, letting his legs fall down the face of the Wall. His feet touched holds in its surface. Soon he was flat against the side of the Wall, his fingers holding on to the top.

He swung his feet away from their holds. All his fingers were clenched on to the scabbed, damp rock. It would be just the same to let go and drop. His nose touched a thatch of moss. He could again smell his whisky breath, pumping up his body. It would be easy.

Then he laughed. His fingers were sweating and he crabbed them along to get a better grip. It might be drizzle or it might be sweat on his face. His feet dangled, way down. He would see how long he could hold on.

He began to sing. Not very loudly. In perfect tune and time.

> *'For he's a jolly good fellow*
> *For he's a jolly good fellow*
> *For he's a jolly good fe-e-llow.*
> *And so say all of us.'*

He repeated the verse twice and then stopped. Silence. No one had heard. Then he pulled himself back on to the Wall. It was stupid.

EIGHT

'You're very mean.'

Arthur did not look up. But he closed his book. Reassured, Patricia came into the room and sat in the only other chair. They were in the summerhouse, claimed by Arthur as his 'den' since he'd been about eleven. It stood at the end of what had been a well-preserved ornamental garden – now overgrown through lack of labour – well away from the house, and overlooking the bottom field of Wall-End Farm. In it, besides Arthur's piano and two large armchairs, there was little else but books and 'curios'. This latter word – insisted upon by Arthur – covered a rather tentative collection of Roman glass, two small Persian vases, dry-point drawings, silks. Right across one of the walls, there was an enormous tapestry – a cheap reproduction, but nevertheless warm and beautiful – representing a courtly hunt, with all those gentlemen not on horseback standing in elegant cross-legged pose at the side of long dimpled ladies.

This den was private.

'You've locked yourself away ever since you came back,' she went on.

'I thought that everybody would want to be on their own . . .'

'At a time like this,' she concluded for him, and giggled.

'Did Mummy tell you?' she asked.

'What?'

'How it happened.'

'No.'

'It was awful.'

She knew her brother was offended by what she was saying. For this reason, she continued:

'He was drunk, of course. He'd been on the drink all the afternoon – Mummy pretending not to know – that's how she's been doing it the last few months, you know – and anyway she was saddled with some stupid nuts-and-bolts man. He was up at Rosley – took him there myself as a matter of fact – then he seems to have tried to ride back on Foster's pony – and ended it all by letting Andrei drag him home. Terrible!' Then, affectionately, she added: 'Poor old thing.'

'Thank you,' Arthur replied.

'Why didn't you come home right away?' she demanded.

'I did. I caught the first train after your telegram.'

'I don't mean that.'

Arthur was silent. He resented being the excuse for his sister's callousness about their father.

'Why didn't you come back as soon as you'd resigned your commission?'

'You must have read my letter.'

'Yes. But you could have thought things over up here. I should have thought that London would have been the last place for that.'

'There were some people I wanted to see.'

'Oh.'

Patricia was halted in full bustle. While talking to Arthur, the tense privacy of her bearing had softened to a mistimed excitement. Her hands signalled out of rhythm with the emphasis in her speech; she let her body droop when speaking fiercely – made as if to jump to her feet in the middle of an even sentence or silence. And Arthur, never looking at her, withdrew into precision and coldness.

'What did you decide?' she asked.

'I haven't yet made up my mind.'

'What are the alternatives?'

'Obviously, I'll have to stay here for a while.'

'And then?'

'I think I'll go away.'

'Where?'

He shrugged his shoulders. The notion was so fragile in his

own mind. He did not want it to be destroyed through mis-handling at such an unprepared stage.

'I suppose you want to trot off to Sarawak or some such hold and do good and look at sunsets and be inconspicuous all at once.'

Arthur took out a packet of Players – withdrew one of the anonymous white tubes from the carton – and flicked on his lighter.

'Have you heard from Oliver?' she asked him.

He lit the cigarette. He ought never to have told her about Oliver.

'In fact, I thought you'd go with him. Why didn't you?'

Arthur shook his head. That was enough. Patricia gave up, slumped back in her large armchair, and looked past him, out of the window. Arthur turned towards her and they began to talk about their friends in the area.

'How long will you stay?' asked Mrs Langley, later.

'Until everything is cleared up,' Arthur replied.

'That may take a long time,' his mother went on. 'Your father,' she paused, 'there are debts'.

'I know.'

'Oh?'

'Williams told me. I went to see him yesterday.'

'I see.' Mrs Langley nodded, giving him her permission for having gone to the family solicitor without consulting her and, at the same time, indicating her gratitude for his command of affairs.

They were sitting in the long drawing-room. Annie had served tea and Mrs Langley's conversation was given the gracious aid of useful action. Besides the almost constant reshuffling of tiny plates, cups, the sugar and milk bowl, the teapot – all this directed her nervousness into something which absorbed it undemandingly.

The room itself was surprising. Not for the heavy, solid generation-tasted furniture which lay about it like an emblem of gracious country-house comfort, but for the touches, light – two eighteenth-century copies of Italian primitives – delicate – a supple Tudor chest, dark oak enravishingly carved, in its setting, a flight, an indulgence – yet strong touches which had been laid by Arthur's father and himself and gave the stable room an elevation, a disturbance – contradicting the unquestioning assumption of its values – a detachment.

'And so you may settle down here,' Mrs Langley went on.

'I don't think so.'

'But you will be here for a while?'

'Yes, Mother.'

His unresigned patience jerked her into a realisation of her coercion.

'Did Williams suggest what we might do?'

'Yes. It will have to be something rather drastic.'

'Sell?'

'Yes.'

'Did he suggest what?'

'He did, but I didn't quite agree with him. I would like to sell Foster his farm.'

'But that's – could he afford it?'

'Williams seemed to think he might be able to.'

'We get a good rent from him now, you know. He persuaded your father to install many things at Wall-End.'

'I don't know yet,' Arthur said. Then, to conclude something he did not want to talk about for fear that its cause might be brought up and exposed – to the pain both of his mother and himself – he went on: 'We'll see about it, anyway. There's no great hurry.'

'I'm glad you've decided to hunt,' she went on, as happy to change a subject as to remain with it. 'You'll be able to pick things up again quite easily that way.'

He knew what she meant – and felt obliged to challenge her so that his silence might not later be taken for agreement.

'I'm hunting for the sport, Mother,' he replied. 'Not for the invitations.'

'But they'll come all the same, dear,' she answered him.

'And if they come as a condition of the hunt, then I shall stop hunting.'

'That would be rather unreasonable, wouldn't it?'

'It would be perfectly reasonable – given my own reasons.'

'You haven't told me what those reasons are.'

'To do it for the sport, Mother.'

He smiled, gently, and Mrs Langley was relieved. She expressed this relief in a mime of tea-pouring and plate-patting, again seeming to suit the action to some phrases she might once have spoken. Her fingers were deft. Arthur noticed how firm the skin still was on her hands.

Then, she stopped; there was no conclusion. Arthur felt that he was playing a tentative charade. It was his duty to guess what his mother was about to say and to be prepared to reassure her while not committing himself, through sympathy, to answers which would encumber him with later obligations.

She began to talk about the army. About his father's career, his own postings, dwelling on his successes, nudging him towards regret.

'Why are you so insistent?' he asked. 'Did you expect me to stay in the army all my life?'

'I would not have been unhappy if you had done so,' she replied. 'At the very least it gave you a career. I can't see what you are going to do now. You may have plans – but you never tell me of them and I won't ask – unless you wish it. But there is little for you to do here.'

'Father found enough to occupy himself with.'

'He was ill and old enough to have retired,' she answered, nervously. 'And you are young and healthy.'

'Would it make you feel better if I told you that I did have plans?'

'My feelings are unimportant.'

Immediately, she appeared to forget what they had been saying. Returning to her mime, she gave no indication of being either answered or satisfied. Nor did she show concern. Arthur waited for her next jump, but when she did speak, it was to make a trivial request. He could see that all they had talked about, even though unconcluded, was now dismissed. She was considering her next move. Each morning, she made a list of activities, visits and general arrangements – all neatly pencilled on blue note-paper – and she worked through the day according to these declarations, concerned only to spread out her preoccupations over the necessary length of time. Since her husband's death, she had been as an unsupported web.

After tea, and after Arthur had self-consciously helped Annie with the washing-up, he went to the summerhouse. Pat was out taking back a relative to the station at Newcastle and so he would be undisturbed. Before going into the garden which led to his den, he waited until Andrei, walking towards him, caught him up. The two men went along the weed-bulging path, talking about the new tractor which Andrei had been proposing, discreetly, since Arthur's return.

He was writing his diary when Annie came to announce the Reverend Craddock. The old vicar was waiting for him in the drawing-room. After civilities, he began:

'I won't try to disguise the purport of this visit. I came to ask you about your interest in the Wall.'

Arthur was puzzled at this unexpected task.

'The Roman Wall. Hadrian's, or more exactly, Agricola's Wall – though even that is not quite accurate.'

He paused, peeping over his glasses to see if his scholastic sally had met with a response which might be encouraging to one of an academic turn.

'You see,' he went on, 'your dear father was – Honorary President.'

'Of what?'

'Of,' the dry fingers fluttered into patterns of exclusive self-indulgence, 'of our Society.'

'To preserve it?'

'To explore it,' the vicar corrected. 'To keep the spirit of its builders alive with the formalin of scholarship.' Again, the mouse-peep; this time, a smile; sufficient for him to continue: 'Your – the Colonel did not disclose the extent of his concern over our work to many; but I know that it was very close to him. He was a man who believed that certain things were worth doing, whatever the labour, whatever the cost.' This time, he pushed back his glasses on to the top of his nose, and looked squarely at Arthur. 'The cost was always reasonable, of course, very reasonable. But even had it been twice what it was I'm sure your father would have paid. Indeed he used to say that, as President of the Society, his chief function was Treasurer. His joke, you know. I am the Treasurer.'

'I see.'

'Yes,' the vicar concluded. Then, as if he had unaccountably caught himself out telling a white lie, the old man blushed and bobbed away. He had put his case clearly – and the Society meant a considerable amount to him – but he realised his rudeness in so artlessly articulating his hopes. The Society meant so much to him, however, that he could not contain his worry for its future one day longer.

'I would like to join your Society,' said Arthur. 'Could I?'

'But we'd be delighted!'

'I'm afraid I know nothing about archaeology. Or about the Romans.'

'But here's your chance.' The vicar was moved to an agitated foot-fussing which threatened to break into an Anglican war-dance. 'Here's your chance!'

'Of course,' said Arthur, gently, 'I shall be only too honoured to continue any – relationship which might have existed between the Society and my father.'

'We can elect you. We can decide . . .'

'As an ordinary member,' Arthur interrupted, 'what would be my function?'

The Reverend Craddock looked abashed for a moment. Everything had worked so perfectly – even to the hope beyond all planning that Arthur might refuse the post of president. Mr Stoneman, who had written articles for the Cumberland & Westmorland Archaeological and Antiquarian Society's quarterly publication, had long emphasised the importance of the leadership residing in the right place; in this case, as he put it, 'in the ditches!' Now – he could be offered the post, with nothing lost.

'What would I do?' Arthur repeated.

Whipping off his spectacles with an agile swipe from his left hand, the old vicar thrust out his right hand and cried:

'Dig! . . . Dig! Dig! Dig!'

Arthur walked the vicar to the gate and saw him on to his ancient 150-c.c. motor cycle. Then, instead of returning to the

summerhouse to write, instead of returning to the house to be
met by his mother's enquiries about his social movements – and,
perhaps, be pestered by Pat, he decided to walk over to the
Wall.

This path took him past the Foster farm. He wanted to sell
to Nelson Foster. He admired the way he had worked with his
son – forcing his way through all the slow manoeuvres of rural
acquisition. And it would be so much easier than all the binding
strategy needed to hold things together while the debts were
paid. Throw it aside! There was something in the very unwisdom
of selling which was attractive. Lighten the inheritance! He
wanted neither to display a monument for the present, nor to
erect a line which would tie him to posterity. Let Foster have
it.

He walked up the hill and then dropped down the little slope
which went to the stream. Nothing but gorse bushes, heather,
wet-grey little peep-stones of rock – a no-man's wilderness
with unplumed trees posted to guard a safe return for the
spring. Arthur walked down to the stream and jumped it – his
foot sinking heavily in the mossy mire on its farther bank.
Then, surrounded by nothing, not a sound which broke the
boundless space of silence, he climbed to the Wall. To his left
was that part which rose out of Foster's end field and
marked his boundary. There was the sheer drop. It was almost
dark.

Where Arthur stood, the Wall was no more than a dishevelled
furrow of large, hand-chipped stones. Yet, even abandoned from
their original position and lost of all the purpose of their first
function, the stones had a distinction which, Arthur could easily
understand, might move the Reverend Craddock to turn them
over for ever.

It would be pleasant to work with the old man and his Society.
He could do so or not, as he wished. He felt so free that the
comprehension that he could do as he wished seemed partly
exotic, partly oppressive. At his father's funeral, around the
grave, there had been people he had known since his childhood.
Yet he did not want to press old contacts into new moulds of
friendship. He was glad that there was no one in the neighbour-

hood sufficiently close to his adult experiences to claim that common interest which politeness always prodded to acquaintanceship, and isolation tended to foster as intimacy. It was unsociable of him – but he was pleased with it. It would be pleasant to discover his own whims, to act out of selfishness.

He would hunt. They kept two hunters – besides Bonnie, Pat's horse – and although they were not young, they were serviceable and well cared for by Ted, the groom and odd-job man, Annie's brother. And the Border Hunt was not such a grand, dressy affair. It was rather poor, in fact, he reflected contentedly, comparatively small, very unsettled, drawing its numbers from an unfashionable area. Its difficulties and unambitious working mitigated the guilt which its still privileged enjoyment gave him.

Guilt and Oliver. The same side of the same coin. Even the slightest thought of Oliver could change his mood.

He had to make everything pointless.

He was surprised to discover that he had been walking while revising his plans in his mind. He had recollection neither of having begun to walk, nor of having moved. Yet he had gone through the village, past the pub; he must have passed people. Now he was no more than two hundred yards from the drive leading to his house. He had completed a circuit covering about three miles.

He would have to do better than that! He would write to Oliver. It need compromise him in no way. He had not written him an honest letter since his return. There was a great deal he could ask him, and Oliver's practical experiences were important. Yes. He must find out what was in front of him. That was no more than sensible.

He went into the house to change his wet boots and get a drink. Pat was in the drawing-room.

'I've been waiting for you,' she began. Then she paused to stretch into a long yawn which lifted the length of her body as it lay along the big settee and brimmed her fresh, air-smacked face with burnished warmth. She had changed for bed and her hair swung down on to the silken breasts of her dressing-gown.

'Where've you been?'

'Walking,' Arthur replied grimly and went over to get himself a drink. He did not want to exhaust the determination he had gained in his walk by arguing with her.

'I'll have one too,' she called out.

He poured two whiskies and took her glass over to her. As he came towards where she was lying, she raised her legs and swung herself up and around into a sitting position, bouncing out the soft cushions as she finished the movement, leaving half the seat free.

'Sit down here,' she said, before taking the glass.

'I want to do something in the den.'

In attitude, standing with two glasses out in front of him at the end of stiff arms, and in manner, somehow forced to arch brotherly brusqueness, he was both uncomfortable and conscious of looking ridiculous.

'In the den!' Pat repeated, gruffly. 'In the jolly old den!' She laughed.

Arthur smiled and held out her drink.

'Here it is.'

'Aren't you going to stay and drink with me? It's so comfortable in here.'

The fire was tumbling about ember bridges in the huge grate; there was a stand light beside an armchair in the corner. That was all. The room seemed enclosed in ample, intimate, browsing.

'Really,' he pleaded, 'I want to write something rather urgently. Look. Please take this drink.'

She took it from him and sipped at it, as if obediently. He was caught in the slightly offensive absurdity of his own demand.

'Please stay,' she asked him, quietly. 'We haven't really talked together for such a long time.'

'That's not true.'

'Not really – like we used to.' Her voice was even softer now. And purer. But whispering through the ash-red and golden room like the cold ringing glow of glass.

'Stay,' she repeated.

Arthur felt the warmth from the fire push against his legs.

Pat nudged herself a little farther along, to give him more room.

He sat beside her and leaned back into the thick support of embroidered cushions.

NINE

'Your boots?' Lizzie shouted.
  'No.'
  'Leggings?'
  'No, woman.'
  'It is wet. Wellingtons?'
  'No! Have you no sense at all?'
  'Shoes, then?'
  'Yes.'
  'Your good shoes?'
  'His only shoes.'
  'Bring them in and stop clackin' . . .'
Nelson was being dressed for signing the contract. Straddled in a rocking-chair, with his shirt drying in front of the fire from the steam-wet ironing, his suit hanging from the picture rail like a strip of fancy dress just waiting to show what it could do, socks which had split into potato holes at the first yank over the shin, hair already plaster-combed and set with cold water, face briny bright and scrubbed beetroot – there he sat, the master of the house, soon to be the master of the farm and own it. There, with his wife scuddling around him like a little seamstress, risking even to tease on such a royal occasion – pretending he did not want to wear his brogues! – and his two daughters – the one with iron held at the ready, the other examining all garments from every angle and taking a pinch at this, a dab at that – the dog outside caught in the family's turning big wheel – kitchen blaring with lights – John perched on the edge of the settle whistling 'Tipperary' – all, all for the great event.
  'Yes! Yes!' Nelson shouted. 'It's my own place now, eh?
PRIVATE PROPERTY. TRESPASSERS WILL BE PROSECUTED BY ORDER OF THE BLOODY

OWNER. ME. NELSON FOSTER ESQUIRE. There's nowt they can do now, eh? Come on with them shoes, woman! It's only feet that's going into them.'

'The first thing they look at!' Lizzie shouted from the kitchen.

'Well, if they've nowt better to look at, I've nowt much to worry about! Eh?'

'Now,' said Avril, mincingly. 'Have you a pen?'

'What for?'

'To sign everything. You must have a pen.'

'Mr Bloody What's-his-name should have a pen. He should give us half a dozen with what I'm paying him.'

'You can't go without a pen,' said Avril, severely. Then with a big smile: 'I'll lend you mine.' And she disappeared upstairs.

'Anything more to press?' Shirley demanded, iron up to her head.

'Just my knees!'

'You'll need a suitcase,' said John.

'Eh?'

'A suitcase!'

'What for?'

'To take all that money with you.'

Nelson frowned. Then:

'It's all right, my lad. I'll get that munny back. Just you wait!'

He even allowed himself to swear without private penalties. 'By bugger I will,' he muttered.

'Here they are!' Lizzie arrived with the shoes thrust out in front of her like a hot plate.

'Clothes-horse!' John bellowed.

Nelson stood up in vest and second-best trousers. The high clothes-horse was brought and placed in front of the fire like a large guard.

Nelson looked at John and Shirley. They laughed.

'Out!' he ordered. And they went into the kitchen. A few moments later, Avril followed them, biting off their enquiries on her flushed face by snorting 'Manners!'

'You can come out now!' Lizzie said.

She came to the door and opened it for them, her hands

rubbing through the thick apron which seemed the natural outer layer of her old dress.

'Well then?' Nelson demanded.

He pulled himself up straight. From the bright gleam of his hard toe-caps to the smart shine of his hair, he was:

'Perfect,' said Shirley.

Avril dashed forward.

'Just a minute.' She pulled a small, correctly wrapped handkerchief out of her pocket and patted it into her father's breast-pocket. He peered over his stiff collar to look at it.

'This just for ornament?'

'A finishing touch,' said Avril.

'Not to be used except in a fix,' said John.

'Oh, no!' Avril replied to her brother. 'There are several occasions on which it can be used. If Mrs Langley should spill her tea, for example . . .'

'On her dress?'

'Anywhere.'

'I wipe it off with this?' Nelson enquired.

'Yes,' Avril stated firmly. 'And, say Captain Langley – well – runs out . . .' She stopped. Nelson was raising the stiff-ironed sleeve of his brown suit to his nose and threatening to wipe. He paused, arm still bent across his face.

'My God and she thought I would. Eh?' He laughed at John. 'Everyone outside a bank's a barbarian.'

'And everybody inside makes jokes all day,' John replied.

'Well?' said Nelson, dismissing the digression. 'So I'm OK. Am I?'

John nodded. In fact, strapped in his grey three-piece suit – 'Same one I got married in!' – Nelson looked unmistakably clean and dressed-up – as if the long confinement to leggings and old breeches had fomented an accumulation of dandyism which now surged forward to grab its one opportunity for expression.

Outside, the van – washed by Shirley – was drawn up just beside the door. Quietly, almost shyly, Nelson clambered into it and left.

Shirley went to start the milking. Avril dodged back indoors.

'Didn't you fancy going with him?' John asked his mother.

'No. He would be put out if I was there.'

'Why?'

'Case he made any mistakes and I saw them.'

'But you needn't tell him.'

'It wouldn't matter.'

She was still watching the gate through which the car had disappeared. John put his arm around her shoulders and felt the huddle of her sparse body under the sacked bundle of clothes.

'Are you pleased about it?' he asked.

'Your dad is.'

'But what about you?'

'Oh! I like him to be pleased. It's what he's wanted ever since he started. Somewhere of his own.'

Still, she watched the gate. John heard the clanking of cans as Shirley set about her job; he should be helping her, but he wanted to stay with his mother. It was only rarely that they had such accidental moments of rest together – and, though the pause assured him only of some ancient treasured pain between them he loved to relish it, almost to brand it on his mind.

'You know,' she began, 'I wish you weren't so restless with your father. He didn't have an easy time. He looks to you to pass things on.'

'I know.'

'And he isn't what he used to be. I can see it – I can see it more than any of you can.' She looked at John and he could not bear the guileless, simple look. He turned away. 'He isn't an easy man,' she went on. 'I know he loses his temper a bit and he's a bit bossy, and maybe he doesn't see much outside of what he does. But it all means a lot to him. You have to remember that.'

'I know, Mam,' said John. 'But it doesn't mean as much to me. Sometimes I don't think it means anything to me.'

'You'll just have to settle down.'

'I don't know that I want to farm all my life.'

Mrs Foster began to move towards the door; time enough had been spent on talking. She stopped only for one second longer, to touch John's arm and say:

'You couldn't do anything else, you know. You should have made up your mind about that a long time ago.'

John went to help Shirley. She chattered away jocundly, coaxing the animals, quietly addressing the cans, gossiping to John – saying nothing that had not been said before one hundred times a month and now it was as gentle as the lapping of water on sliding stones. She was dressed in old corduroy trousers, a thick grey shirt and a heavy blue fisherman's knit sweater which she had made herself; as usual, her calves and feet were jammed into long wellingtons. She was like Nelson, heavy, strong, graceless except in her work which gave her body a purpose and lightened its movements to ease. John was lean like his mother. He had to crack himself into work, as if ropes bound his body each time he rested and sliced through his will. When he did work hard, he went with a speed which betrayed both his anxiety to get the job finished quickly and his fear that he might not be able to finish at all. When she told him of her date that evening, he tried to dissuade her.

'But I promised to go,' Shirley said.

'Is it the same fellow you met – you were with – last time?'

'No. It's Alec Mackintosh. He's a friend of Alan's.' It was John who blushed.

'But can't you stay in?' he asked. 'I mean, Dad'll want us all to be there when he comes back.'

'I'll stay till he comes back.' Then, 'It's no good staying in all the time. You should go out. You should enjoy yourself.'

'Do I look all that miserable?'

They were outside the door. Darkness was rolling up the short December day and Shirley's face spread into the soft grained speckles of half-light so that she looked half-hidden in its innocent graveness.

'Sometimes,' she replied. 'And sometimes I wish you would go around. Go – *with* someone.'

He opened the door and they went into the dark lobby. Shirley went right through to help her mother. John went to the sink to wash.

He could go down to the pub in the village. To Mrs Eliot the landlady who would pull his pint before he asked for it and arch her pencil-slit eyebrows when he handed over the money, overlaying his hand with her own and scooping off the coin with her rubbing finger-nails. 'Not got yourself a girlfriend yet? A good-looking lad like you?' With a deep-sunk dimple on her red left cheek and a flounce of the hair that dropped permanently on her forehead. And her husband, walking around the three bars on duty like a policeman with a nod for all and a word to no one unless heavily pressed for the time or the price of a large order. It was she who kept the place alive. He was more interested in his ferrets. Old men who had always known his father – at least since he had moved up here – and charted the progress of the farm with the obsessed lack of real curiosity which matched their observations of the pendulum on the clock. Darts, Dominoes, Fives and Threes. No cards. Gambling for money not allowed. Money under the table. Maybe some of the young men, married or waiting to be married, dodging the wife or on the way to the girl, stopping for a quick pint which ran to two or three or four. Mr Flowers – he was always there – 'Always here,' he would say – always drinking his regular gills in the same way on his usual seat at the ritual time. The postman, Mr Harrison, who carried the mouth-organ in his breast-pocket and could suck it and blow without using his hands. A small red brick big-backsided pub at the far end of the village built for hope of growth which never showed and trickling with custom that would never have paid but for the pigs at the back, which Mr Eliot got to after the ferrets, and the brood hens of Mrs Eliot, dimple-winged and plump like herself. An ugly pub and a cold pub even in summer, but still the thatched centre of the football team and Saturday nights – and so for John while he had been in those things; but that was never very often and never at all since his holiday. He went into Aldeby and got drunk on his own. The earth-smacking evening sweat of tired, caked customers was like fur which John rubbed the wrong way when he went in and he knew that after it he would hound for action.

'Is he back?'

Dickie stumped through the door, past John unfolding the tucked-in collar of his shirt, wet in spite of the precaution. He followed him into the kitchen. Shirley and his mother were laying the table for tea – a tea which would include at least one hot course – and Avril helping occasionally but spending most of the time hanging out her toe-nails to dry.

'Well?' Dickie said, chest full of a new brown cardboard box. 'Is it all done?'

'Can't be,' Lizzie replied.

'Maybe he's stopped for a drink,' Dickie suggested.

'Yes.'

'That must be it,' he went on. 'It's so cold outside. You need a drink to keep you going.'

He nodded. Then, to show that he could survive the failure to take his hints, Dickie plonked the cardboard box on the table.

'I've fetched them.'

Lizzie approached the box carefully. First, she wiped her hands on her apron, then she sat down in front of the box. Her shyness piqued the curiosity of all three children.

'Ten bob exact,' Dickie said. 'No change.'

She nodded, and, delicately, she opened the interfolded leaves at the top. Then, in silence, she brought out Christmas decorations, one by one. Green and yellow bells, lush pink streamers and red rolled crêpe which could be twisted and stretched to cover all the walls.

No one spoke until they were all on the table. Then:

'Christ,' said John. 'I'd forgotten we were as near as that.'

'Well, we are,' his mother nodded, her hands buried in the rich paper, 'we are. And I thought, this time – we'll have decorations.'

The rawly coloured decorations made the kitchen look melancholy. John could never remember any new furniture having been bought, or forget the times new clothes had been bought. Nelson's austerity kept everything mean. Only Avril dared extravagance, and her new skirt and dresses were like the sign of what everything might end as – unless . . . Now, John saw the distressed joy of his mother at the simple garlands; now he was ashamed of doing anything which would hurt in any way the chrysalis so patiently self-restrained and so fragile in its rare vellications.

'Right!' he said. 'Let's get them all up before he gets back!'

'Yes,' replied his mother. 'We'd better do that.' She stood up and took Dickie's hand:

'And I'll get you a bottle of beer.'

With Dickie on a stool in the corner, and Avril picking from an old children's paint-box to decorate strips of brown paper with 'Merry Christmas' and 'A Happy New Year', Shirley clomping on to chairs in thick woollen-stockinged feet, John twisting the crêpe with his mother – one at either end of the kitchen holding the crinkly red paper between them, and, more than anything, Lizzie gazing at each daub of brightness as it was fastened on to the wall, spinning out the few baubles into a whole festival, they worked together.

They were nearly finished when Nelson came in. He stopped at the kitchen door. Everyone waited for his explosion.

'All this for me?' he demanded.

'For Christmas,' Lizzie replied, truthfully.

He looked around. Shirley was on the edge of the tables reaching up to pin the end of a streamer into the top corner. Avril was cross-legged on the floor, paint-box to one side of her, brown paper the other. John was at the table with his mother, clipping open the furly paper bells. Dickie, glass behind his stool and bottle out of sight, looked at Nelson with an enquiry which suggested that the whole purpose of the long and bothersome journey to the farm had been no more than the honest interest of a brother in a brother's affairs.

'All fixed up?' he asked.

Nelson nodded. Then, accepting the decorations as part of his own great day, he relaxed and nodded again, a great smile running across his large red face.

'Ay,' he said, quietly. 'Barrin' a bit to t' Bank – she's mine.'

Lizzie smiled with him – John smiled at her – Avril giggled with pleasure at the new achievement – Shirley laughed with relief and Dickie chuckled out:

'I knew it! Knew you'd beat all o' them. Knew you'd get there!'

'What were they all like?' Avril asked.

Nelson was pleased at her recognition of the importance of all aspects of his excursion and he settled down in the rocking-chair before he answered.

'What was their place like, first?'

'Well,' he said, 'they'll never starve. You needn't worry about that. And they'll never have any trouble about where to put things – I haven't seen as many drawers and carry-ons since I was at your mother's father's house before you were all thought of.'

'But what sort of things do they have?' Avril persisted.

'Oh! All kinds. Pictures, pots – all kinds.' He turned to Lizzie. 'Grand big rooms. You would like their rooms. You could play five-a-side in that sitting-room of theirs.'

'Is old Annie there?' Dickie demanded. 'Cross-eyed old Annie?'

'Ay. She's there. I don't know why. She's as daft as a brush.' He spread his arms out comfortably on to the chair-rests. 'We had tea, you see. Oh, yes,' his voice rose into a clownish imitation of elegance, 'we all had tea. That's what they called it, anyway. Not a sit-up-and-beg job, at all. One of them carry-ons where everybody sits on their own chairs with their knees together and tries to eat nowt to show they aren't hungry. Anyway, old Annie cuffuffles in wid this trolley – Mrs L. picks up t' pot – out it comes – nowt but water! T' old besum had forgotten to put 'tea in!'

John saw in his father's gleam at this story the assurance which the mistake had given him.

'And what were they all like?' Avril persisted.

'Well,' said Nelson, 'that takes some thinking out. I liked *him* . . .'

'Captain Langley?'

'Ay, but I think he's stopped that Captain caper. He's finished wid t' army, so he tells me. He was all right. Nay fuss or showin' off.'

'He looks nice,' said Lizzie.

'Hmm,' her husband replied – but he decided to ignore the question which, on another occasion, he would have asked immediately.

'Kind,' Lizzie added.

'What was she like?' Avril asked.

'Well. T' mother wasn't so bad, a bit quiet, not much to say for herself. That other . . .'

'Patricia?'

'Ay. I didn't fancy her at all. She was one of them sarcastic types.'

'She's beautiful.'

'Maybe. But she could use a good husband to tell her what's what.'

'So everything went off all right?' John asked.

'Yes,' Nelson replied, proudly. 'Yes. I didn't disgrace you all. And – it's mine now.'

Tea, the table cleared, Nelson out to have his last look around, returning just in time to see his two daughters about to leave. Avril, who had spent all the afternoon before Dickie's arrival in minutely elaborate preparation, now held up her arms, had her mother help her slip on her dress, pushed her feet into stiletto-heeled shoes – and was suddenly primed. Even her expression seemed to change, to switch from 'steady' to 'go'. Her boyfriend was going to pick her up at the end of the track leading to the farm; he had not yet been allowed into the house and his existence was recognised only by Avril and her mother. Shirley, too, had changed to go out, ignoring John's hints and dissuading glances. She would bike down into the village where Alec Mackintosh, who was hired on a farm the other side of Aldeby, would be waiting with his motor bike. Dickie had cadged a grudged promise of transport from Avril.

Nelson watched them go out with a consenting complacency which suggested not only the greatest good humour but the generosity of discovered tolerance; they went with his per-mission.

John did not know whether to stay or go. His father, still in his suit, was spread the length of the armchair, his slippered feet stuck on a small copy which balanced on the thick fender. His mother was up and down, now picking at a cuff or collar with her needle, now rapidly pottering about the kitchen, rearranging, storing, working. Between the replete and the attendant, between the proudly recumbent and the tacking readiness, between satisfaction, congratulation and new visions and expectant, nerve-ended pliancy – the two garlanded with crêpe chains and hung about with gushing colours against the submissive brown – between the rare stillness of his mother and father, John was at once reduced to negligible dependency or forced to dominating intrusion.

He excused himself abruptly and went to his bedroom. There, he took up the book he was reading and slumped on to the narrow bed. He lay on his back, holding the book against the light, reading quickly but breaking off for long periods, either to consider what had been written, or to daydream. It was *The Scarlet Letter* by Nathaniel Hawthorne. A book he had read once before. It was a whole-patterned world, and in it, he could imagine the completeness which, though undiscovered as yet, lay behind his own disparate acts. Usually, reading could close off the farm, his father. Now it seemed to incite him to a denser restlessness.

Shirley would be at the dance. He hated to see her pulled against someone, pressed, flat against them, her breasts flattened, skirt slapped against her belly and legs, one palm damply pressing between her shoulder-blades, the other dangling, with hidden wrist-force, pushing into the small of her back. He shivered. Why did he have to think of it that way? And Avril, with her ambitions as elastically snappy and accommodating as her knicker-tops. Why like that?

He felt dirty. His thumbs had released the held pages of the book and its leaves swung above his face. Gently he closed it and went to the door. Before turning off the light, he looked around his bedroom. It was small and now, for some reason, it looked mean. There were books piled high in the old Welsh dresser, books on a small table, books on the floor. Two coat-hangers on a rail, one carrying a suit, the other, an old sports jacket. A small chest of drawers. Cramped. No carpet. Lino.

'I was just making some tea – would you like some?' his mother asked.

'No thank you.'

'Sure?'

'Yes.'

He caught his father looking at him. Nelson beamed. His mother intercepted the sudden signal and took confidence.

'Have something with us,' she urged. 'It'll do you good. We were just going to have something.'

'No. Thank you.'

'Come on,' Nelson encouraged him, jauntily, 'let's drink to me – with a cup of tea.' He guffawed. 'That's it! "Drink to me/With a cup of tea/That's what I call/Po – et – ry!"'

Lizzie laughed at John, encouraging him to humour his father, wanting him to join in, be a part of, add to – nothing. He was ashamed of his coolness, but there was no game to be played; no more than one more move to eliminate the present position.

'It'll just take a minute,' Lizzie began again.

It was stupid.

'I don't want any!' he retorted.

'Don't you speak to your mother like that.' Nelson was admonitory, prepared to be outraged.

'Sorry.'

Lizzie smiled. It would be all right.

'Good,' she replied. 'I'll get you some this second. Sit down and talk to your father.'

'I'm going out.'

'At this time?' John saw that it was nearly ten.

'It isn't all that late,' he replied.

'It is for them as works,' Nelson grunted.

Lizzie saw the eclipse of Nelson's stuffed and peacefully self-contented good humour, and wanted to prevent it. She saw John's impatience and wanted to check it. They were rarely unanxiously together.

'Stay just for a moment,' she whispered. 'Please.'

'No.' He was too restless even to stand still as she spoke to him.

'No?'

'No!'

She started away from his exclamation. She gave up.

Quickly, he went into the back kitchen, took down his gun and a torch, called for Ben in the yard and, with the dog padding in rapid, wending tracks before him, made for the mile-castle which was beyond the farm, on the side away from the Langley's and the village. There were usually quite a few rabbits about near the little wood up there.

He had been offensive towards his mother for no good reason. Everything she did was done with such care and came from so true a feeling that whatever she worked at, he felt, could never be wholly bad because of what she herself was. Conscientious, good, gentle. He was a marauder beside her, with taboos for his loot; the fear of what he did; the fear of what he had never done. He had frightened her. Not much, but enough for him to be afraid of what could happen if he allowed the cause of that effect to fester. Yet its cause was something he did not know how to comprehend.

Arriving at the broken square of stones, he sat down and took out a cigarette. His home, the village, the Aldeby where he had gone to school, they were submerged before him under a thickened carpet of blackness, pricked only by the faintest glimmering of blurred electric lights. Around and about was endless high land, bare, made for winds to swoop over, snow to lie on for weeks on end, rocks to break and fall.

He flicked on the torch and beamed it in front of him. There was no movement. Ben was skirmishing in the small wood nearby. It was a poor place to land up on a Saturday night. His mother had told him that, if he had wanted to do something else but farm, then he ought to have made up his mind long before. He was twenty; yet, he believed her.

He went over to the wood. Lizzie had been so tremendously moved by that cardboard box of paper chains. Just a few rolls of coloured paper; and he had walked out despite her wishes. He had wanted to do something against her. He had been conscious of his antagonism – even of the emerging thrill of a will to go totally against her, hurt her – and yet he had not restrained it.

He was in the wood. Putting down his gun, he found and grasped the rough, slim trunk of a small fir tree. Slowly, he pulled against it, loosening it from the ground. It was tough, and by the time he had shifted it into a steady rhythm, his sweat had broken. He wiped his hands, took a fresh grip, and swung it around faster – leaning his weight against it and letting the needling swish of the branches push into his face. It was slack. He held it lower down and screwed it into its own circle as hard as he could. The bark flaked in his hands. This would be for his mother. He could feel it leaving the ground. For Christmas. The small outside roots snapped. He bent down and dug his hands under the top roots, then, doubled up, he swung and heaved at the same time. It would complete her decorations. It was coming. Suddenly, it tore out of its earth, and the bushy coronal lifted into his face.

He heard himself gasping for breath. That would be all he would do. He would neither fight nor look for trouble any more. He was afraid of his own viciousness.

His father had bought the farm. That ought to be enough. He would work and forget what had happened. He put the tree over his shoulder and went home.

TEN

'There can be no doubt,' said the Reverend Craddock, with a dab at the beaded cluster of perspiration which had delicately arisen on his brow, 'no doubt at all that it is a marvellous day for a dig.'

'Marvellous,' Arthur echoed, glad to stand up and leave his spade deep in the sticky grave which still managed to be wet despite the drying day.

'Gratifying,' the Reverend Craddock continued, working up the conversation. 'Benevolent,' he added. 'Encouraging. Heart-warming!' He beamed.

Arthur laughed and pulled out a packet of cigarettes which he offered the vicar, whose fingers pecked at them. He was enjoying his afternoon's work. There were five besides the Reverend Craddock and himself. The others, under their new president, Mr Stoneman, were deep in a grave of their own digging on the other side of the mile-castle just out of sight.

'Good place for a dig,' repeated the vicar staunchly, heaving at the cigarette with all the ancient muscles of his face. 'Quiet place. Nice place.'

Arthur agreed with him. They were at the mile-castle which John had used to walk up to. In two hours they had been disturbed only three times; once by a small bi-plane which had circled low above them and called out the Reverend Craddock's vocabulary of speculation for a full ten minutes after it had disappeared from sight; the second time by three boy scouts who had declared to the vicar that they were walking the length of the Wall and who, for that enthusiasm, were stopped in their journey a quarter of an hour while he explained to them the precise geography of their route; and lastly, by a solitary hiker,

age about sixty, who loomed over the rise in skiing hat and
khaki shorts and suddenly decided on an enormous diversion
down the hill when he saw the Reverend Craddock approaching
him.

'Bit of a change from army life, eh?' he asked with military
brusqueness.

'Yes,' Arthur replied.

'Always a pleasure to do work you really enjoy.'

'Yes,' said Arthur. Then, 'It's surprising how you can work
away without interruption for hours on end.'

'Exactly!' The Reverend Craddock nodded vigorously and sat
down. 'That's what I always say. All work for no pay – provided
you enjoy it – proves that Jack's a bit of a gay dog! Eh?'

'And you become utterly absorbed in such work,' Arthur
added.

'Precisely!' declared the vicar – and he stretched back to rest
himself more comfortably against a convenient stone.

Arthur gave up. He was never more than half-hearted in his
teasing of the old man. He had spent too many pleasant afternoons with him not to appreciate his lazy delights. Delights in
which he himself shared with the irresponsible relish of someone
doing what he thinks is entirely irrelevant to his main purpose
but can yet be afforded for sufficient reasons.

'Tell me, Arthur,' the vicar began, 'are you going to take over
the management of your – your mother's – the farms and things?
I've seen you working away like billy-o this last month or two.
You looked very happy in it. Does the idea of farming appeal to
you, now you've tried it?'

'It always did,' Arthur replied. 'In fact, sometimes when I was
– overseas or something like that – I could think of nothing
better than a day's work around here.'

'Yes. It's a good life. Hard work. Fresh air. Dull. But good
enough for anybody sensible enough to take advantage of it.'
The Reverend Craddock paused, hoping that his companion
would ramble into the sort of personal divulgences that he
enjoyed hearing above all things in life.

'I was surprised to hear that you'd resigned your commission,
you know,' he suggested, pointedly.

'Oh, Why?'

'Well,' he pulled the cigarette to its last millimetre. 'Well,' he repeated, 'I thought you wouldn't.' Satisfied with this neat qualification, he again waited for his gossip.

'Twelve years was enough.'

'I *see*,' said the Reverend Craddock, swiftly, meaningfully. Uselessly. Arthur had gone back into the hole to dig.

He preferred not to lubricate the vicar's curiosity even though he accepted it as the necessary price of his way of living. A negligible cost. For such enquiries were part of the spread stillness of the stretched summer afternoon, and both were part of a pattern which he had consciously allowed to grow around him. Peaceful, empty, singular, with the edge taken off any mystery by discretion. And so, although he had been home for almost a year, though he had worked with the vicar, seen him at jumble sales and fêtes, listened to him in the church and been with him when his mother had entertained him to tea – he had told him nothing. Thus forcing him back time and again to a most superficial and meatless inquisitiveness.

He had made the decision not to join Oliver in his lay-missionary work abroad until he had straightened matters out and allowed his mother the benefit of his present support, and it seemed that the decision had suspended him so comfortably that he need never take another. Indeed, he often thought of it as the only decision he had ever taken. School and the army had been designations. His experiment with Oliver, an inspiration drawn from restlessness, admiration and sorrow; no binding reasons – no duty, no pleasure, no necessity. To stay here had been his decision – and his stay, while, perhaps, seeming uneventful, had also been undisturbing though neither placid nor entirely without qualms.

'Everything was all right.' It was not a trumpeting conclusion and it hardly pleased him, but for the moment he was satisfied. What had happened was that he had allowed time that was past to recede until it had all become part of his youth. Whenever he felt particularly uneasy about what he was doing – this occurred rarely – then he would tell himself that he was preparing.

As a too-strong, too-important counterpoint to the way he

was living came Oliver's letters. Often, in fairness, in answer
to his own letters which took refuge in a plaintive confusion of
attitude.

Oliver was extremely certain. 'I do not believe that it truly
represents you,' he had written. 'In this I may be wrong. But I
feel certain that you will soon do that which you believe you
have to do. It requires only a word, a push – something! I am
convinced that you will join me here before the year is out.'
When Arthur had read that, he had almost raced to his diary to
discover exactly how much time that gave him. 'To make my
position as truthful as I can,' Oliver had gone on, 'let me tell you
how I am myself. At first, I found the work uncongenial and,
even, at times, revolting. It is an unpleasant word to use and I
feel ashamed of it, but I am afraid that it described my feelings.
Moreover what I could achieve seemed to be so superfluous as
to be almost useless. I was more homesick than ever I have
been since my first day at school and for a while I was properly
ill. Now, I am well and happy. For no magical reason, for no
great success, for no sudden friendship. (I live alone and go for
weeks without civilized conversation – which probably accounts
for the preposterous length of this letter!) For no other reasons,
in fact, than the one which originally decided me to do the work.
I realised that I was doing it; that this was what I wanted to do;
and that my miseries were no more than preliminary incon-
veniences which I had not bargained for.'

The letters made Arthur regret that Oliver was not on hand
to talk to. Yet they did not move him. At first, he had been
unhappy about his indifference, it had seemed shallow and even
cynical. Now, he was as far removed from such a judgement as
the judgement itself from its evidence. The slow-working of his
life already seeming to entrust him to the easeful round of nicely
encrusted habit, threw off, or rather, glided past, any disturbing
intrusions.

There he was. Taking an afternoon off, with a good morning's
work behind him – plenty to do in front of him – with no
conscience-prickling tendrils of obligation to make him reconsider the advantages of country life – with a glorious day,
interests, a use. Perhaps his usefulness was a little of his own

imagining, without much to do with a real assessment of his contribution to his mother's or his own affairs. Still, he had disentangled the wreathed remainders of his father's last few years; that had been useful.

He was heavily jostled by the vicar's sudden leap into the ditch.

'Stoneman,' he muttered, and lanced his spade into a pile of earth already loosened by Arthur. 'I suppose he's come to tell us he's found something!'

The resentment contained in the vicar's mild-mouthed remark could be explained by Mr Stoneman's organisation of the work. It was complicated and lacked neither generalisations on life nor references to the trenches, the state of the English countryside and the habits of the Romans, but what it meant, in the end, was that he, Mr Stoneman, went for the most profitable areas while the vicar dug at that point at which most decently coincided distance, politeness and lack of prospects.

The Reverend Craddock waited until the shadow of his president lay over him before easing himself into the upright with his right hand supporting the dedicated, aching, small of his back.

'Discovered anything?' he enquired.

'Vicar!' Mr Stoneman boomed. 'I am an antiquarian – not an explorer!'

The heavy socks which rolled majestically from battered brogues to meet the muddy knees of sagging jodhpurs, quivered with respect for their wearer's distinction.

'Well,' the vicar went on, rather petulantly, 'what did you want to tell us?'

'I came,' said Mr Stoneman, with apostolic emphasis, 'to chat to young Langley.'

Arthur squinted up at him. With his back to the sun and the thickened wad of stomach-chest-neck pressing upwards like a stuffed suitcase, his head jolted back as if dislocated, the President of the Society was straining mightily to assume a philanthropic expression.

'What about?' the Reverend Craddock demanded.

'No need to be concerned, Craddock,' the president replied. 'I won't interrupt your work! Dig away!'

'Hm!' The vicar gave a little snort of independence which, though almost mouse-like, registered, somewhere, in the bush of Mr Stoneman's ears.

'I,' he said, 'am resting myself for five minutes!' He pulled out a watch from the waistcoat whose poor, over-strained buttons stood on a constant guard. 'British Army!' he explained to Arthur, confidentially.

'Where?' asked the vicar.

This time it was Mr Stoneman who snorted; the snort of an elephant demanding a tiger for tea.

'Marching!' he thundered. 'March for fifty-five, rest for five! Best system in the world! Am I right, Langley?'

Deep in his hole, Arthur nodded. He dared not trust himself to speak.

The Reverend Craddock accepted that he had been out-manoeuvred, or rather out-gunned, and permitted himself to be sufficiently interested in what Mr Stoneman might impart to leave his work and listen.

'Queer people, the Romans!' Mr Stoneman began. 'That's why I got myself interested in all this business.' A large hand lifted into the air and then dropped into its usual niche behind the back.

'Odd!' he bellowed, warming up a little. 'Always building walls. Damned good walls they were too. Could teach us a thing or two. But that's what I asked myself.' He looked at the watch to make sure that it was sticking to its job. 'Why in God's name did they do it?'

Arthur nodded to mark his understanding of the human motives behind dry scholarship.

'And then one thing led to another!' Mr Stoneman concluded. His words, at this juncture, in the mouth of anyone not endowed with the lungs of a dinosaur, might have appeared sentimental. For, with this final punctuation, his head jerked seventy-five degrees forward to incline on his neck where it rested pensively.

'Have you seen the museum at Housesteads?' the vicar asked Arthur, to broaden the discussion a little.

'I went there once,' Arthur replied.

'Ah!' the questioner was disappointed.

'And it was closed.'

'Ah!' The Reverend Craddock beamed. 'It must have been after four o'clock. Or at a weekend. Or on a holiday,' he concluded. Then, 'Or maybe old Barlow was out somewhere.'

Arthur acknowledged the weight of these probabilities.

'Well, you must go some time,' the vicar went on. 'Marvellous place. All sorts of people have worked at Housesteads, you know.' He paused, to show respect. 'W. G. Collingwood – that is, R. G. Collingwood's father – he worked there. And his son went along with him on the digs. Professor Richmond at Durham University is the man in charge of things up there now.'

The Reverend Craddock's lecture was stilled by a crash of oaths which cascaded from Mr Stoneman and gave everyone within a radius of five miles to understand that he was unhappy with that state of affairs.

'They ought to get on with the encampment!' he roared. 'Camp life! That's what we want to know about. Whores!' The Reverend Craddock blinked. 'Harlots!' Jumped. 'Jezebels!' Spluttered. 'All ten feet under and not a man with a spade to dig for them!' The vicar protested, formally.

Arthur left them to it. He would walk back by the Wall. Taking leave of his two-patrons – who were sufficiently moved by this to break off their argument for the length of two seconds – he took up his jacket, slung it over his arm, and set off. He wore light slacks and a white silk shirt, the sleeves folded up over his elbows. The sun on his already sunburnt arms and face made him cheerful, and that was enough. Any thought of the effort of despair or deep consideration seemed too forced, too cultivated. He was lucky, and altogether as physically pleased with himself as he had ever been.

He walked rapidly along the path which twisted in the shadow of the Wall. He would never tire of this countryside. Every day its sane tranquility made episodes like his work in the Welfare Society seem unbalanced and phrenetically dangerous. The army was still in his walk; his back, stiff as a cane, his steps, moderately, efficiently paced for brisk endurance.

He came to the one dark spot in the whole summer country-side afternoon. The sheer drop at the point where the Wall bordered Foster's farm. He stopped and looked down at the black pool which always seemed cold. It looked as though it had been there for ever and not once tempted either man or beast to drink or sport.

'It's easily the best place around here.'

He turned. Pat was no more than two yards away from him.

'To jump,' she explained.

Arthur shivered.

'Are you so determined to cheer me up?' he asked.

'That would be useless,' she replied, 'since you appear to be so extravagantly cheerful that the best anyone can hope for is to bring you down.'

She smiled at him. Her smile turned his placidity to melancholy. Her solitude, her ceaseless, lonely rambling on horse or, as now, on foot, her unexpected entrances and exits, these were beginning to jolt him. She acted as if he had never left home in the first place, and behaved as if he ought to understand all that had happened to her since they had last known each other really well, that is, as children. What most intrigued him was what she did on these solitary walks. He had challenged her about it a few weeks after his return.

'Where do you go?' he had asked her, abruptly.

'Anywhere.'

He hesitated, curious to know, wary about the consequences.

'Come on,' he teased her. 'You're out almost every day.'

'That's the point.'

'What?'

'To get out.'

'But you come back.'

She smiled at him.

'Yes,' she said. 'I come back.'

He dared not go on. He knew what she wanted him to ask, but he was too unsure of his position in the house since his return to have the strength to ask it and so be told the truth. She came on him so suddenly; even when he knew that she would be in a room and, going in, expected a response from her, there was an unnerving indeterminate lurch about her remarks.

Now, he felt that he had entered into her own territory, somehow trespassed. His place was the summerhouse.

'Mummy's anxious about you,' she said. 'She was afraid you might have set out for China. I told her not to worry.'

'You both knew perfectly well what I was doing.'

'Yes. But did we know *why*?' She peered at him in mock interrogation.

'I should have thought that obvious,' he answered irritably.

She stared at him, and he looked away.

They walked back to the house together. In the yard, she slipped away from him as suddenly as she had arrived. Arthur liked the yard; with the hay thickly stacked in the small barn, nicely mounded cow-packs, trail of straw and mossy felt of soft stone, the small water-trough, the four stables and, on one side, the unexpected border of a garden which led through to the summerhouse – with all this, he felt himself to be in the middle of a painted landscape, one of Gaugin's Breton farms. It was so ripely settled, layer on layer.

He decided not to go in to see his mother and turned towards the garden. He felt slightly guilty at not going to see her.

But it slipped off when he went into the summerhouse.

He took up the letter where he had left off the previous night.

'Dear Oliver,

'Thank you for your letter. I have just as much time and inclination to write to you at the length at which you wrote to me; yet I find it difficult even to begin.

'To begin with, we now seem to be discussing my actions with such a limited relevance to their complication as to make of any argument no more than an exercise in scissors and paste. Not that it is – and not that I treat your comments as cavalierly as that might imply. Nor am I suggesting that my position is so unique in its complexity that ordinary considerations do not apply. Only – on paper – everything seems so straightforward, so comprehensive, so obviously correct – and so irrelevant. It is as if the statement of a position thereby rendered it untrue; or so generally true as to be unhelpful. Sentences of decision ring like old bells calling no one to church any more. There is an abstract coolness in the openly admitted justification for action which makes it no more than a code drawn up to reassure those who have quit.

'I don't know why I scribble this nonsense . . .'

It went on in much the same way for eight pages and it was still unfinished. Reading it, he was amazed at the implied spurning of Oliver's decision of life. He knew that he liked and respected Oliver more than anyone; that only in his company had he ever, in his life, been brought alive to action whose grooves had not been heavily furred by the long previous tread of others like him. Yet it was simply that he was not in the mood to face up to what joining Oliver would entail.

He tore up the letter carefully, folding it and refolding it into tiny squares. Then he dropped the white stained confetti into the unlit fire. The windows were open and he sat facing the Foster land, feet on the sill, neck cupped in his hands, looking out at the slow then steep run of land which reared to the Wall and cut it into the sky. In the fields in front of him, two men were working. Fosters, father and son. He envied them.

With a sigh which was an end to any threatening complication, he took out a cigarette and reached for a book. It was a faultless English summer day.

Oliver was probably sweltering with arid heat; teaching, building. He looked at the title of his book: *The Civilization of the Renaissance in Italy* by Jacob Burckhardt. It was absurd as well as being complicated.

He would write no more.

ELEVEN

The scooter was far from new, but it was new to Avril and she drove it with valued care. The two-and-a-half miles from Aldeby to the village was a deserted journey in most weathers, a lonely one always.

It had threatened thunder all day. Clouds had boiled up and their quick changes of density had flattened the light so that fields and hedges, roads and trees seemed to stand in a different relationship to each other. The road seemed to be higher, the trees lifted as if their roots were stretching their tips, the fields shortened, near enough to touch.

It was more or less straight for the next few hundred yards.

'Ask him tonight,' Tony had urged.

'Yes.'

'Promise?'

'Yes.'

'Tonight.'

She would! It was not right that their father let Shirley go around the place as she did – even if he didn't know of it – and yet refused to have anything to do with Tony.

'How much can you save a week?' he had asked.

Avril had already worked it out. Thirty shillings a week to her mother (who kept it by for her – without telling Nelson, nor would Avril tell Tony, not even let herself add it up, keep it as a surprise), twelve-and-six for cigarettes, about fifteen shillings for new stockings and one thing and another, seven-and-six for petrol – she had paid for the scooter outright – she would make do with shoes, no new coat, only a dress for something really special.

'Three pounds ten.'

He looked pleased.

'Now, if I can manage five – that's – 52 eights is – 416 and 26 makes – we can have £442 this time next year.' He paused. 'Not allowing for any rises.'

'I would want to keep on working for a bit,' Avril warned him. He grabbed her, gently.

'We'll see about that.'

Tony seemed to consider her whatever they did together. Sometimes, when she imitated her father or John to him – grunting her words and banging on the table, scowling – then she would realise that she was as much urging him to do as they did as trying to make him laugh. But he was so nice to her.

'They tell me he's in insurance,' John said.

'Well, what of it?'

'I hope he's well covered for sudden death – if he comes and sees Dad!'

'Don't be so nasty,' Avril shouted. 'You lot and your damned farms! I'm not going to be stuck in the middle of a field all my life – I can tell you.'

'Got a car an' all, eh?'

'Well. At least he isn't frightened to spend a bob or two now and then. Anyway!' she raised her voice even louder. 'You just leave him alone and look after yourself. If you can manage it.' John laughed at her. 'At least he isn't too frightened to take a girl to a dance!'

That had been the previous evening, and she remembered with embarrassment the sudden glare which had answered her taunt. She shuddered slightly and turned the throttle to speed up and get home to get her question asked and go and tell Tony. Sometimes she was as scared of John as she was of her father.

At the corner she leaned over slightly too far and her pedal caught the ground. She tried to twist the scooter into an upright position, but the handlebars swivelled too quickly and she was off.

It was not a nasty fall, but her ankle hurt and, more important, she could not get the scooter to start. And it was all uphill.

After pushing it for about ten minutes, she had to stop. Her ankle was smarting badly, and when she felt it, her fingers touched painfully on its soft puttiness.

'Damn and hell!'

There was not a building in sight. She would not be able to get any sort of help until she got to the village. The grey bright thundery weather which had been so fine to ride through was now alarming. Only when she stopped could she sense the immensity of the solitude all around her, brushed only by the lonely whine of wind through telegraph wires and its brief rustle through thick hedges. There had been no rain all day – and yet its hiss seemed to spread in from the fields – and pass over her – leaving her even more isolated than before. As far as she could see in any direction, there was nothing human, nothing to help.

She spun around as soon as she heard the engine, and waved to slow it down. Arthur got out of the van, put the scooter in the back, and drove towards the farm. Avril settled down beside him in the front.

'That you I've seen with Mr Stoneman and all that lot?' she began, cosy in her good luck.

'Yes.'

'What are they all looking for?'

Arthur considered.

'Nothing in particular,' he replied, 'just traces of the Wall and Roman settlement.'

'I see.' She began to giggle. 'What do they do with the traces when they find them?'

'Write about them.'

'For other people to read and go and dig some traces up themselves?'

'Yes.'

'Huh.'

Both of them laughed. Normally, Avril would have considered such questions 'tasteless' and Arthur might have been a little more whimsical about his answers; but the accident of their encounter, with himself the stray rescuer and Avril the stranded desolate, had happily jolted them towards the opposite of their normal behaviour.

Arthur usually drove rapidly. Now he steered the car circumspectly as if Avril's ankle were actually hanging outside the door in imminent danger of being bumped. She, who would usually be wary of what she said to people of whom she was unsure, now bubbled away like a spout. She compared him with Tony, and easily admitted that he was more handsome, looked more intelligent and dressed more elegantly than her boyfriend, reserving Tony's superiority only in the undefined area of personal-particular attraction. Arthur was refreshed by her open confidence, and there was a warmth about her which unfroze the chilled set of his manner with Pat and his mother.

The van bumped across the yard, and Arthur dashed around to help her to the door. The rest had allowed the sprain to stiffen and Avril had to put her arm around his shoulders to hobble into the house.

Mrs Foster attended to it quickly, and within five minutes, Avril was sitting beside a blazing fire, bandaged foot on a stool, shawl around her shoulders, cup of hot milk in her hand, cushions settled.

'I was just makin' supper,' Lizzie said to Arthur. 'Would you care for some?'

'I don't want to put you to any trouble,' he replied anxiously.

'Doesn't bother her,' Avril burbled, cup to mouth. 'She likes straining herself,' and she heaved herself into a yet more comfortable pose.

'Don't listen to her, Mr Langley,' Lizzie answered. 'She just wants to shame you. It'll be no trouble at all.' She bobbed to the kitchen door, then popped her head around the frame. 'But thank you for considering it,' she added.

'You'd better watch out,' Avril whispered, loudly, 'if she takes a fancy to anybody – she packs them up with so much cake that they have to stay for a fortnight to sleep it off.'

'I think I would enjoy being packed with your mother's cake,' he replied.

Avril opened her eyes widely and shook her head in wonder.

'Well, sit yourself down,' said Lizzie, bustling in with plates growing out of every finger.

'Ay!' Avril shouted. 'Sit down before you're knocked down! Hello! Make way for Mother Trouble.' Her accent broadened as she instinctively moved to that part of her personality which, she could see, most amused Arthur.

'Isn't she awful, Mr Langley?' said Lizzie, biting her bottom lip and clucking happily. 'I wonder you bothered to stop and pick her up.'

'He couldn't help it,' Avril replied grimly. 'It was either that – or run me down!'

'Well,' Lizzie countered. 'I know what I would have done.'

'There you are!' said Avril. 'No mother-love whatsoever. I tell you,' she continued broadly, 'you've come to the right place here. It's only because there's a visitor in the house that she hasn't put a crutch in my hand and sent me down to feed her chickens.'

'Shirley's doing that,' her mother answered. 'I don't know why we pretend it's your job, anyway. You're never back in time.'

'I take good care not to be!'

Lizzie grimaced and trotted back on that endless relay to and from the back kitchen and Arthur, not realising that he was the cause of what seemed to him to be such a natural familial exchange, sat rather shyly in the corner of the bosky, unlit room. Avril, with her back to the window, was silhouetted against the eastern reflection of the sliding light and her face seemed the same dark, rich-stained colour as her hair. In front of her, Avril saw the rough elegant clothes of someone who looked younger than John; she had calculated Arthur's age in the car and yet with his unlaboured sunburn against a white shirt, he appeared no older than someone just out of school.

'I hope I'm not being too nosy,' said Lizzie on her return, 'but we did hear that Mrs Langley had taken bad.'

'Oh!' Arthur replied. 'Oh! She's quite well again now, thank you, Mrs Foster.'

'Good.'

'Yes,' he continued, boldly polite, 'Dr Barwise seems to think that she'll be almost as fit as she was before.'

'Well,' Lizzie answered, 'I'm sure I'm relieved to hear it.'

Again, as when he had listened to the exchange between mother and daughter, Arthur was entranced by the unforced warm-heartedness in Mrs Foster's words. The plain furniture, the strong, sweet trail of food, the crackling fire shining more light than the glazed grey evening, the accent rounded as water-stones and burred with easy use – all this draped him with a rich feeling of serenity.

'The last time I was here,' he announced, suddenly, 'was when you were moving in.'

Avril stared at him.

'Well!' said Lizzie. 'I didn't think you'd remember *that*.' She laughed. 'There was a fine old mess, that day. I bet you thought you'd come across a tribe of savages!'

'No,' Arthur replied, quietly, 'I think – I remember I wanted to stay.'

'Good job you didn't!' Avril grunted. 'They would've had you out with a pick and shovel before you'd known where you were!'

The outside door shook on its hinges as if someone wanted to shake it off them.

'Supper up?' John bellowed. 'I'm famished!'

'Enter the head-hunters,' Avril whispered.

'And I'm bloody caked,' he added, clumping into the kitchen. Arthur was boxed out of his sight in the corner. 'Hurry up, woman,' he went on, cheerfully, to his mother, 'let's have something to eat and then I'll away for a swim and clean up a bit.'

His jeans shone with shiny pressure and palm sweat; they were held tightly with a thick leather belt over which flopped the belly of his shirt eased out for comfort. From his massed pile of hair to the turned-down wellingtons into which the bottoms of his jeans were stuffed, he glistened with a shivering energy which seemed to attract all the light in the room to itself leaving the rest empty in pale shadow.

'I think you need a wash before you swim!' said Avril.

He turned to her.

'What the hell's happened to you?'

'Fell off a pavement.'

'Thrown off more likely!'

Then he saw Arthur and stopped talking. Lizzie explained what had happened and introduced John to Arthur who muttered something about it being silly they had not met before. Shirley came in and was manoeuvred into a muffled cross-exchange by Avril whose position was made difficult by John, now sitting on the end of a bench beside her and listening to an A-Z account of the whole affair while flipping through a book. Nelson's entry needed no repeat performance, and after he had heard out Arthur's reason for being there, he engaged him in conscientious conversation about local affairs.

On his own ground, Nelson was king, and his solidity gave the supper table a sounding board without which it might have scattered to hastily pocketed silences. Shirley ghosted her mother; John ate quickly, and over-loudly cursed at both his sisters. Lizzie was happy at the round pleasantness of the meal, and Arthur felt himself quickened by the rapid variety of fresh nuances.

It was Shirley who went to answer the knock at the door. She was away for a few minutes, and the noise around the table dropped as everyone leaned back to listen.

'It was Teddy Langholm,' she said. 'His dad wants to know if you can give him a hand getting everything in. He says if he doesn't get it in tonight – he never will.'

'He's right there,' John muttered.

Nelson looked grim. Arthur's presence, for the first time, annoyed him. He did not like to appear ungenerous among strangers.

'How many men did he want?' he asked.

'As many as can manage,' she replied. 'Two from here, I suppose.'

Nelson chucked in irritation.

'I wanted to mix all me feed tonight,' he said. 'And if I don't get it finished – that's *another* thing that'll never be done.'

He snorted, testingly, at Arthur, to show his dilemma.

'I'll go, anyway,' John announced.

He looked away from his father.

'I can come as well,' said Arthur, quickly. 'Then Mr Foster can stay here to do his work.'

This was shortly considered, tested, twice, against Arthur's true willingess, and then accepted. John and Arthur went off to

help with the harvest and, when they had gone, Nelson paused
for no more than a minute, before getting up to go out himself.

Avril had watched Arthur's exit carefully. Then, while the
four of them who remained sat quietly around the table, she
had thought over her promise.

Her father was at the door.

'Just a minute, Dad,' she said, 'I want to ask you something.'
With her mouth set grimly, she looked just like him.

They went to the Langholm farm in Arthur's van, stopping only
for a few minutes at his house where he dashed in to tell his
mother where he was going.

Nothing much was said between them, and when one or the
other did make a remark, it lodged uncomfortably in the centre
of distrustful caution. Arthur drove rapidly.

They soon found where the work was and were immediately
given their place in it. Arthur's appearance was unexpected and
provoked a moment's quizzical pause from Mr Langholm who
was reassured by John's explanation that he had stood in for
Nelson. From then on there was too much to do to worry about
why people were doing it.

From fields to the great barn the track and land sprouted
labour, moving with tractors and trailers mowing the long,
bowed stalks of stained gold corn, baling, threshing, lifting over
the whole area a simmer of steady, hurried effort. The grey
clouds, still unbroken as an arc, drew all the light into their own
darkening fall; the sky leant down slowly to the earth as if to
overlay it with smothering pressure of brooding weight. Thunder
had been released in other parts, and now it rolled up slowly
above the vaporous bank faintly, further off as yet, but soon to
come and slash the steady lines once and for all, that day. On
the ground, men were made to scuttle and the corn, already
wilting before the outburst, had the sodden look of crops about
to be ruined. There would be no more harvesting for weeks, if
ever, that season.

The lights were turned on. In the farmyard the house, bed-
rooms and all, was switched bright and the open-curtained
windows shone out their bulbs like sideshows. The tractors

turned on their lights and their twin yellow globes probed the field and track like peering antennae. Cars were brought into the field and lined up at the top of it – and their headlights were switched on to help the workers. Bare cable was looped from byre and loft and the naked bulbs hung a safe distance from the barn.

The farm was way down from John's, in the opposite direction to Aldeby, right in the neck of a valley whose river spread from thereon to join the Tyne. Way above it, like the crest of a frozen wave, was the Wall, showing its power far more at this distance than it did near to. And around, in all directions, for miles in all directions – nothing more than a clump of farm buildings, an escarpment of cottages, the long accumulation of a small, gritty town – the land riding free.

Arthur was put to help on the thresher. He had to fork up, and soon his skin reeked with the luxurious sweat of ripe grain. It was work which jolted his back and forced his arms to a stiffness which would turn sore the following morning. The corn swished up from the ravelled pile – up to be hooked on another's hoist which fed it to the machine. Men all around him, their faces comically flecked with the tag ends of stalk and seeds. A barrel of a man sacking the final product against his open waistcoated belly, then humping it away and another taking his place.

But the important thing was to get all in. John had been given Mr Langholm's tractor while the farmer went away to see to the lights, and he drew the glinting rolling blades down the field with a great sweep. He worked within moss-green hedges which stroked the darkness like felt on silk and withdrew into black centres rustling with the scatter of field-mice and the crawl of animals. John was in his element; drunk and late home the previous night – as in the old days – he had gone through most of the day encircled by a tight hangover which had made every large movement a delicate pinpoint of balance; now, with the alcohol sweated out, and the strange lowering night to prod him on, he opened up to warring action and pulled through the work with an energy which at once annoyed and amused those who were with him.

The two of them saw each other rarely, but when John brought his whooping tractor up to the barn, he would shout out to Arthur just as he shouted out to everyone – and Arthur began to respond, enjoying the brawling, half-lit intimacy of it all. And whenever he did go near John, he saw himself treated as a fellow among neighbours. The two of them had come together to a different place. At least while they were there, they would act together.

The harvesting went on for about three hours – everyone certain that it would rain the next minute. But though the clouds sank so near to the ground that they seemed ready to jolt against it there was no rain. Soon the countryside was pitch black; the glow and arc of headlights at the Langholm farm were the only traces of people; no glow of town or village, no separation of shades by hidden lamped streets – nothing but darkness.

Arthur by this time was working so mechanically to keep up with the others that he wheeled around as if threatened when John banged him on the shoulder.

'T' best part of it's done,' John announced. 'They can manage just as well without us now. We can bugger off.'

Arthur took his word for it and they went down to the field for the van. They said good-night to Mr Langholm – refused his invitation to stay on for something to eat, and left.

He drove quickly. Something in John's moving, unsettled beside him in the cooped closeness of the van, made him take risks.

'Slow down!' John shouted. Then, lowering his voice, 'Please . . . this bridge.' Arthur saw the small stone bridge in front of them. 'This is where I swim.' The van stopped. John got out. 'You needn't wait,' he said. 'I'll make my own way back.' Then, awkwardly, politely, he added: 'Come if you like. I've brought a towel.'

As Arthur went down the deep-walled steps to the path which led alongside the gorge-bottom river, the pasty coat of his cooling sweat lifted from his skin at the hiss of long-suspended rain. A large, fat raindrop plopped on to his bare neck. It was perfectly still. Even the flutter of the water over the rocks seemed like the noiseless rolling of oil across steel. No birds, nor rustle, no sharp squeak or crack; a held breath.

They were at a small clearing. Vaguely, in the darkness which flowed over them like a liquid mist, spreading over and sealing everything, he saw John strip off.

'Put your clothes under some of these big stones,' John said. Then, 'Here she comes!' he shouted.

The clouds eased back and let in some light as they gathered their belly weight of rain. Arthur, struggling, rapidly, out of his clothes, saw John marching towards a large pool, formed by a high circle of tumbled rocks giving the appearance of the tip of a crater. The plump raindrops drummed faster, stinging the ripe ground with quick smells.

John dived in. Arthur heard him thrashing the water.

'Hurry up!' he bellowed. 'It's marvellous in here.'

Then it poured.

TWELVE

By complicated manoeuvring Arthur had managed to arrange it so that they arrived at the Coxe's with both the van and the car. He had been even more reluctant than usual about going to the Coxe's private dance. Before coming:

'I think that you are being most ungracious,' his mother reproved him. Dressed in a short, heavy evening dress of thickly draping grey silk, Mrs Langley rose to her appearance and attacked where, until now, she had prevaricated.

'I'm being honest, Mother,' Arthur replied sulkily. 'If that is ungracious – then I am prepared to accept your description.'

'And now you're being silly,' she retorted.

He stood at the mantelpiece in the large drawing-room, then, feeling the antique formality of this pose, he crossed the room, using the whisky decanter as his objective.

'I think that you have kept yourself to yourself for quite long enough,' Mrs Langley continued, shifting slowly round to reface him. 'You scarcely go out, and no one has been invited here since you came home. Surely there must be someone you would like to see. I have long ceased to expect anything of that kind from your sister – but I certainly expected a different attitude from you.' Arthur poured himself a drink and contained himself against a reply. He realised the limitations of his mother's strictures. Only once or twice since her illness had she leapt into such a strait-jacket of consistent and vehement expression; and now, as on the previous occasions, he was aware of her brittle effort – the raising of a curtain on what she cared about most but rarely had the energy to propose; and he was afraid to contradict her too harshly lest he jammed something, locked her or upset her, took her away from the balanced quietness of ordered and restrained living. 'Why don't you take your place in things in the country?' she demanded. 'Your father was part of everything. So was my father. You can't waste your time alone.'

'I enjoy it.'

'It doesn't appear so.'

'Please, Mother. I work all day – I like to be alone in the evenings.'

'Don't you understand that if you never do anything – she'll never do anything? You ought to take her out. I don't know what she does. She does nothing at all.'

Mrs Langley was now straining at her speech. The words came out through a mouth which seemed to chop at them as they passed.

'Mother,' said Arthur firmly, 'each of us is perfectly content.'

'You are both selfish!'

'Perhaps we are. But that is no reason for you to be so concerned.'

'Patricia does nothing. What does she do? And you don't help her. You should help her, Arthur.'

Pat came into the room with a modesty which confirmed Arthur's suspicion that she had been listening at the door. She walked across towards him, bowing slightly at her mother, swinging her bare shoulders in a dress which – though Arthur guessed it to be out of date – lifted her to a startling beauty. He turned to pour her a drink.

'Are you sure that you wouldn't like something, Mother?' Arthur asked.

'No thank you.'

Mrs Langley spoke meekly, her eyes clinging to Pat's face almost cravenly.

'Well,' said Pat, spinning out the loose pleats of her dress as she turned from Arthur to her mother, 'have you been talking about anything interesting?'

'No,' Mrs Langley replied quickly. 'I was encouraging Arthur to join in more.'

'Join in what, Mother?'

Mrs Langley looked around her, seeming to find the few feet which separated her from a chair an uncrossable gulf.

'Join in what?'

The old woman smiled, vaguely, at her daughter and stretched out her right hand, feeling for a support which would lead her to a chair. Pat had both interrupted her, cutting her off when nothing was resolved, and made her aware of possible reaction to what she was saying.

'We'd better be going,' Arthur suggested, briskly.

'Yes,' said Pat. 'I hate to be late for anything like this.' She smiled.

Arthur ushered his mother out of the room and helped her into her coat. Understanding neither the proper requirements nor the sudden switches of mood in his mother, he was concerned only that she should be treated as a partial, but permanent, invalid; this way he would be safe.

Pat stood in front of the small oval mirror in the hall, still with her drink in her hand. He took her coat and held it out for her. Slowly, she put out her arms in such a way that he had to take the sleeve carefully across her hand and awkwardly pull it towards her shoulders. When it was almost on, she swung around to him, her face suddenly riveted on his.

'Why *don't* you go out?' she whispered.

Arthur dropped his arms to his side and shook his head.

'Are you ready?' Mrs Langley enquired.

'Always,' Pat replied – and she went to her mother, taking her through the door and into the yard.

He followed, determined to arrange things so that he would have independent means of transport. Already, he was weary with the evening's entertainment.

Yet, as soon as he entered the Long Room at the Coxe's, in which the dance was taking place, he was aware of a feeling of relief. Within the comfortably lined walls, the floor, unfussily cleared for dancing, the small Scottish band at the far end of the room, the conversation pleasant and friendly, this was the unforced milieu in which he could so easily take such an enjoyable place.

Pat was soon dancing, and Arthur watched her. Why had she not chosen to play her proper role? Her solitary walks, her long disappearances – these seemed at once monstrous and pointless in the well-lit elegance of the Long Room. More than that, like his own private burrowing, they seemed absurd. No one, he thought, coming freshly into this room, would even believe when told, let alone guess for himself, that Pat's attendances at such functions were limited to arbitrary, whimsical impulses which fell so far short of common politeness that invitations were sent her more out of tolerance than affection. She stared across at him and he turned away. Yet he could not resist looking up at her again, and again she caught him. This time she laughed and her partner followed the direction of her laugh to nod at Arthur who moved off.

He was ashamed of his nervousness which came, he was sure, from knowing so few of the people there. In one way, he knew all of them. Mr Herbert, his wife and their three young daughters, all of whom lived and worked at the large eighteenth-century country-house which was open to the public and run, as Mr Herbert would say, half-modestly, half-sadly 'as a business'. Major Hill (ret.) and his wife with one son still at school, another in the City. Sir Norman Hunt, a director of a large shipping company in Newcastle; with him his wife, son and daughter. The Martlands, Terraines, Collinses, Grants, Oakshotts – all, somehow, phantoms to Arthur as he had given no life to them through friendship. For he was the real friend of none of them. Even during his holidays from school, Pat and himself had stayed firmly apart, participating when essential – but mostly apart.

He passed by his mother, sitting with Mrs Coxe and Mr and Mrs Onslow. She nodded to him, calmly. The talk was of flowers. Detailed, technical talk which reminded him of his mother's assurance when, as often, she worked in the garden. Here, as there, she was exactly as she ought to be. As with Pat, seeing her as she was now, he could barely imagine her other than poised, settled, part of this society.

He had kept to himself too much. This, in reality, was the proper life of both Pat and his mother. The death of his father and his own morose return had caused a change which he had wrongly come to regard as the normal state of affairs. It was his years away in the army which had made him insensitive to the rhythm which was here, now, being taken up.

'Cigarette?'

Arthur started away from the slim case.

'Thank you. Yes.' He took one. Duncan Collins. About two years younger than he was.

'You haven't been out much the last few weeks.'

The Hunt. Duncan's father was one of the wealthier farmers and either he or his son hunted at least once a week.

'No,' Arthur replied, almost apologised, 'I've been busy.'

'How do you enjoy running the estate?'

Arthur smiled, recognising the shyness which underlay Duncan's use of the word 'estate'.

'It could hardly be called an "estate",' he said. 'What we have around the house isn't much more than a smallholding. Then there's Drummond's farm – and that's about it as far as the land goes. Still,' he added, to prevent any impression of a snub, 'I am working on our part of it – and I must say I enjoy it very much.'

'The more you have the more you have to enjoy,' Duncan retorted – bringing out the stoutly inherited slogan like a warning. 'I must say,' he continued, severely, 'I was very surprised that you sold that other place of yours to Foster. He's made it into quite a property, you know.'

'Yes. I'm glad. My father seemed to let him get on with it while we still had it.'

'Good investment with a man like that,' Duncan interrupted. 'As long as he put up the rent with it.'

'And so I felt that the farm was almost his anyway.'

Duncan's eyes misted slightly, as if he was deliberately forcing himself not to look at something he found rather disturbingly distasteful.

'Besides,' Arthur added, as a corrective, 'I had to sell something.'

'Never sell land!' said Duncan, brusquely. This was followed, however, by a nod which told Arthur that he understood his difficulties – what with his father and one thing and another – and this made Arthur regret having provided the opening for condolences he so resented.

They talked a little more. Stiltedly, but not uncomfortably.

He envied the way that Duncan fitted himself so firmly into what was going on. He liked him – even, he discovered, took pleasure in his company. And why not? Duncan was exactly the man with whom he ought to be friendly. They spoke so little before and after a hunt – but Arthur recalled one or two sentences which had suggested a sketch of Duncan's habits. Cars; trips to London; evenings with some of the army officers at Hexham and Carlisle; shooting; parties. He set these in front of himself in the most tempting, desirable way he possibly could; yet while he felt that he was missing something, he could not feel envious.

'Well,' Duncan concluded, 'see you later I expect.' He nodded and walked across to a group of friends.

Arthur realised that he had heard nothing of Duncan's last remarks.

The music had stopped and Pat was being led towards him. She nodded to her escort a few paces away from her brother. He noticed that she was cool, almost weary; whatever feeling had excited her to sparkle in her dress had already been replaced by one which obviously caused her to react against the whole affair.

'Are you ready to go?' she demanded, quickly.

'I'm rather enjoying myself,' he replied. 'I think I've been missing a lot – staying in all the time.'

She looked to discover whether he was serious. Then, not finding what she wanted, she said, fiercely:

'I think you've been bloody stupid since you came back!'

The band began to play the Gay Gordons. Pat noticed someone moving towards her.

'Even you can dance this,' she said to Arthur and using her rudeness in cutting the intended partner to cover Arthur with such embarrassment that he was confused into following her, she led him on to the floor.

She flung herself into the skipping dance. He held out his arm for her, and she took his hand, twirling beneath it, her hair lifting off her neck and showing a skin so ivory cream that he wanted to let his hand rest on it, to discover its real texture. She gave the appearance of relishing the jig enormously, her eyes catching his own with pleasure every time she completed her circle, whooping at the appropriate places, dashing down the length of the floor in the leading section. It was only towards the end of the dance that Arthur became sufficiently unaware of his clumsiness to enjoy it. Then the music stopped.

They were in the middle of the floor. She curtsied to him and, stiffly, he bowed. He led her to one side of the room.

'You can go, now that you've done your duty,' said Pat.

'I don't mind.'

'Well, as you seem to be frothing with enthusiasm, do you think you could offer me a cigarette?'

Arthur reached for his case and held it out to her. As he struck a match to light it, the band began to play a breathy accordion version of a pop song with the drums plodding through the beats like horses' hooves on mud-tracks. She hunched forward and pulled at the tail of yellow flame: no one came to ask her to dance. Duncan was chatting to some of the younger women – talking forcefully, he observed, and he concluded that the subject must be political, or in some other way removed from the centre of their interests. Mrs Coxe had moved on to Sir Norman Hunt and family, prising into them like a lever into four wedged panels of wood. Jane Martland, who hunted occasionally, was the only one to catch his eye, and he nodded to her briefly, returning immediately to Pat. Away from the dance floor, she was yet attached to it; she gazed at the twisting figures with intense concentration. Arthur realised that Pat must be the oldest unmarried woman in the room; the realisation shocked him to a distaste for a situation which could impel it. He was sorry for her.

'Would you like to dance again?'

She looked at the cigarette, barely spoiled with the faintest rim of ash; then she turned towards the floor which was the stage for the only two couples of the party who could perform the required routine.

'Are you sure of what you're saying?' she asked.

He followed her glance, and his knees clenched with dismay.

'No!' he replied, abruptly.

She laughed and Arthur, glad to have his sympathy dispelled before it developed to an action which would commit him too far, laughed with her.

'Jane Martland,' Pat whispered. She smiled at Arthur. 'I'll spare you,' she said.

Jane, almost on them, found Pat sandwiched between herself and Arthur.

'I was just going out for a moment,' Pat announced to her. 'Would you come with me? There's something I would like to talk to you about.'

With no more than a nod to Arthur, Jane went away with Pat. Shielded from what had not disconcerted him in the least, embarrassed by Pat's obvious strategy, suddenly alone with no objective even remotely akin to a prospect, Arthur determined to leave.

It was five past ten. Too early to persuade his mother to go. Inexcusable for him to leave her and Pat to stay on and be forced to return home without him. He stood in the hall for a few moments, uncertain of what he should do. Then he went back to the drawing-room and told his mother that he had forgotten something. He would be away for not more than an hour. She was unenquiring, unperturbed.

It seemed mean to take his own van – too forceful a reminder of his earlier lack of faith. He went to the car.

'I knew you'd take this,' said Pat.

He wanted to drag her out of the seat – throw her away.

'You were very quick,' he said, calmly.

'Yes.' She was nervous. 'I'm as happy to leave as you are yourself.' She smiled.

'I'm not leaving,' he replied.

'Then neither am I.' She stared through the windscreen and waited.

Arthur turned and set off for the van. The car door slammed hard and she ran up to him.

'Pat, you're behaving stupidly!'

'So are you.' She laughed. 'If we leave – we leave together.'

'Please stop being so silly.' Still he spoke quietly.

They stood, at the door of the van. Very deliberately, Arthur

reached across in front of Pat and opened the door. She began
to get in. He grabbed her arm and stopped her.

'If you don't leave me alone I shall pack and go tomorrow! I
didn't come back here to be treated as if we were children.
Now,' he bit his words, 'get out of the way!'

She stared at him. He held her look without yielding to it.
Then she shook off his arm and went away.

He drove down the gravel drive slowly. The house, noisy and
well-lit behind him, seemed more real now that he was outside
it than it had done when he had been inside. He did not look
back at Pat. He pressed all thought of her out of his mind and
called up the mood which had taken him into the house. At first,
he went towards the pool under the bridge where he had swum
with John two nights previously. There was an aimless shallow
wash of detached melancholy which he could not throw off; as
the house had seemed lively only when he had left it, so that
evening with John seemed more real than anything which had
happened to him since, or for months before. Real? It was stupid
to question a word when he knew what it referred to in himself.
Real. Open. True. No past. Carrying no balances of others'
fortunes or opinions. Oliver was no longer real. The letters
were no more than encouragement to stand still. Oliver's last
letter was still unanswered. For how many months? It was all
playing. He wanted something to happen.

He reached the bridge and slowed down. Then he remembered something, turned the van towards the Foster farm, and
moved off quickly.

It was a perfect setting. Arthur decided – and he was a perfect
fool.

The moon was big, almost grainy, heavily lodged in the black
sky, chalkily unthickening the shadows. Arthur could clearly see
the Wall curving and dipping, an old skin trailing across pocked
and knotted bark. Always being there; useless, lasting, sliding
along its course with no more effort, no purpose but to be
preserved. Yet Arthur felt no power from it, nothing to invoke,
nothing to disturb, only interest. Another interest fastened on
to another relic.

He had scrambled up the hillside like a fugitive. Cursing his stupidity with every slip, every false foothold, and going faster, running towards his own idiotic impulse as if fleeing from a terrible accident, submerging his reason under inexplicable suffusions of need.

It was all extremely foolish.

He lit a cigarette, smoothed down his dinner-jacket and looked around him with the eye of someone admiring the countryside. 'Fine night for a stroll.' Yes. 'Thought I'd pop out.' Lovely country. Fresh air.

He walked towards the mile-castle before the wood.

'Who's that?'

Arthur stopped, sharply. His tongue suddenly thickened against his teeth. He would go away without answering.

'Langley.'

'Oh.'

John's voice was indifferent, almost antagonistic – yet somehow this settled Arthur's panic and encouraged him to go over to him. He was sitting on one of the brokendown walls.

'Fine night,' said John.

Arthur shut his mouth quickly to prevent a giggle.

'Yes,' he replied.

He realised that, left to himself, John would say nothing, that he probably understood him to be out for a walk and expected him to pass on. Standing, almost posing – to assure all onlookers of the casual irrelevance, mere politeness, of his words – he asked:

'Could you tell me the name of that place we swam at the other night?'

'Hm?'

'Where we went swimming.' He was a fool to have come. 'The name.'

'It hasn't a name that I can think of.'

'Nice place.'

He would pause for another twenty seconds – to give balance to his words – to show that they were not a nubbed overture but a slight rustle across completely self-assured silence – and then he would leave.

'Is your sister better?' He barked.

'Avril? Better enough to go out anyway.'

'She had quite a nasty fall.'

'Oh – she was probably dreaming or something daft like that.'

'You speak of dreaming as if you despised it,' said Arthur, desperately.

'No,' John answered. 'It's all right when you've no distance to fall.'

Then he laughed.

'Down with dreams,' he muttered.

For the first time, he looked at Arthur. Standing, ready to go, ready to leave, in his jet-black dinner-jacket with the silks faintly glossy in the moonlight. His rough answers seemed comical. Arthur so obviously wanted a friendly chat.

'I've seen you working here with old Stoneman and the vicar, haven't I?' he began.

'Probably, yes.' Everybody for miles around had seen that. It was his label.

'Do you really enjoy doing that sort of thing?'

'Yes, I do rather.'

'What is it exactly that you like about it?'

Arthur immediately rejected his stock reply to this question.

'I suppose I like to pretend I'm learning something,' he said, eventually.

'Why "pretend"?'

'All right,' Arthur laughed. 'I do learn things. Whether I like it or not! It's very pleasant as well.'

'I can see that. Old Stoneman's a joker for a start.'

Arthur liked both John's curiosity and his gentleness. It would have been so easy to have spoken nastily of Mr Stoneman.

They began to talk about the Wall. At first, the conversation was question and answer, with John doggedly pressing Arthur on recent finds, what they meant, what they added to what was already known, how they changed it. Arthur's lack of adequate replies to many of the questions encouraged John's interest. And as they went on, John began to refer to information of his own.

'I'm sure you know more about it than I do,' Arthur commented.

'Nothing like.' He paused. 'We once went around Chesters and the Housesteads. Then they gave us a pamphlet. I meant to follow it up, but I never did.'

'I have a few books which you can look at,' Arthur volunteered. 'I don't know whether they'll be much good – but you might like to glance at them.'

'No. You needn't bother yourself. Just tell me what they're called and I'll get them out of the library. Thank you.'

'It would be no trouble, really. I'll let you have them the next time I see you.'

'Well,' said John, brusquely. 'Thank you. Very kind of you.'

Arthur was relieved. His work was done. The link had been made and now it could go on or not, as he wished. He would have to be getting back. He must not spoil anything.

'Well then,' John began, awkwardly, 'I'll have to be off. Thanks again for the offer.' He hoisted himself to his feet. 'Good-night.'

'Good-night.'

Arthur did not stay to watch him go, but set off in the opposite direction right away.

John was flattered by Arthur's action. It was obvious that he had sought him out. He had enjoyed talking with him – not that much had been said, but he felt that, with Arthur, he might be able to talk in a way he had never done before. If they had anything to say. At least it would be a change.

THIRTEEN

For two days John purposefully refrained from working near the Langleys' place.

Then he had to go down. He did what he had to do slowly, keeping near the hedge which bordered the field. Ten times he decided that he was wasting his time; but he stayed.

Arthur called him and they went into the summerhouse. 'Here are the books,' Arthur said. 'That one by Collingwood is really more a total history of the Romans in Britain. But you might find it useful if the other becomes too parochial.'

'Thanks.'

He took the books carefully. In the strangely shaped room, with its odd harmony of things which, on their own, he would either have overlooked completely or dismissed as 'tat', he felt uncomfortably clumsy. He had wiped his feet loudly at the door, but he imagined a trail of thick-ribbed wellington footprints behind him. And his working-clothes refused to ease into anything in the room, pointing his uncertain stance with their obvious utility.

'Do you mind – could I have a look at your books?' John asked.

'Please.'

Arthur jumped aside although he was far from being in John's way.

'Go ahead,' he added.

The books were in large open shelves which covered two walls of the octagon. Even in their display there was something attractive and John admired the few calf-bound books – occasionally a set of four or six – which mellowed the bright spines of the other volumes, giving the whole collection a treasured appearance. His eye skimmed the titles quickly, picking out only what was familiar, or what was odd. A set of Dickens, bound in green leather with two or three books in each volume. Aldous Huxley – many of his – D. H. Lawrence, Somerset Maugham, John Steinbeck, Ernest Hemingway, Albert Camus, P. G. Wodehouse, Graham Greene. There was a fat book entitled *Stubb's Sermons*, a book of Francis Bacon's Essays, another with the quaint name *Lark Rise to Candleford*, a set of small volumes labelled *The British Plutarch*. And he passed names he had read in reference but never in fact; Laurence Sterne, Jonathan Swift, Thackeray, Chaucer. There were hundreds of books.

While John was looking at his shelves, Arthur busied himself by poking the fire and stacking on more coal. Then he put on a small stove apparatus which supported a glass bulb of coffee, and spread himself over one of the armchairs, lighting a cigarette.

'I haven't read all of them of course. Or even most of them,' he explained, nervous in the muzzled intimacy of which John appeared unaware. 'The books I have are those I want to read.'

John did not reply. Finally, he turned towards Arthur and whistled admiringly.

'You've enough here to last a century,' he said.

'Probably take me that time to read them all.'

'Hm.'

'Would you like some coffee? Sorry I can't offer you tea. It's too much trouble to make it down here.'

'No,' John answered, detachedly. 'Thank you very much. I'll have to get back.'

Arthur nodded.

John returned the books at about the same time in the afternoon a week later. The clocks had gone back and it was almost dark. He had finished his work, washed rapidly, and changed out of his working-clothes. Arthur had been in the barn with Andrei and was dirty, dressed in old grey flannels, an ancient shirt and a battered sports jacket.

'Sit down,' he said. 'Won't take me a minute to get this fire going.'

Deftly, he pulled out a cardboard box from a small cupboard under a window seat, screwed some newspapers into loose twists, crossed cleanly-axed kindling on top of them and then took some coal out of the large scuttle, settled it carefully, and lit it.

'It won't take long,' he muttered.

Then he stood up.

'I don't let anyone come in here, so there's only a fire if I make it. You were lucky last time. I took the afternoon off.'

This time it had been planned. He had guessed that John would return at about the same time in the afternoon, and each day had made it his business to be within sight of the Fosters' bottom field.

'Coffee?'

'Yes please.' John had sat down in one of the armchairs while Arthur was at the fire. He had taken up a book which had been lying on the floor, and was flicking through it.

'It looks grim in here,' Arthur observed. And again, with efficient concern, he snapped on two side lights and knocked off the main switch, shuffled some loose papers on his desk into a heap, swung the other armchair around so that it was facing the fire, put on two or three pieces of coal, brought out a low table – a short scrubbed bench with squat legs – and placed cups, sugar and milk on it.

'That's better.'

John looked up. The room was a series of arcs from the two lights, each thinning slowly to shade, flowing up the walls and on to the segmented ceiling. As the light from the bulbs went upwards, the area in front of the fire – between Arthur and John – seemed lit only by the yellow flames which looped up and out from the splitting coal. Objects which had laid underneath his immediate memory, half imagined, now struck him vividly; the strange green glass, the little stone mummy figures, also green, the prints on the wall, the silk spread across a small chest and draping it around like a funeral flag, the long tapestry which filled one of the walls full length. John nodded at these things – to show how much they affected him.

'Do you play – that?' he asked, pointing at the piano.

'Not now. I used to play it a lot. As a matter of fact, I meant

to do something about it when I came back. Haven't got round
to it yet.'

'Your sister – does she play?'

'No.'

He turned around to the coffee.

'It's nearly intolerable in this glass construction,' he announced, gruffly. 'Still – with or without milk?'

'With milk.'

'Me too. Keeps the taste down.'

He poured attentively and both of them took sugar and milk.

'Were the books any use to you?'

John took a mouthful of coffee before replying. He hesitated:

'Not really. You have to know so much before you start with
those kind of books.'

'They are a bit dull,' Arthur responded.

'I'm sure they know what they're talking about and all that.
But they didn't put over any picture of what it was like.' He felt
his way.

'Oh, I don't know. They seem to give you plenty to go on.
The rest's up to you.'

'I suppose so,' John replied, cautiously.

'I prefer them to historical novels or reconstructions or whatever you call them anyway,' Arthur went on quickly. 'They're
usually so ordinary that you end up by thinking that everyone's
always been the same.'

'I haven't read any. But they can't be much worse than those
that you lent me. They're just like somebody wanting to find
out how we lived now – and reading a dictionary to do it!'

'What should he read?'

'I don't know. Maybe newspapers.'

'They always look like an accountant's lists a few years after
they've been printed. Impenetrable!'

'Well,' John hesitated, 'books then. Novels. At least there's
some life in them.'

'I would still prefer histories. But contemporary histories.'

'They'd be no better than newspapers!'

'At least they might have some facts in them,' Arthur
answered, smiling at the quick cancellation of his argument.

'Most novels I read seem to take it for granted that everyone knows about everything. You never read about how someone works or makes his money or reacts to the news or things like that.'

'Well, those books you lent me are full of those sort of facts – and as far as I'm concerned they might as well have been ape men walking backwards and forwards on that Wall.' Then, after a brief pause, he added: 'You can't really tell me that facts – just facts – can make you feel that you understand what any particular time in history was like. You've got to be able to imagine it!'

He took a deep breath. He had come prepared to talk, and even though his voice sounded parrot-like and so odd as to belong to someone else, he put his head down and forced his way on.

'Take *For whom the Bell Tolls* as an example,' he continued. 'I knew nothing about that civil war in Spain – but I did when I was reading that book . . . And you've got Charles Dickens' books there. Well, if you read *Oliver Twist* – you'll know what it was like to be an orphan in a workhouse. I bet you what you like that anybody writing a history of it would make it sound like some kind of awful ancient monument.'

'You ought to read Mayhew . . .'

'Who?'

'Mayhew. Henry Mayhew. *London Labour and the London Poor*. Then you wouldn't say that. I have it somewhere.' He went across to his books. 'It's in four volumes,' he said. 'Just take the first.'

'And if I like it – read on!' John grinned.

'That's right,' Arthur replied, and he dropped the book in John's lap as he went past him and back to his chair.

Over the next three or four weeks, they saw each other about half-a-dozen times. Twice when one or the other hailed from a bordering field and they left their work for a few minutes to talk – the other times in the summerhouse. Once, in the summer-house, they were interrupted by Pat who walked in, stopped to be introduced, stood with her back to them for about five minutes, and then left without a word just as John was about to produce an excuse for his own exit. Another time, outside,

Arthur stopped for no more than a minute, leaving when Andrei called out to him.

'He's a queer bugger,' said John the next time they met.

'Andrei? No. It's just that he's got so used to living on his own in that cottage that he seems odd. It's sad really. He seems to have to make such an effort to live – just to get by – in England, that he has no energy left for anything else.'

'I didn't mean queer,' John corrected himself. 'I meant miserable.' He wanted Arthur to talk about himself through Andrei.

'Yes. I think he is miserable. And I've talked with him about returning to Poland – but he won't go.'

'He never seems to go out.'

'Hardly at all. He has a television. He looks at that.' Arthur spoke dispassionately.

'Poor bugger.' He had failed: it was better to know nothing.

'Yes, and it's so strange the effect he has. Because he has none. Every time I meet him I know no more and no less about him than I did the first time. He goes away at the end of an afternoon – and I'm not sure that he'll come back,' he laughed. 'I'm never really sure he ever was there.'

'What do you mean?' In so dismissing Andrei, Arthur appeared to dismiss everything.

'Well. Like some things that have happened to me. They might have happened. They might not. I can't really remember.'

'I can,' John replied.

'I mean I can't see that they have influenced me one way or the other.'

John wanted to ask him for examples. He knew so little even of the outline of Arthur's life. Yet he was afraid to press him.

They sat in silence. At first, when such a hiatus had occurred, John had wavered between instant departure and desperate talk of anything. Now he accepted and enjoyed it. It was a relief, part of the pleasures of such a friendship.

FOURTEEN

'You don't shoot as if you'd been in the bloody army!'

Arthur grinned at him and guided the long barrel around steadily. The rooks had already scattered and lifted; now, those that were there either darted into a nest or moved restlessly from one tree to another. One of them settled in the cranny of branch and trunk. Arthur took careful aim.

John swung up his gun and fired. The bird lifted and flew away.

'Bad luck!' he said. Arthur brought down his gun.

'Thank you.'

'Pleasure,' John replied. 'I thought it might fall asleep before you got round to pulling that trigger.'

'Good of you to wake it up.'

'No trouble!' John answered. 'No trouble at all!'

They went on through the wood. The ground was dry and comfortable on the surface, but it soon broke to a quagmire. A Sunday afternoon in winter. The paths – hardly paths, looping ribbons of brushed grass – were now piled with leaves, again seeming light and harmless, but concealing soaking layers.

'I wonder how these leaves ever get tidied up?' Arthur said.

'They just rot.'

They were the only two out for miles around. These two hours after the middle of the day on Sunday were the only daytime natural break in the farmer's week. To be spent in sleep. Even Nelson had begun to concede that – and although he still announced that he was going to see to his expenses, and took out the long municipal looking black ledgers in which he kept his accounts, he would doze off after five or ten minutes, throw back his head over the chair, and snore loudly.

His mother had followed him into the back kitchen and watched him take his gun.

'Are you going out shooting?' she had asked.

'Just about,' he replied.

'We don't see much of you these days,' she said.

'Be thankful while you can!'

Lizzie tittered – and John knew that it came from unhappy nervousness.

'I'm all right, now,' he said, softly. 'You needn't worry about me.'

'But I do worry.'

'Why?'

She bit her lower lip; the action made her look incongruously girlish.

'Because I think you're being swept away,' she replied. 'I think you might be let down.'

'Now why do you say that? You've met Arthur. He's not a snob or anything.'

'No, he's a nice lad. I like him.'

'Well then. Why worry?'

'I don't know.' Then she lowered her voice, but spoke more firmly. 'For one thing I don't like the way you treat your father. He needn't be your father. It hurts him the way you go on.'

'Go on what?'

'Well – take no interest. He cares about that sort of thing.'

'What do you want me to do?'

'I don't know.'

She stood, waiting for him to reach out to her. He was late as it was. He left – knowing he could do nothing by staying – unable to throw off the guilt his mother had passed on to him, until he met Arthur. His preoccupation had led him to forget to bring Ben.

They were near the edge of the small wood.

'Look,' said Arthur. 'Neither of us seems to be passionate about slaughtering animals today – why don't you come back and have a quick coffee?'

John looked at his watch.

'It'll have to be quick.' Then, 'Yes. That'd be fine.'

He must be careful not to complicate his position with Arthur. Lately, a hesitation would be treated as disinclination and could lead to endless probing of 'real feelings'.

Once in the summerhouse, John took up a cue and began to play on the small billiard-table which Arthur had had brought in from the house. The room was so crowded with objects that it gave the appearance of a totally self-containing bolt-hole. With the books, Arthur's 'junk', the piano, billiard-table, chairs, coffee, it had a density which seemed at once desirable and unnecessary.

'I'll be with you in a minute,' Arthur said.

John played his shots idly, using the table as an excuse for looking at Arthur. He could still not get used to Arthur's efficiency in domestic arrangements. When he had joked about it, Arthur had jumped into a blushing excuse about the army, speaking like clipping-scissors, 'only thing I learnt', 'keep myself tidy', 'make a snack', 'lived on snacks', 'useful for that'. He did not talk much about the army, or about his family, nor did John press him to do so. Both of them avoided reference to what lay outside the context of what they had built for themselves. Sometimes, when they had talked for a while and John was tired of the effort, they would read or Arthur would self-consciously suggest that he might like to play cards – then he would want to know something of Arthur's past life, so that he could chew easy gossip between the gulps of conversations. Yet he desisted from asking anything. Once he had suggested that they go out for a drink, but the pub had been too empty and obtrusive, their isolation around a small iron-legged table awkward, the game of darts spiritless. It was better to be confined by the summer-house.

'Have you ever been to Edinburgh?' Arthur asked.

'That's to the point, anyway,' John replied.

Arthur grimaced. He knew no way to broach a subject with John but with both feet forward and jump. He was aware of the inelegance, even the comic aspect of this, and yet he could do no other.

'A beautiful city,' he mumbled.

John took careful aim and sliced his shot.

'Damn!' He scowled at the cloth. 'I can't even aim a cue these days.' He looked across at Arthur. 'Why?' he went on. 'Are you going up there or something?'

'I was thinking of driving up next Saturday.'

'What time would you have to set off?'

'Late morning. It wouldn't be worth it after lunch.'

'Hm. I would like to come. I've never been there. Stupid, isn't it?'

Still he stood beside the table, and they faced each other like men on either bank of a stream; this physical recognition, a wariness or uneased intimacy, would often bang down between them.

Arthur poured out some coffee.

'Is there a cup for me?'

Pat closed the door behind her as quietly as she had opened it.

'Certainly,' Arthur replied, with patently affected pleasantness. 'How would you like it?'

'Black.'

'Black as hell,' John whispered under his breath.

'Did I hear you say that you were going to Edinburgh?' she asked.

'If you were listening at the door you did – yes,' Arthur replied, politely.

'Of course I was listening,' she chided him.

'Sorry,' Arthur said. 'I shouldn't have doubted it.'

'I'm sure you didn't. But it's as well to preserve appearances in front of your visitor.'

'Please, Pat!'

'Thank you, Arthur.' She went and took the coffee from him.

When she turned and came across to him, John could see that she was enjoying every minute of it. So was he, he noted. Even a fortnight earlier, he would have disappeared into confusion and emerged only to look for the door. Now, he smiled.

'I'm so pleased you're enjoying yourself,' she said. 'You must come and meet the family some time. Then you'll really be entertained.'

Square in front of her, with her eyes staring into his, John felt his smile loosening to a silly grin, and he fumbled for a reply, unsuccessfully.

'You ought to bring him into the house,' she went on, still looking at John. 'We're house-trained. I think we could be civilized enough for him.'

'Pat!' Arthur's voice rose sharply.

John kept his eyes on Pat. He was not going to let her walk over him.

'Of course,' she continued, chattily, 'I know that I'm interrupting some terribly serious tête-à-tête between you two. But you see, I can't bear to think that my brother should cast all his pearls before – just one person.'

'I didn't think that you were so particular,' said Arthur. Both John and Pat turned in surprise at the sneer in his words. 'But if you want to hear my words so badly, then please have the good manners to wait your turn!' He paused. 'I think you ought to go.'

'No!' she snapped. Then, calmly, 'I would like to hear what you talk about.'

'For God's sake, Pat, stop acting so melodramatically! It's perfectly obvious that you aren't welcome here and I can't tolerate your silly dramas!'

'I'm leaving, anyway,' said John.

'No, please.'

Arthur came forward to him.

'No, no,' John continued, waving him away. 'I don't want to cause any trouble,' choosing his words nicely, and speaking to Pat. 'Your sister wants me to go and I'll go. But not out of embarrassment. I'm going because it's the easiest solution.'

'Of course!' she replied.

'But I choose to go,' he went on. 'And if you think you've kicked me out – you're mistaken. I'm going to save you being kicked out yourself.'

'Many thanks.'

'A pleasure.'

'Don't be absurd!' she retorted.

'I find it difficult not to be as things are,' he replied. He went to the door, and turned, making his deliberation clearly obvious.

'I'll leave you to your,' he pronounced the words carefully, 'tête-à-tête.'

Arthur turned his back on her and stared out of the window.

'You'll have to move across the room if you want to see him going up the field,' Pat began. 'Or maybe you have some special route worked out – and he walks around all the windows twice before leaving!'

'Pat, you're being very silly,' he answered, calmly. 'Childish.'

'You needn't talk,' she said.

He ignored her.

'If you go to Edinburgh,' she went on, 'I'm coming with you.'

'As you wish.'

'And I'm coming down here whenever I want to from now on. Childish? You're the one who's childish with your little private play-pen.'

'Whatever you say.'

Pat turned away. Arthur was afraid that she might be crying. The thought frightened him. Her hair loose, shoulders slightly bent, she might have been a young girl.

'Let's not quarrel,' he said.

'We've done nothing else since you came back. I thought that . . .' she paused.

'Yes?'

Pat swung around to look him straight in the eyes.

'I thought it might be the same as before.'

'I know.' Arthur's voice was dry. He tried to make it as casual as he could. 'But that was all over with, long ago.'

'I can understand your wanting to see him,' Pat went on slowly, 'but you see him so often. You act as though you can't bear to see anyone else.'

'That's not true.'

'Yes, it is.'

John would be well on his way by now. It was too late to run after him and bring him back.

'You must understand that we've both changed,' Arthur continued, lamely.

'I haven't.'

'Yes, you have. We both have. I – it isn't the same as it was before. It can't ever be the same again.'

Pat stood quite still. Then she sprang at him, slapped his face, and rushed out. The slap was cold on his cheek. It did not sting.

Arthur stayed in the summerhouse until way after midnight. He neither went into dinner nor bothered to turn on the lights when it grew dark.

He had been to John's home only twice since they had harvested together. He envied them. There was warmth and openness; John's mother so sweetly simple. Shirley so wary, Avril chirpy – his own house, by comparison, appeared melancholy. Long corridors barely lit, too many rooms too large. Pat and his mother circling the passages, winding through those rooms in endless spirals of involuted self-concern. Each concerned to preserve, the one what was past, the other what she had saved from the past.

Arthur longed to see John again. He had to prevent himself from bounding out to follow him. But he stayed where he was, determined to think through the position in which he had placed himself.

He was aware of many difficulties. There was something unbalanced, strained about his meetings with John. A liaison based on his own true but fragile affection for books, facility in mild expositions, and John's sudden discovery that books could exist on the surface of his life – this seemed at once feeble and unsatisfying. It was capable of no extension; he would serve John's purpose – or vice versa, though he could not imagine it – and that would be that. He wanted more.

He was conscious of the protected complacency of a life which could call 'work' that which was superfluous. Andrei and Ted had managed the few fields, the stock and horses before his arrival, and they could do so again without him – were already doing so, in fact, as his initial interest in the job faded. Of the selfishness which could ignore even those little things it was his plain duty to make a pleasure of in the country. Conscious that his return had done Pat no good and was quickly affecting her with real harm; aware that he had little impact on his mother but to puzzle her.

From a practical point of view it was ridiculous for someone of his age and opportunities to quit what at least was a useful – even promising – career, for such useless introspective refuge.

Conscious – above all – that he had let lapse an aim which had once been firmer within him than anything he had felt before or since. He smiled when he thought of Oliver, patronisingly, witlessly.

He had to keep himself still. To let the friendship between himself and John take its own way. To wait.

FIFTEEN

'Have some tea?' Lizzie asked.

'No thanks.'

'Cocoa then. It won't take a minute.'

Nelson waved his hand; he would not be bothered to reply.

'You've got to get something into you,' Lizzie persisted. 'Something nice and hot.'

She stood beside him, ready to fly off to the kitchen. But slumped in his crumpled waistcoat with his legs drooping on to the floor, missing the fender – he ignored her poised attention as he ignored her questions.

Hesitating, looking at her husband constantly so as not to miss the slightest demand he might make, Lizzie moved over to the seat which faced him and sat down, feeling totally helpless.

They were alone, Saturday evening. Avril with her boyfriend at a country pub; Shirley at the pictures in Aldeby with the two daughters of Mr Townsley from the next farm; John taken off after the afternoon clearing. All of them away before the dizziness which had suddenly overwhelmed their father.

'It's lucky you were in here,' Lizzie said.

Her words shuttled woodenly across the quiet room.

'Are you sure you're all right?' she continued. 'You don't want a doctor?'

Nelson lifted his right hand to his face, lifted it curiously as if he were only hoping for the action, not directing it, and fumbled his fingers across his eyes, wiping, pulling at the cobweb of fragility which seemed to have been laid on his face to mark it.

'I'll be fine,' he muttered. 'Just get us somethin' to drink.'

Lizzie darted to the kitchen and began to make some tea. While she was out of the room, Nelson gripped the arms of the chair and stood up. Not until he was firmly sure of his footing, testing his strength by pressing what little there was of it into his legs, not until then did he let go the chair. All the blood that was in him thinned to nothing, and he closed his eyes to be steady. His chipped ruddy skin moistened and was pale. Inside his clothes his frame seemed reduced, withering. He held himself upright until the muzzy swirling had passed, then he bent his knees slightly to reassure himself.

When Lizzie came in with the tray, he was back in the chair, his head against its high back, legs tensed, pushing just a little on the floor to move the rockers.

'Put somethin' on that fire, will you, lass?'

She left the tea on the table and took some logs from the scuttle, these were eased into the ember flames, not too hard, to keep the warmth up while they added to it.

She poured tea in one of the small, white china cups which had come to them from her father, and after she had seen Nelson sip from this, she passed him the egg sandwiches and flushed with pleasure when he took one.

'Any better?'

He nodded, then fumbled with the tiny chocks of egg which crowded his mouth as he tried to speak. Lizzie laughed and, after he had swallowed the sandwich with a large poking of his Adam's apple, he smiled back at her.

'You're all right, then?'

'Don't keep on, woman,' he answered, mock-severely. 'I can eat your sandwiches, can't I?' He paused. 'Well?' he demanded.

'Yes.'

'Then I'm fit for anything!'

Again, they laughed together, and in the unique half-hour or so of truce with work which followed, they chatted through more sentences of pleasant gossip than the scraps of a whole month on end would show most times. And all the time Lizzie watched for the slightest trembling or wilt of listlessness.

'Well,' said Nelson, with frail aplomb, 'I won't do any more tonight. No.' He shook his head, grimly. 'No,' he repeated. 'I'll just take it easy tonight. What there is to do can wait. And what had to be done on the nail – that'll just have to wait as well.'

With this, he stretched himself into the memorable freedom of a period of absolute indolence. His heels lifted from the floor, holding up the two slippers like two brown pennants, he unbuttoned his waistcoat and unbuckled the thick leather belt.

Lizzie began to clear up so that there would be nothing untidy in the room to spoil it.

'Nothing,' said Nelson.

'Anyway,' Lizzie responded, as she piled the tray neatly, 'John can do anything you really need doing when he gets back.'

Her voice slowly dropped as the sentence concluded. She had ruined it.

'He'll be lucky if he can find his way back,' Nelson replied savagely. 'If he stinks at night like he stinks of a mornin', he'll be lucky if he can do enough to get out of bed.'

Lizzie started to go to the kitchen. If she said no more – she might just save it.

'Know what he had the cheek to say this afternoon?' Nelson demanded. Lizzie stopped, her back to him. 'Bloody hypocrite.' She turned.

'Please, Nelson,' she said. 'Please don't upset yourself. You're not well.'

He twisted his head away from her look and stared into the fire. She paused to say something else, then gave up and went into the kitchen.

Nelson looked at the charring wood with the delicate coil of grey smoke which lifted on the edge of the yellow flame. He was too tired to tell the story to Lizzie, but he could not prevent it from sliding up into his mind.

They had been forking hay down from the loft to the stalls underneath. He had felt sick, somehow, even then, and John had noticed.

'Sure you're feeling all right?' John asked.

Nelson did not reply – but he found that he had stopped the regular swing of his fork.

'You go in for a minute,' said John. 'I can manage this.' It would mean missing Edinburgh.

'You can manage nowt.'

They worked on. Then:

'Look,' John urged, 'I don't mind. You look badly. Go in. I'll finish up tonight as well. Go and have yourself a sit-down.'

'Tonight!' Nelson sneered. 'I won't see you for dust.'

'Don't be daft. Just let me do it all and go and look after yourself.'

Nelson stared at his son for a moment, and then, in a voice which he imagined to be a shout:

'Just you do the work you're paid for!' he said. 'That's all I want from you. No more. The rest's for me to do. I know what it's worth.' And though John had stayed out a long morning, it was done.

Lizzie sat down in her chair and looked at him while her fingers worked slowly on turning a shirt collar. Nelson was muttering to himself. 'Let me do it all, he says. Let me do it all . . . Huh!' She wanted him to rest.

SIXTEEN

'I hope she didn't appear too melodramatic,' Arthur began.

'Who?' John had considered his behaviour at some length, and concluded that he had been rude to her.

'Pat.' Arthur smiled. He had introduced her only to introduce what he himself wanted to say, but John's withdrawn caution threatened to extend the prologue throughout the play. 'The other day,' he went on, patiently. 'When she came in and "took over".'

'Oh. Then.'

'Yes.' He paused. 'I hope that you didn't think her over-dramatic.'

'Why should I?'

'Come on, John. You know what I mean. I thought she was, anyway.'

'It's her place.'

'What does that mean?'

'She can do what she wants in it,' John replied.

Arthur was stuck. To disentangle the assumption of that one sentence would take him most of the evening. He would let the subject drop.

'No,' said John, argumentatively, 'I wouldn't have said she was melodramatic.' He considered: in such a corner of confidence, even private disturbances which reflected badly on himself could be unloosed. 'In fact, if anything, I think that I was a bit – over-reached myself a bit.' The casual confession stumbled slightly, for want of a ready formula, but nevertheless he felt that his manner had carried his intent.

'Not at all,' Arthur retorted, briskly. 'You had every right to be amazed. She was damned rude.'

'No,' John answered, happily, 'I wouldn't have said she was "rude" exactly. More – "peculiar".' The last word delivered emphatically. He had already used it several times, to himself, when revising the encounter.

'She's certainly that,' Arthur replied, seeing a suitable punctuation. But this agreement, once uttered, sounded not only ungallant and unaffectionate, but disloyal. 'I mean, I'm sure that what you said just about sums up her – attitude – on that particular occasion.' Not much better. He began again: 'I'm sure . . .'

'Yes,' John interrupted him. 'That's what I thought. But she has a right to be. I haven't. It's her place.'

'I can't see that property has much to do with manners,' said Arthur, rather testily.

'Maybe it hasn't,' John replied. 'But I would say that she was right about calling me a visitor. And a visitor can't say just whatever he likes.'

'Why not?' Arthur demanded impatiently.

'Or he'll be sent off,' John grinned. 'Like I was.'

'But that's ridiculous. I thought that, if anything, you sent her off.'

'Just in time. And all I was doing was to make the best of a bad job. No. She won.' Then, 'She was straightforward enough about it, anyway.' Carefully, 'Is she always like that?'

'Of course she isn't!'

'Oh.'

Silence.

'Just that I think she's had rather a rough time lately,' Arthur continued. 'Since our father died, that is.'

'I see.'

John wanted to hear no more. That subject was the one he would do anything to avoid in Arthur's presence.

'I don't know,' Arthur went on. 'I think that she's disappointed in me, as well.' He watched John's face closely; no response. That dissatisfied him. He had noticed John's enlarged care when he added the general enquiry about Pat, and guessed its motive. It was better to go on as if he had understood none of this. 'You see, it's amazing but she doesn't have many friends around here,' he continued, 'even though she's lived here all her life.'

'Well, she wouldn't, would she?'

'Why not?'

'Well, there aren't many around here that would – fit in with her.'

Arthur was shocked.

'Yes, it must be very difficult for somebody like her,' John added, stolidly.

'I can't understand why you should say that,' Arthur replied. 'I simply can't understand it. Apart from anything else – apart from the question of Pat's "specialness" with which I agree but, I'm sure, for entirely different reasons – there are plenty of people she knows in the area. She's meeting people all the time.'

'What are you worried about, then?'

'I'm not worried.' He paused. 'I'm bewildered.'

John examined him for a while to test his statement against his appearance and then, finding that they tallied, he leaned forward with an eagerness which unnerved Arthur further, and began:

'I know what you're thinking. And you're half right, half wrong. But the fact that *we* can get on together has nothing to do with her. Just because *you* take people as you find them doesn't mean that everybody else does. And you needn't be – "bewildered" as you call it – that's just ignoring facts. Your sister's being more straightforward – no, more normal – than you are when she tries to look down on me. Mind you, she can stuff that! But I don't think it's the real reason. She just likes to be on her own as far as I can see, she doesn't like mixing very much.'

'You seem to have had the opportunity of observing her quite closely.'

'That one time in here was the first time I have ever spoke to her,' John replied.

'A quick impression.'

'It had to be quick!'

They were silent. In showing such a reaction, Arthur had opened that which he wished permanently closed. The way he had – unusually – deliberately asked John to come down this evening, the care he had taken to extricate himself from all possible commitments which might lead to intrusion, even the way the summerhouse was prepared – large fire, side lights, some drink in (all, he hoped, unnoticed by John, and all done with a shamefaced nervousness which tried to deny the affection it concealed) – all this had been a preparation for the one thing he really wanted to confirm; something elusive, indiscoverable, impossible to elucidate, and, once known, by that very fact probably made the less true; yet he needed to find out. He needed to know that John was enjoying their friendship and would continue it. It would not be easy to do this.

Ridiculous! It was obvious that John enjoyed it. That was a simplification – insinuating that distributed goods, even in the wrappings of friendship, had somehow been given just reward in the coinage of 'enjoyment'; Arthur knew that John had absorbed himself in these encounters. He could see that he was happy, hear that he was delighted. But, still, he could not be sure, not certain, not absolutely at ease.

'You were going to say something about Pat,' John encouraged him.

'Was I?'

'That's the impression I got!'

'What was I going to say?'

'Look,' John replied. 'I'm not trying to force you into anything. Let's drop it if it makes you feel like that.'

Like what? Arthur longed to ask; longed to pull out every minute assessment and investigation of motive and feeling.

'I was just – I suppose – going to excuse by explaining her,' he answered.

'There are no excuses needed,' John murmured.

Arthur could see that the subject was set in his mind.

'You see,' he went on, detachedly, 'there isn't much to tell except that we were all very close when we were young – and, I suppose, in a way, she's expected us to – stay as we were then. Impossible of course.'

'Why?'

'Just impossible.' Arthur was calmer now. John's question had at last touched on the impulse which was usually checked when about to allow any investigation of this question. Still, he must be honest. 'I mean, quite simply, because we've all changed. Even when my father was alive – it was better then, perhaps he allowed her to pretend for too long – but even when he was alive it was impossible. And I can't explain to her . . .'

'Why not?'

Arthur shook his head. No further. Self-preservation prohibited that. He was too aware of the entwined ambivalence of his own attitude and action, public and private, the encouragement, the indecision, the joy, the fear. No further.

'You get the same sort of thing, to a greater or lesser extent, in all families. All large ones,' he concluded.

John wanted to ask what sort of thing that might be, but he withheld the question.

'The way you were talking the other night about the army,' John began, consciously switching the subject but doing so, as he noticed, with Arthur's gratitude, 'I wonder you ever left it.'

'It's easy to glamorise what's over and done with.'

'It's just as easy not to.'

Arthur laughed.

'Yes,' he replied. 'I suppose it is. And I did like it, until the last year or so.'

Gradually, guided and prodded by John's demands, he described some part of his service. He liked this not because he particularly relished reminiscence, but because it gave John's interest an object which was within easy reach. Moreover, Arthur found that now – or it might have been to do with circumstances rather than time – with John he was happy to spin out his army days. Sometimes he caught the wash of *A Soldier's Memoirs* churning on ahead of him, but, more often, the mere reconstruction of his service rehabilitated its importance in his mind and so resettled its position in his life. The life which had followed his resignation had been too shattering for him to do anything but forget what had gone before it. Now he was glad to remember it, though perhaps such an effort was undertaken only as a conscious levelling – wanting to sweep clean and clear the path behind him so that he could go on purposefully, and be seen to be doing so. John must not think that their friendship was based on a whimsical reaction to inertia.

He mentioned Oliver, but even in trying to be fair towards him, he cheated. For though he was quite open in cataloguing a list of his virtues, this was done in accents which suggested a commendable accumulation of admirable properties rather than any remarkable mixture of goodness and courage. He could not speak warmly. And in fact, what warmth there was in his descriptions was associated with those towards whom he had felt little but apprehensive respect while with them. Strong men; men, as he said, with a faintly amused seriousness, of decision and authority. Men who would set a target and reach it; declare an aim and achieve it; plan an objective and take it.

'That's why I admire your father so tremendously,' he went on. 'I'm sure you won't be offended if I say that it seems to me that, starting from nothing, or very little, he has done wonderfully. Not spectacularly.' Conscious, as always with John, that his words could congeal to a pasty sermon or thicken to rotund patronage, he spoke gruffly, thus clearly intimating that which he feared and so, he hoped, by drawing attention to the delivery rather than the content, giving free passage to what he had to say. 'In fact I'm glad he hasn't been spectacular,' he continued. 'That nearly always means that there's a hell of a mess been left behind somewhere. No, he goes on, doing the thing he likes, knowing what he wants, taking all his opportunities, not forcing anything, on the other hand, not letting anything pass him by. That's the sort of strength I admire. A strength which reaches its ends without breaking anything – without destroying bridges and ravaging countryside to be militantly metaphorical – the sort of strength which can weigh its own resources, balance them against desires, consider others besides itself, remain true to its own pleasure – and yet achieve what it set out to achieve.'

'I'll pass this on to my father,' John replied, laughing. 'He'll probably ask you to put it all down on paper so that he can send it to the bank the next time he wants a loan.'

'But you know what I mean.'

'Yes. I just think that your example isn't so good, that's all. No,' he went on, as Arthur prepared to contradict him, 'I don't want to go into it.' He paused. 'But what appears straightforward from your side doesn't – anyway. It's always seemed to me – I say "always", I haven't been around long enough to say that – never mind; it seems to me that people who know what they want so clearly, so exactly, aren't to be admired – well, as much as you seem to admire them anyway. It's all right if they *arrive* at something great – wanting to be one step nearer to it all their lives and pushing for near and immediate aims all the time. Then they have time to live; they have time to enjoy a victory and relax for a year or a month or whatever it is. They have time to spread themselves slowly – because if you want something which is not too far away then you know that you don't have to strain everything to get it – they can allow themselves to consider other things and perhaps, in doing that, discover new aims, stronger ideas, a bigger prize to go for. Then, if they do that, maybe they'll have the opportunity to think about other people besides themselves. And, as for those who suddenly decide that they're going to be a great this or that when they're about ten – well, they give nobody any rest until they make it. All of them really,' he concluded. 'I don't care much for any of them!'

'I disagree,' Arthur replied, mildly. 'I do admire anyone who decides that he wants to do something – and then does it. Not if what they want to do is stupid or harmful – of course not. But it seems to me to be a good bargain; to decide that you are going to do everything you can to realise an ambition which means all that you desire. That is, of course, if you keep within certain rules – otherwise, I agree, I would be forced to admire dictators and any slick grub who wriggles his way to the top – but if you do keep within those rules, do what you always wanted to do, achieve what you set out to achieve, and yet leave intact – in fact, help – the people and institutions which help you – then I can see no better way to live.'

'Do you think that you can ever keep one idea, one single idea, in your mind all your life – and still enjoy everything?'

'Maybe the only way to "enjoy everything" is to do one thing.'

'Like work as a farm-labourer for sixty years.'

'Maybe.'

'Just maybe!' John retorted. 'I can't see any satisfaction in doing one thing because you've got to do it.'

'Some of the best and happiest people have been forced into the lives they led.'

'Well, they were lucky. They were happy in spite of it.'

'I don't know,' Arthur replied.

'Nobody can. But I'll take a bet!'

'So you don't think that it's any good to have a single ambition!' Arthur continued, after a pause.

'Not if it excludes as much as most ambitions do.'

'Again, I disagree. It seems to me that those who get the most out of life – in every way – are those who drive themselves towards one end and do it with such force that they suck in all that's around them, like a whirlpool.'

'Or a hurricane.'

'You'd rather sit on a lake,' Arthur suggested.

'On a boat, yes.'

'Perfectly still.'

'If I wanted to be,' answered John.

'Going nowhere.'

'Oh. Going here and there. Now and then, you know!'

'Really just to drift around for the rest of your life.'

'You've got a cheerful way of putting it, I'll say that for you,' John responded. 'And I don't exactly think that I'd be asleep all the time – which is what you seem to imagine. No. I'd just have a pleasant life. Do what I wanted when I wanted.'

'And no more?'

'What else is there?' Arthur shook his head. John was irritated by this seemingly disparaging repudiation. 'What do *you* want to do, anyway?'

'That's it. I'm afraid that I don't want anything very much.' He looked at John, knowing that it was the wrong moment to approach the subject he had determined to raise in some way, and yet fearing that this opportunity lost might leave no other. 'In fact, I would like to carry on much as I am doing at the moment.'

'Well then!'

'It isn't particularly inspired, I know that.'

'But you like it, don't you?' John demanded. 'You're well off, as far as I can see, and what's wrong with staying like that? There are thousands would jump at what you have.' Arthur looked dismayed; John grinned at him. 'I wouldn't mind changing places with you, for one.'

'Oh?' Arthur brightened open. 'And what do you think you would gain by the exchange?'

'Oh, I don't know,' he was unwilling to invent the objects of an envy he did not feel; if anything, his affection for Arthur was always overlaid by a thin settling of uncertainty which hardened occasionally to pity; yet he wanted to cheer him up. 'We were talking about the people whose lives we admired,' he began, eventually, 'and, in a way, I suppose that I admire yours. You're free to work or not to work and yet you choose to do it – and since you know you've chosen to do it, you must enjoy it more than – me, for example: I do my work because it's the only thing I'm any good at. But I suppose I could change if I got fed up . . . Then there's this place you've fitted out for yourself – that's all right; and you've horses and – none of these things might seem to matter to you very much – but they mean that at least you can be miserable in comfort. But *we're* not exactly starving either. Even though you might mistake us for a family coming out of a famine, I suppose that there isn't all that much difference. I mean, the difference between you and me is nothing, compared with that between both of us and most of the rest of the world . . .'

'I agree,' Arthur murmured.

'We could be twins to a Chinese,' John went on; he waited for a laugh; he was trying, anyway; nothing. 'No. So it isn't that.'

'Well then?' Arthur spread out his hands; he would wait and hope. And yet, it seemed silly to demand acknowledgement of what so obviously existed.

'I suppose I admire you because you've read all those books. Or, at least, if you haven't read them, you know about them in some way. That's more important, perhaps, than having read them. You've grown up with things around you that I would have liked. Let's leave it at that.'

'I could say the same of you.' Arthur caught up the brief

silence and bundled it into more talk along the line which would
lead, he hoped, to his own satisfaction. He was tired of his
persistence over such a childish need for a token. 'I envy your
having always done work that was obviously useful and yet
demanding. *And*, it has enabled you to remain firm in one area
all your life. Those things must give you a tremendous strength.
To say nothing of working with your father.'

'Nothing at all,' John muttered.

'As for the books and the house and all that sort of thing,'
Arthur went on, excitedly, 'I think you're wrong; totally and
utterly wrong! It's much better to come at these things as you
do – making demands on them, forcing them to give you what
you expect, forcing yourself to look for what you most want. I
accept them – and, in fact, I do no more, the effort has been
made. They have been put there for me – one way and another
– and I accept them and do no more. My act is to receive, not
to discover. I am given things, I don't find them. And it's
pleasant, it's nice, it's agreeable, it's congenial, it's cheerful, it's
charming, it's all of that and it can so soften one's mind that such
a well-lined existence can appear pointless. Why shouldn't life
be conducted at paddle-pace between any two poles that are
ever erected anywhere? Why should I question answers which
have served? Withdraw from situations which have pleased? It
seems, in one way, to be no more than a petty spite against
nothing more substantial than one's own delightfully inflicted
good fortune. Yet all of this could go! I value more the talks,
the fact that we meet and are amused by each other's company.
I value this much, much more than anything I might have either
learnt or inherited.'

He stopped. He could see that John was tilting into embarrassment.

'The rest could go tomorrow,' he added, sensing that it was
he who had to speak.

'Not today?' John saw a way out.

'No.' Arthur steadied himself, smiled. 'Not today.'

He was irritated by his lack of restraint. It was disagreeable
to him that he should find such seeking for assurance necessary;
its very proclamation seemed to invalidate its hope. Arthur had

never before been in such a position. Always, he had moved to someone's reciprocated trust and admiration out of an established community of interest and taste, either within his family, at school, or in the army. And this sort of an association had, for him, become essential, not in the sense that he needed it in order to feel himself complete – it appeared in a less positive way than that. Without such a friendship he feared despair – a meaningless despair because he was never so unaware of his relationship to others as to be able to allow himself to imagine that his despair could be justifiable. Yet, that it was meaningless made it the more disturbing.

He did not know John. He was never sure. In every pause there was a tapping reminder of difference; and in each acknowledged notice of this, a further proof of that which Arthur most wanted to ignore – and, was convinced, could be ignored; and perhaps his persistence grew from a delight in the near possibility of estrangement; and perhaps he imposed the task of being certain of John's feelings as a test of his own amiability, or as a limited operation along the lines which Oliver had often suggested – to start with whatever was nearest in practising the attitude which represented the values you wished to live by; a reaction away from his family, from his own meagreness.

These arguments creaked on top of his contained self-sufficiency like clumsy mills straddling a river. Sometimes, he became so absorbed in their workings that he thought himself free from their source – one quick encounter with John destroyed that.

For this was the centre of it. He demanded an affection of which, he was convinced, John was unaware; repeating insults to himself, drilling this need until a rush of longing had turned into a routine of concealed stratagems, constantly refreshed by being with John. He wanted the trust so that the tumbled force, the unchained willingness and inexperienced readiness to anything, could properly be attached to him. Sometimes, he would think that it was nothing but the unbalanced construction of confusion, exhaustion, self-pity. Or that it was no more than the inevitable obsessive digression of someone temporarily displaced. It had led to no loss of dignity – no padding along

lanes in the hope of a view – except the once; no conflict with
his mother or with Pat – except the once; no great closing-off
of opportunities – except the one.

'You're wrong there.'

'Yes?'

'Yes,' John repeated, glad of however tepid an interest in
what he hoped would change the subject without offending
Arthur by appearing to do so. 'What you were saying about
someone – well, like me, you said – "coming to books" and
doing this and that with them. It isn't true. I like reading – well,
I don't know exactly why. But it doesn't go much further than
that. I'm not dying to read everything ever written. I've no
desire to know everything there is to know, see all that should
be seen and talk it all out into big ideas. I might be quite happy
doing it, but that's a different thing.'

'The fact that you don't want to read everything doesn't mean
that I was wrong in what I said. You find things because you
decide to look for them. That's all I meant.'

'Yes, but, whereas you would read and talk wherever you
were, I might read – if I felt like it – and I would never want to
talk about it.'

'I don't consider that to be proof of anything. Constantly using
books as a basis of conversation might prove nothing more than
that you have nothing much to say for yourself. Anyway, you
do talk.' Arthur was gruff, encouraging.

'*Here* I do. But nowhere else. If you decided to go away next
week – I'd probably never talk about a book again as long as I
lived. And never want to.'

'I don't believe you. God knows, you're a damned sight more
earnest in the matter of book-talk – or any talk – than I ever
have been or ever will be.'

'But don't you see,' John insisted, 'you're kidding yourself?
There's this place here, the summerhouse, and for some reason
or other we settled down and go on about this or that – but it's
nothing to do with what I'm like most of the time.'

'Maybe it is. Maybe this is . . .'

'No. Wait a minute,' John interrupted him. 'You don't understand. I don't want you to build up these visions of what you

think I do, what I act like, what I think about – just from what happens in here. Because you do – and you mix it up with some grand idea of what farm-work is like – and then you're away! But it just isn't true.' He hesitated. 'If we hadn't got to know each other – then I would have none of this. If you went, it would vanish with you.'

'But why should I go?' Arthur asked, carefully.

'Oh, I don't know.' John stretched back in his seat. It was late. 'You're bound to push off some day.'

'Why do you say that?'

'You are, that's all.' He looked at his watch. Nearly midnight, up at half-past five.

'But I enjoy working – living here,' Arthur continued, doggedly.

'For the moment, yes. But there can't be much to hold you here for long.' He stood up. Still seated, Arthur shoved his face up towards John, afraid, it seemed, that standing up would break some spell.

'I believe I have never been happier than I am now,' he said.

'Good,' John replied, moving towards the door.

'And a great part of that is due to you,' Arthur went on, evenly.

'Good again!' He was at the door. 'I'll have to be off. No,' Arthur had been about to speak, 'no coffee, fags, booze or arguments. I'm away.'

Arthur was still in his chair. A large wing armchair. His hands gripped the arms. He looked miserable. John did not want to be held up for any longer.

'Good-night then,' he said.

'Good-night,' Arthur replied.

John fumbled with the handle, unnecessarily. Then he opened the door.

'It would suit me if you stayed, anyway,' he said, and left.

He walked quickly. The night was black but he did not feel out one step. He needed sleep.

He was glad that he had told Arthur about their meetings being isolated in his life. Somehow, the idea that he might be thought of as always the same as he appeared in the summerhouse had made him feel that he was in some way cheating, lying.

A light was still on in the kitchen and he winced in irritation at his mother's invariable concern.

'I was just going to bed,' she announced brightly, anticipating his reproach.

'You look as though you've just woken up,' he replied.

Her eyes were slackened with the tense relaxation of snatched sleep. She had flopped in a chair with a sewing bag on her lap, the apron still, as always, around her waist, hair lank across her forehead, too heavy to push back yet again.

'Let me get you some tea.'

Hoisting herself up, with a painful determination which showed plainly the differing capabilities of her mind and body, she smiled at him and went towards the kitchen. John let her go.

'Did you have a nice time?' she asked, from the other room.

'Yes, thank you.'

Visits to Arthur were always treated as formal expeditions.

'How was Mrs Langley?'

'I didn't see her.'

'Oh. Did you see his sister, then?'

'No.'

'Did you go out anywhere tonight?'

Trying to follow, trying to embrace John's privacy to herself. To be friendly.

'No.'

Silence.

'We just stayed in his summerhouse place and talked,' he added. 'And we played billiards. He's put in a billiard-table.'

'I didn't know you could play billiards.'

He could not see her. He had sat down with his back to the kitchen. The fire was mouldering grey, dead.

'Where did you learn to play billiards?' she went on.

'With Dickie.'

'Oh.' She laughed. 'Trust your Uncle Dickie to teach you that.'

'What's wrong with it?'

'Nothing.'

She came in with teapot, cups, sugar and milk, biscuits and cakes on a tray. Setting the tray on the broad fender, she began to pour quickly, so as not to jangle the crockery. They had talked to each other in whispers.

'What did you talk about, then?' she asked, passing him the tea.

'Nothing much.'

She puckered her mouth, unbelievingly.

'You were there long enough,' she continued.

'What if I was?'

'I'm glad you were. But you must have talked about something.'

'I can't remember.'

Nor could he, the effort closed his memory. He noticed that his mother had pricked the middle finger of her right hand. It was bleeding.

'How did you do that?'

Following his look, she saw the blood.

'I don't know.' She paused, still looking at the finger. It was pasted with blood, as if the skin had been carefully stripped off to show the flesh underneath.

'Maybe it happened when I dozed off.'

'You should have gone to bed.'

'I had some things to finish,' she replied, quickly.

'You were waiting up for me,' John contradicted her roughly. He hated her to wait up for him, tire herself, wear herself out.

She was on her knees in front of the fender. Gaily, she looked up at him.

'Well?' she demanded. 'What if I was? I like to see you.'

'You should get some sleep. You'll be up again before you close both eyes. I don't need waiting up for.'

'I think you do,' she replied.

It was useless.

'But it's not worth it,' he persisted. 'It just isn't worth it.'

'I think you're worth it.'

Silence.

She got up and went to clean her finger under the cold water tap. John was ashamed of himself – but the guilt which caused this was not of his making.

'Your dad finished that trough tonight,' she said, as she came back in.

'Did he?'

'Yes. Shirley helped him.'

She looked at him. He could not bear it. To do nothing, ever, that she would not totally approve. That was the only way.

'You mean, I should have stayed on to help him.'

'I didn't say that.'

'D'you want to know why I didn't?'

'No, I'm sure you had your reasons.'

She took up her tea. As she drank it, her eyes moved slowly around the never-changed room, tired, sad.

SEVENTEEN

Pat slept with the curtains and windows wide open, winter and summer. Now, when she woke up, she felt her face stiff with cold. As she leant over to turn on the bedside light the patchwork quilt which she had made herself crackled, as if frost had bitten into its surface. The weak light scarcely drove away the darkness, filtered through it rather, wanly lapping against the black rush.

She lay awake in bed for a few minutes; as usual, she was too early. But Arthur had promised that he would hunt with her, and although they had been out together once or twice recently, this promise had about it the nature of a return to what they had once been.

The room was large, like most of the many rooms in the sprawling house. It had belonged to her since her sixth birthday, and still now, with the show-jumping cups on the girlishly stacked bookcase, the pictures of hunters cut out of *The Field*, once pinned to the walls, now scattered on what was intended to be used as a dressing-table, with the school photographs, the set of three small hand-carved ponies which Arthur had brought her, the rosettes, tennis racquet, an eighteenth-century stone-carved head which she had found in a ditch while riding and gone back for in the car, an old map of the 'Northern Contys of England and the Southern Contys of Scotland' – with all this, it was still a young girl's room. Even the wallpaper – put up by herself, to her mother's annoyance – was pretty, careless, unwomanly. In fact, the room appeared to have been visited by a woman only rarely, and then, briefly; a stub of lipstick beside a tatty powder box – almost as large as a cash box – three pairs of high-heeled shoes, none of them new, littered under a massive mahogany wardrobe; a pink petticoat over a chair, the ashtray on the bedside table piled with butts. Her father had made it a rule that both Arthur and herself must look after their own rooms; Annie was not to touch them.

There was a door facing the end of the bed which led directly to what had been Arthur's bedroom. While he had been home on a leave, three years before, his mother had invited her sister and husband and two daughters to stay with them for two or three weeks. Arthur had given up his room at that time, moved to a vast, peculiarly-shaped bedroom on the other side of the house, and declared himself so pleased with it that it had remained his room ever since. Now, this adjoining room was empty.

Outside, she could hear the soft putter of Foster's electricity; however early she might get up, she was always later than that farm. Below her window, in the yard, she listened to Ted and Andrei chatting, first to each other, then, as they reached the stables, to the horses.

She got out of bed and dressed for riding. There was a large, ornate Victorian jug and basin in which she washed; cold water; she would change it later in the day. She went across to the window – and cursed.

On the yard, lit by the windows beneath her, over through the orchard, up the fields which led to Foster's farm and beyond it to the Wall – now greyly illuminated by the first pale push of morning light – everything was covered with snow. It lay in a little ridge on the open window-sill in front of her and spilled on to the floor. She picked up a handful; it was still soft, powdery; perhaps it was no more than a top sprinkle which would clear by mid-morning without having harmed the ground. Robert Oakshott, the Hunt Secretary, would phone if the meet were cancelled.

She had waited in her room so long – in order not to be first to breakfast – that she discovered herself to be late. They had breakfast in the dining-room, as with the other meals, but somehow this early morning gathering had always a bleak, huddled look, as if the half-panelled room and the handsome oak table refused to be drawn into such an unimportant drama. It had been much worse when her father had been alive. With almost malicious expectedness he had disappeared behind stretches of newspaper. Sometimes, Pat would eat her breakfast in about three minutes and then, unnoticed, rush out of the room – to be in her own silence, afraid of her parents' inert indifference to the beginning of a day.

Arthur tended to imitate his father's papered seclusion. But she could bring his attention to her whenever she wished.

Out of the window she could see the snow on the long front lawn pouched white on the dark, sagging yew-trees, smoothing the rockery to a soft even bank; only the long wall which bordered the road was untouched – and its mottled grey side, distempered by crusty lichens and trailed ribs of feeble ivy, the splashed cream scars of new cement where it had been patched up – this reflected exactly the straggly morning light. It was April: spring.

'It looks as if your day's sport will be lost,' said Mrs Langley.

'Robert will phone if it is,' Pat replied.

'But it does seem rather hopeless,' her mother went on.

'We'll know soon enough.'

'Do you have any alternative plans?'

'None.'

'Margaret said that she might come over this afternoon. If that interests you.'

'I'm afraid it doesn't.'

'Well, you'll have to find something to do. Arthur won't be able to go, now.'

'Why not?' Pat turned to him. He shrugged.

'He has some business to attend to,' Mrs Langley announced, happily.

Pat raised her head then, in a way, butting her mother out of the conversation, knocking aside her complacent interference.

'What is it you have to do?' she asked Arthur.

'Oh, nothing!' he mumbled. 'Williams wants me to go and see him about something . . .'

'*And* he wants to discuss everything with you,' his mother interrupted. She addressed Pat. 'He wants Arthur to go around all the property – everywhere. "To review the whole situation."' She was excited by it.

'Why does it need a review?' Pat demanded.

'Oh, it always does, darling,' her mother murmured. 'These things always have to be reviewed from time to time.'

'Well?' Pat enquired of Arthur, ignoring her mother's flutter.

'Williams is an old woman!' said Arthur.

'Father never used to listen to him,' Pat answered.

'But your father was . . .' Mrs Langley paused, looked for a conclusion to son and then to daughter; none came. 'Different,' she concluded, softly.

Pat knew that Arthur had been taking less and less interest in their affairs since those first few months after his return. And while there was little to be concerned over, she guessed that Williams was anxious to avoid yet another slither to financial danger in the Langley family.

'You're not going, are you?' she asked, after a look which, she saw, carried her hinted threat of blackmail to its target.

'I can't see us having much sport today, anyway,' he muttered.

'That wasn't my question.'

Arthur shrugged. He had agreed half-heartedly with his mother before Pat's arrival. For some reason, she had appeared delighted by the letter, insistent that he should go. He liked to indulge her, and he was not too unhappy about an excuse to miss the hunt.

'I know that you are making tremendous sacrifices anyway,' Pat said, 'even in considering to spend the day with me. Would it be asking too much to put Williams on the altar with all the rest?'

'It's far too cold to ride today,' said Mrs Langley, briskly.

'You know nothing about it!'

'Pat!' Arthur glared at her. 'Please!'

'Why don't you want to come?'

He did not answer.

'Well? Can't you be bothered to speak outside your precious "den" – ever?'

Arthur was reading the paper.

There was no sound in the room. Mrs Langley, her breakfast finished, sat stiff in her chair, held up, it seemed, by the pressure of her wrists on the table, waiting to see breakfast properly out so that the move to her next station was not made too soon.

Pat snatched the paper out of Arthur's hand. His fingers clutched at it. The large sheets ripped across. Mrs Langley cried out, softly; she never interfered now.

Arthur handed over his retained portion of the paper to his sister and then, as calmly as he could, he took up his cup and went out of the room. Pat threw the torn sheets on to the floor. Mrs Langley was afraid to say a word.

The telephone rang as Pat was coming downstairs with her jug of dirty washing water. She let Arthur go to it. It was Oakshott. The hunt was off. Arthur looked up the stairs at her.

'So there was no need for a scene after all,' he said, emptily.

'None at all,' she replied and went past him.

Outside, she had been walking for no more than half-an-hour when the sun came out. Suddenly, it cut away all the pinched grey and threw its light on to the thinly laying snow. She strode along, wellingtons hidden under a long trenchcoat, a dark green silk square fastened around her hair. Although her face was free of any sag or stroke of age – tightly fresh, rather, with the weather smacking hard against it; although her walk was nimble and strong, her hands, now straight-jammed in her deep pockets, now balancing her walk along rough ground, yet it could be felt that she needed only a dog to seem a settled spinster. In one short leap, she would pass from girl to old maid; now, she walked as if it were daily necessary for her to tramp down a certain amount of secret misery.

Arthur and John went out riding together now. John borrowed one of their horses. Never Bonnie.

She had seen John with the horse. Watched them from the Wall while they had been in a field. Ted was showing him how to break in a wild horse. Making the old hunter jump and rear. John clapped him on, urging Ted to tell more and more lies about his time as a groom at the Front. He had made the horse go around so fast that, in the end, it had jerked into a panic of wildness. Then John had approached it, dared it, jumped on it, bare-back. They had not seen her.

She had seen Arthur around the summerhouse. Circling around it as if it were a shrine. Not wanting to spoil its atmosphere by infecting it with impatient waiting before John came. Smoking, looking across the field to the farm.

Knowing that she would be waiting for him in the house after he had spent the evening with John, Arthur would try to evade her. There were three doors. The kitchen door, the main door, and the french windows. There was also a door from one of the stables which led, through an outhouse, to the scullery. She did not lock any of these doors. If he came in without seeing her, she would always hear him going to bed; his bedroom was above the drawing-room in which she waited, always.

Because he had always been indifferent to the hunt, she had taught herself to be indifferent, also. Now, he appeared to despise it – and all that went with it; she, also.

You would have thought that he had never had a friend till now. When people he had once and always known came to see them he was affably unmoved, uninterested. He had never been much interested. Only in her; then. Or the army. Oliver? 'He's all right,' said Arthur; 'enjoying it.'

John was attractive. She could see that. When he walked with Arthur, it was he who led. He had to slow every pace not to race away. Arthur would talk with a shift, a flicked side-glance, looking out; John – thrusting at him. She heard them laugh and turned away.

And he was going to stay on and stay the same. He wanted nothing to change. To repeat each day on the day following was all.

Whenever she went to them they stopped, at once. John was always pleasant. Even Arthur, now, was not uneasy in front of her.

So they were friends who found each other's company amusing, tended to be exclusive, were meeting now for transitory and particular reasons – nothing to do with any great common bias of affection – it would go, John would go. She could go on as before, and why should that make her so fiercely miserable that all things hurt her wherever she went?

The sun swiftly pressed away the thin sheet of snow and the ground soon became slushy because it was hardly frozen. She arrived back for lunch, deliberately late, and hovered in her bedroom until Arthur's van took him away to Williams and the review. Then lunch, alone.

There were many things she could do and many more she could have done. In the country, around the village, there was a waving tuft of loose-ended enterprises fluttering for some agent to neatly knot and arrange them. In the county, there was the structure of family known to family, parties, visits, horses, committees, arrangements, engagements, excursions spontaneously decided on ending up at inevitably pretty pubs, views, houses; Margaret had come after lunch to talk with Mrs Langley, no doubt, about her dreams.

Pat went to her own room and flopped on to her unmade bed with self-conscious ungainliness; as though, alone, she had more need to emphasise her role, to remind herself of what she was so that she would not scatter after something which would take effort. The lapses between actions always required an effort of which she was nervous. It was against her attitude to do nothing unless it had, in some defensible way, a purpose; you could laze in the sun in summer because that was idyllic; you could lounge in front of a winter fire, because it was cheerful; chatting with people in the village was fun; she had certain jobs to do and she did them and they were straightforward enough: hunting and show-jumping were sport – walking was pleasant; even mooning around the house was somehow acceptable, it had a fallow charm. It was this self-acknowledged isolation which was intolerable.

She read few books, nor did she elaborate domestic crafts into involved interests. A certain self-sufficient rigour had prohibited the development of close friendships, and a disinclined arrogance had worked against that embroidery of acquaintances which often feeds and protects people better than friendship.

Since her father's death and Arthur's return, she had slowly settled into an awareness of her position. This very fact – that she could regard herself – was uncomfortable enough; and made more so by the results which came from the self-examination.

She was thirty, unmarried, and, as she looked around, unlikely to be married. Her interests had been the extensions of adolescent passions, always somehow temporary, waiting on this or that – on Arthur – to confirm or change them. A simple reckoning. But unbearable. Suddenly, she was part of a system which could ignore her; this short catalogue ripped off the dreaming speciality which she had always assumed to protect her. What basis she had ever had for this, she did not know. It had grown; as she had grown with Arthur: it was there unquestioned until now.

Now she was in danger of double deprivation. It seemed to her that the cocoon had been a strait-jacket and her solitariness destitution. As her analysis was simple, so was her remedy; she had to do something, or what had been withheld would advance to self-inflicted violence.

She smoked a great deal. The small cigarettes were like toy sticks, to be pulled from their neat packet and destroyed. Her room was strange to her. Again, she could not quite believe that she thought that. But there were times when she would come into it – and the walls would seem oddly placed, the bed somehow positioned so that all the relative dimensions of the furniture were changed; there was a gap between the anciently rubbed Persian rug and the wardrobe – and there, the floor seemed like a jutting slab of fashioned wood. It was ridiculous to allow herself to move into such a state and, after staying on for a few minutes to prove to herself that she was leaving not through fear but through a less important inclination, she swung off the bed, went to the door, along the corridor and downstairs, into the yard.

It was now in bright sunshine. Her bedroom faced the sun and yet she had not noticed it. A perfect day for sport too late.

Arthur's van was parked outside the door. She went towards the summerhouse. Beyond it. Arthur and John were talking together at the point where a few yards of rickety fence stood in for the hedge.

They broke off what they were saying.

'Have you just come back from your walk?' Arthur asked.

'Some time ago,' she replied.

John and Pat nodded hello to each other.

'I saw you setting off for your walk,' he said. 'Going like a steam-engine.'

'She's a devil for punishment,' said Arthur.

'You should enter those competitions,' John went on, looking just to one side of her as he spoke. 'We could start a new one. Aldeby to Hawick. All on Shanks's pony.'

'Do you think that we could bring Arthur into it?' Pat asked him.

'No,' John shook his head extravagantly. 'Old Arthur here would have to be carried in a litter with sandwiches and coffee laid on every two minutes.'

'Maybe he could be the starter,' Pat suggested.

'Yes,' John agreed. 'Or he could cart a collection box around.'

'Oh, I don't know. Maybe the pick and shovel brigade. Stoneman and his mountaineers. They need all the charity that's going.'

'And maybe Arthur could present the prizes,' Pat went on.

She kept it up; Arthur was glad to see this play.

'What d'you think he would give?' John asked.

'I don't know.' She paused. 'Maybe some of those bits and pieces he has in his den.'

'I don't think that they would be much appreciated,' John replied. 'I think that people would want something they liked.'

'And why shouldn't they like what I have?' Arthur demanded.

'Well.' John considered for a moment. Pat encouraged him to go on. 'It isn't that they wouldn't like it. It's just that they might think you were trying to get rid of something.'

'They would appreciate the gesture,' said Pat.

'But they would throw it on a rubbish heap,' John concluded.

Arthur laughed and the circle having been formed, they chatted on. John liked to be near Pat; the feeling which lifted off her excited him.

'It must take persistence,' Arthur found himself saying, of the Reverend Craddock's postered announcement of yet another jumble sale. 'And considering the few people there are in this area, the amounts raised are quite impressive.'

'I wish that the means of raising the amounts were as impressive,' said Pat. 'I think that I must have bought fifteen "lucky dolls".'

'I've never been to a jumble sale,' John announced.

'You ought to,' Arthur told him. 'I'm not suggesting that you'll find any resplendent array of Christian virtues – but it is rather remarkable that so many different people can be persuaded to give to – like this – an Indian village they've never heard of and will never see.'

'Maybe it isn't there,' John replied.

'No. No,' Arthur retorted briskly. 'These things are bona fide. Have to be. Couldn't get by if they weren't.'

John smarted a little and came back.

'If they were really desperate about these things, they would force the Government to tax for it. Then they could raise some real money.'

'Oh no,' Arthur protested. 'For one thing, governments have not the time to occupy themselves with all the charities that need help. And, much more important, you've got to admire individuals who, individually, want to give help.'

'I agree with John,' said Pat. 'These jumble sales are harmless, but they're not much good as far as raising money is concerned.'

'I think that they're pretty good at that,' Arthur replied, stiffly.

'Well,' she answered, 'it gives Craddock something to worry about, anyway.'

'That's unfair. He does his job well.'

'And so say all of us,' she murmured.

John laughed and decided to make his move away; he would have been content to stand there for the rest of the afternoon, but it was better to go while he could still carry with him the knowledge that, for the first time, Pat had deliberately been for him. He told them that he was leaving.

'Are you sure you can't make it tonight?' Arthur asked.

'Certain.'

'Oh well.' He paused, knowing Pat to be assessing him. 'I suppose that I'll see you soon.'

'Soon enough, anyway,' John answered, briskly, smiling at Pat. He nodded to her. 'Next time you want to hike off somewhere give us a shout,' he went on, 'maybe I could fix you up with a lift on a tractor or something.'

'Thank you,' she replied. 'I would enjoy that.'

'Then you would have some time to spare to collect for old Arthur's jumble sale.'

'We could collect his den,' she answered.

'Yes. Put Arthur in with it. Lot 93 – one man and his band.'

Arthur stared after him only for a moment.

'We *were* going into Hexham to the pictures,' he explained to Pat.

She controlled her reaction.

'He works very hard you know,' he went on, as if excusing such a frivolity; 'my goodness; he makes me ashamed of the easy way I can live.'

'Tut, tut.' Pat clicked her tongue against her teeth.

'Look,' said Arthur loudly, as if volume would impel his thought with greater sincerity, 'why don't *you* come with me to the pictures?'

'Love to,' Pat replied, sweetly.

'Good,' said Arthur. Then seeing that, somehow, he had contracted an arrangement which would help disoblige him of guilt at his behaviour towards his sister by an action which would demand almost nothing of himself – 'Good,' he repeated.

'So we will go out together after all,' she said, lightly.

'Yes.' He blushed. 'Yes, we will.'

They went to the most awful film that was on. This had been one of their private amusements when Arthur used to come home on leave. Consciously, he had decided to revive it, and, suppressing her annoyance at being so patronisingly indulged, Pat declared herself delighted.

It was an English comedy with people's bottoms for jokes and underwear for humour, with bluster for wit and deceit for intrigue and, above all, with loveless, lineless, listless actors for people.

They enjoyed it enormously. Arthur relished its banality and pried open all its faults with exclamations of gratitude that anything could be quite as bad, quite as tasteless, quite as absurdly fifth-rate.

Driving back home, Pat could have imagined things to be as they had formerly been and as she had always wanted them to be. Around them was the open, empty countryside she loved. Their house was safe, the area would never be spoilt, they would always be able to hunt, to have shows, to have a village. No effort, but a long reliance on what had always been established and, though it might alter, would not much change. Whenever she had been to any other part of England, she had found the comparisons all to the overwhelming advantage of that part she lived in. And the Wall, no more than a graceful line of stones carelessly scattered across a bare contour – yet there, something unique, expressing the ageless particularity of its borders.

Arthur was happy. The evening had gone well; Pat's hard rigour had fallen to a pliant comfortableness. He had forgotten that she could be such good company.

Pat let him rest in his contentment. She was not willing to disrupt it while it so completely enabled her to work out her own plan. This was how it had been. But this was the shadow only, and there would be no substance; this was the sign where there was no longer feeling; this, the headless, bodyless plume.

For the moment, let Arthur believe that he was getting away with it.

EIGHTEEN

The three of them went riding. Pat had known of their plans, saddled Bonnie as John had arrived and then led him into the yard where Ted was fitting the saddles with Arthur's help.

John had helped her with her saddling.

'Which way are you going?' she asked.

'I thought we might go towards Langholm's place,' Arthur replied, warily.

She nodded.

'And you?' he added.

'Oh,' she shrugged. 'I'll just go up towards the Cross and then over to Hendersons, near the point-to-point course. It should be lovely there.'

'Yes,' said Arthur, happily.

'Why don't you come with us?'

John wanted her to come and he saw that he could ask under the appearance of smoothing a friction within the family. Pat looked enquiringly at Arthur who glared at the ground.

'Are you sure that you wouldn't mind?'

Arthur shook his head, refusing to commit himself.

'That's all right then,' said John, 'it's settled. And we'll go your way; I would like to go through that wood.'

This was the reason for her choice. Beyond the Cross which stood on the Scottish side of the Wall – a small stump of stone once the marker of a seventh-century celebration of faith – was a small wood which, being sheltered by a steep bank on the north and east sides, contained a remarkably lush display of trees. The buds were just now broken open and the delicate green, fresh-coloured leaves pushed into the air. The narrow path along which the horses walked sprouted primroses, crocuses, bluebells, daffodils. Inside the wood, away from the path, the withheld density of winter crackled and eased to a first scurry of spring. Branches, bent by rain and wind, swung into their faces, but the season seemed to make them light, so that they were easy to brush gently aside. The wood was warm, splashed and stroked by so many colours, so many tints of green, of brown, a streak of yellow, the sparkling of a silver birch, chestnut blossom, the thudded bark of beech, black ash, a tangle of thorned briar which would rise to a nave of wild roses, the thickly bronzed shine of copper beech. Saturday afternoon and, as always, no one there, no one anywhere but confined to job or hobby for miles around; the three of them were undisturbed.

They rode in single file with Pat in the middle, Arthur at the head, John at the rear. Coming out of Langley's place, they had ridden abreast. John had seen his father and Shirley moving around the yard: he had wanted to duck down. It was his first afternoon off for weeks, but Nelson was even more truculent since the farm had become his sole property. He grudged everything – time, money, talk, meals, sleep, inclinations – everything that was not to do with building up his farm. And John knew that his father was working far too hard, straining himself deliberately as if to prove, every minute, to everybody who might be observing him from anywhere, that he would work until he dropped before allowing the land to be one degree less productive and attractive than he knew it could be. He was besotted with his own missionary self-interest. He talked to John only to demonstrate, to urge on, or to complain. John worked hard – partly because it was the easiest way to keep the peace and to prevent those nightly carpings or explosions which ground down and battered his mother; partly because the knowledge of his father's strain forced him to help, to be there if anything happened, to absolve himself of responsibility in advance. And the work – this work from half-past five in the morning until, usually, hours past that time in the evening – that was a daily challenge round which pressed every inch of his body to stretched effort.

But that which tired him also strengthened him, depressing

him to fatigue but also urging him to a further compression of power. Now, at the entry into his twenty-second year, he was as strong as he would ever be. He dared himself every day; to carry two sacks of potatoes, one under each arm; to pull the heavy trailer from the barn to the yard with his hands; to thin the few dozen lines of turnips without allowing himself the slightest break, rising at the end of it with the blood cramped in his thighs, head dizzy; to lift whatever needed two men to lift, to carry what previously had been rolled or dragged along. Whenever he hammered in a stake, or opened the throttle of his tractor on his way to the bottom field, whenever he set to lay cement or shift a load from one spot to another, whenever he did anything which left him alone with any job to do which could be completed more quickly by daring or brute force – then he would fight it as if he were punching against someone. And it was then that he remembered what had before been done by violence; the memories lifted up from the bottom of his mind to be scorched by his present fury.

It was fury. As now. With Pat riding near him up to the Cross, along the ridge, then down the pony track to the wood, with her knees slapping against that magnificent horse, obedient yet demanding mastery, her looks flicking into his eyes like a whip snapped on his shoulders, the open fields, the horses pushing in front of each other. With the feeling that he could yank up the massive weight which carried him and throw it ahead of the others, Pat laughing at him, her hair swirling down from her velvet cap and lacing around her face: Arthur watching him, a free day. With all this, he wanted to open to a final smash of action, and the horror of his guilt which bedded the pain he had received in the most surly repose of his mind, then flew out and demanded expression and retribution. He did not realise until then how closely suppressed his ache of physical shame had been. For, not wanting to be reminded of it in any way, shying away from it with a nervous fear which outleapt the danger by so much that it often threatened of itself to unsettle him, and being more anxious to guard what he wished to reject, to shut it off completely rather than bringing it to however secretive a revision, he had been able to acknowledge his pain and live aside from it.

Now it rushed up within him and, mingled with it, was a new passion which his old shame and fright only sharpened. The out-reaching spring day shot through him and opened him to its rise, its growth, its unopposable beginning. There was Pat.

He pulled up his horse as they cleared the wood, heard himself demand that they stop for a cigarette, ignored Arthur's hint that they should reach Hendersons before a pause, and carried a lighted match to Pat with the excited deliberation of a new lover.

Arthur stayed on his horse.

'Won't you come down and join us?' John demanded, loudly.

'No, thank you. We'll soon be off.' Arthur papered his unease with formality.

John looked around him. Even the leathery clomp of the horses was now gone, and the birds mid-afternoon silent, the wood just a few yards behind them and in front of them a curving mound-leaping roll of hills which led on as far as could be seen. The spot enclosed an immense peace which promised all things.

'I could stay here all day,' he said. 'I would like to stay – just here – just *here*.'

'We'll collect you on our way back,' Arthur retorted.

'What about you?' John asked of Pat.

'Yes,' she nodded. 'I agree. It seems stupid to ride past it all.'

'All what?' Arthur enquired, dryly.

She smiled at him, took off her riding-cap, and sat down on a small bank which lumped from the ground like a grave. John watched everything she did.

'Looks as though *we'll* collect *you* on *your* way back,' he said to Arthur.

'I couldn't give a damn who collects whom!' Arthur replied. 'I thought we were supposed to be going to the point-to-point course.'

'Do you want a race or something?' John asked, calmly.

Arthur did not reply. He fidgeted so much that his horse became restless and he had to let it stomp around in an ungraceful circle. When he turned to them again, they were both lying on the bank.

'Sunbathing?' he asked.

'You could,' John replied.

'We ought to have taken a coach-trip to the sea.'

'That would have been nice,' Pat said.

'Yes.' John laughed. 'Arthur could have done his backstroke.' He looked at Pat. 'Have you seen him doing his backstroke? Very good.'

'He never liked the water to get on to his face,' she replied.

'Maybe he just liked to count his toes.'

Pat laughed and, as Arthur saw them working into a friendship which could prise intimacies from the flattest statements, he began for the first time, to be aware and afraid what Pat might do.

'Well now,' he said, throwing his cigarette on to the ground, speaking pleasantly, smiling, 'let's move on.'

'Tt. Tt!' John went across to the burning stump and screwed it out with his foot.

'First rule of the countryside,' Pat announced, sweetly. 'Don't start forest fires.'

John shook his finger at Arthur and banged his foot on the cigarette end until it was nearly six inches under.

'Don't be absurd,' Arthur retorted. 'The grass is still damp.'

'But it's the principle!' sang John and Pat together; then, looking at each other with delighted amazement, they rolled into outrageous laughter which Arthur found so distasteful that he feared his reaction to it.

They stopped as suddenly as they had started.

'I think he wants to go,' John said to Pat.

'Yes,' she replied, glancing at her brother carefully. 'Yes. I think you may be right there.'

'Well, Squire!' said John, not knowing why, but enjoying Arthur's wince at the word – he had never used it before – 'Well, Squire!' he repeated. 'We'll fall in with your wish.'

'Do as you please,' Arthur answered, quickly.

'Now then.' John held out his hands to Pat, flabbergasted. 'Now what do you make of a man like that? Eh?' She shook her head; he knew that he could go on. 'One minute it's – flee the foul spot and let's get on with the journey – and now it's – "do as you please".'

'If you please,' Pat added.

This time, they suppressed the giggles which pressed into their mouths.

'Right,' said Pat. 'If you'll go, I'll go.'

'After you,' John replied, with elaborated courtesy.

'No. After you.'

'I insist.'

'So do I.'

'I'll go if you go.'

'So will I.'

'You first.'

'No.'

They paused. Talking, they had moved near to each other, almost hovering over the small space between them.

'You,' she said.

'You,' he replied.

'You.'

'You!'

'You!'

Silence.

'Why don't you conduct an experiment in simultaneity?' asked Arthur, detachedly.

Pat broke away and ran to her horse. John's was further away but by throwing himself straight into the saddle without first bothering to find the stirrup, he won.

'Now, we can go on!' he announced.

They were about half-way along the ridge when the first big cloud shuttered the sun. The green all around them dulled. It began to rain – not much, just a light patter of minute drops, passing for a few minutes every so often, settling lightly on clothes and grass, hardly visible.

The point-to-point course was plain only to those who had been there to a meeting, with the bookmakers and small tents marking the top slope of the ridge they were riding along; and below, in the flat valley, the first few artificial jumps glaring out of the bare land, obvious for all to see as obstacles in a race. Yet even without the people, without the jumps, it was easy to trace; there was a narrow beck which had to be jumped, a low stone wall, the fence which oddly circled the few trees through which the riders would disappear for no more than half a minute, emerging at the other side like startled soldiers in retreat; the big hedge was there which was usually flattened down by the first horse and so battered at the same spot by the others that it crumpled to little more than a stack of bracken – even now, if you looked hard, you could see that it was thin at that point; there was the small building – a concrete hut – which served as a turning stake and represented the total construction of the whole area. All of it belonged to Duncan Collins' father who left it free, he said, 'for the sport', although, in his moments of self-lauding commercialism, he would confide that the bloody land wouldn't support a rhubarb patch and any attempt to do anything with it would be more damned trouble than it was worth!

Arthur disliked it. When not in use, it looked desolate, with neither prettiness nor power to distinguish it. At the end of the valley in which the course lay, around a turn – almost like a turn in a large river – was Hendersons, a tiny hamlet called after its one farm, somehow enchanting with two pairs of cottages, three other houses, and a big oak beside a miniature tarn.

His memories of the course were distasteful. He enjoyed hunting and everything that went with it. But racing seemed purposeless; once, the last time he had ridden there, the rider in front of him had been thrown at the hedge; Arthur's horse had only just avoided landing on the man's face.

'Let's race around it,' said Pat.

Arthur ignored her; he knew that she would say that.

'Arthur!' she called again. 'Why don't we all race around it *now*?'

He looked away from her, from her and John. Why didn't they? Over the hills and far away. He was afraid, and his fear was the more jolting because it arrived suddenly fanged. John would be taken away from him.

'How far would it be?' John asked.

He did not want to be against Arthur and yet he could not be with him.

'A mile and a half, once round,' Pat answered.

The drizzle continued. Whereas the land near his own house looked impressive, encouraging, being between the rise of the Solway plain and the uplands, Arthur found this part bleak. The rain wet the brown scrub gorse until it seemed to clot to treacherous rashes on the bald yellow rear of the hills. Dry-stone hedges looped acres of land, running out of sight, feebly patterning that which was slowly heaving them away, not stamping ownership and domination, but pointing the emptiness, marking the barren hoard of unsettlement. Here, the plots of fertile land such as Foster worked were no more than tiny patches, too scattered and too small to be useful, disappearing altogether the further they moved away to bare interfolding of empty hills, sheltering a hamlet only as a passing indulgence. It was too empty for him, for although it was within easy reach by car, although it could be surveyed in an afternoon and travelled over in an evening, yet it felt isolated, it felt unknown, it felt cold. It did not matter that a twentieth century barrage stood forty miles to the east, and others stood against it way off in all directions; it felt withheld. Even the Wall, just a few miles further on from where they were, lost its quaint modern attraction, lost even its sounding proof of other lives and men controlling life, petering under stumpy mounds and tumbling to flattened, featureless plod of stones. There was no security, nor was there the possibility of securing anything.

'It's marvellous,' said John again, speaking through Pat to Arthur, encouraging him, aware of his deception at the beginning of the ride, anxious of its effect. 'I would just like to go on and think that I would never meet anybody.'

Arthur turned to him, smiled. He saw John flicking near Pat, moving all for her, nudging his horse to constant shuffling.

'Well then?' John demanded. 'Let's have a go at it!'

'You two go,' said Arthur steadily. 'No,' he continued, as they were about to protest. 'You two go.'

Trying to avoid petulance, he spoke over-solemnly.

'And off they went!' Pat shouted. 'Far away across the sea,

never to be seen again! Come on! Make up your mind. We'll be drowned sitting here.'

She grinned at John and, going across to him, mumbled something which Arthur could not hear.

'What was that?' he demanded.

John laughed at him.

'Nothing.'

'Nothing seems to please you.'

'It does.'

Arthur held himself back. He was making too much of it all. Soon, the ride would be over, John and himself in the summerhouse, peace, the bedding of the new life, unruffled.

'If you both want to fly around like children, then for goodness' sake do it and get it over with,' he snapped.

'Let's go on to Hendersons then,' said Pat.

'No.'

'Why not?'

'No,' he repeated.

Pat despised her brother's indecision. Each emphatic remark came through patent flurryings of weakness.

'Let's do it,' John said to Pat. 'Come on. Let's go now.'

Arthur saw that John was helping him. Easing. Avoiding him. Best ignored.

'One, two, three, go!' He shouted, violently. His horse pranced up its forelegs, hardly rearing, merely restless.

'Go!' he shouted, again. 'Go on.'

Pat took her horse right around him. Not wheeling to be off, but teasing Arthur, daring him. He wanted her to go, just to go. John was waiting for her. Arthur's horse felt too big beneath him; he was perched on it, not riding it. The polished surge of its neck, damp now, the drizzle settling on the brushed hair like sticky glue, the rod-hard bit, switching reins, heels ready to dig the flanks, huge body lightly shuttling on such slender legs, ready to race, to stay, to trot, walk, gallop, do as anyone wished but never much more than an indulgence, a plaything, noble through its serviceable humility – all this was disturbing, John would stay: he had only to ask him to stay. He could hold on to what he had by a simple accommodation.

'Now!' Pat shouted – and, raising her crop high in the air, she thwacked it against her boots and, leaning far forward over Bonnie's neck, seemed to fly down the hill, the hooves no more than a soft-moistened thrubbing in the wet-sweet grass.

John went after her. He had not even waited for the look from Arthur – permission, apology, acknowledgement, admission – which he knew would come. He was making ground.

They were so small on the bare land. It would help if he could see them as grand, somehow heroic, but even their silent gallop down and across the empty valley, forcing over land that, still now, might never have been walked on, was puny. And yet he had not dared join it. As the fine straggles of rain lay gently across his face, stroke upon stroke, he was covered with suffocating forlornness. It was self-pitying and unjustifiable of him to be so sickeningly enclosed; but this last token awareness held only for a moment against the falling drop of a sheeted melancholy which, at once, enclosed him totally. His life had doddered between privilege and petty enthusiasms; the privilege had so enfeebled him that no enthusiasm had rooted below the level of immediate convenience. All was petty through his measure of it. He had seized on an excuse as a positive alternative and now he saw it as an evasion without even the dignity of a compromise. It had become more than excuse or alternative. In John, he had thought to find a sturdy way which would allow him to conduct himself to purpose as well as enjoyment. The wavering delight had been mingled with a desire to grow firm which was approaching the strength of its ambition. Had been. This invention of defeat flattened his melancholy to a morose unhappiness.

Pat had let him draw level. Already she was uncertain of her harshness towards Arthur. But when John drew up beside her, she did not spurt; the two horses held together, necks rocking like wooden toys. The fields swept up beneath and around them, jarring to new levels, tippling steadily. Together – they were moving across land unmoved, it seemed, even at their instant of impact – more bound in this ravaging traceless scratch than in the clammed intimacy of a tight room – scaring away all that might break in because it was too vast to allow. John too, paced his gallop to match his partner's. It was a race to keep together. They leapt the low wall and rose high above their horses, landing with a single lurch which almost threw them as they twisted to confirm the other's relish. Down another incline and up the bank; horses pushing up like old chargers, knees buckling, haunches shuddering fiercely, reins loose.

She had gained on him, and he pushed his horse on. She went further way from him. Panicking, he twitched the horse's flanks with his crop. Then Pat turned in her saddle, shouted at him; it was all right.

There were no more than two or three hundred yards to go when she slowed down. He stopped beside her. The two horses snorted out grey mushrooms of smoke and shivered with nipped excitement.

'What's wrong?'

'He's gone.'

John looked up to where they had left Arthur. No one. Immediately, he knew that this was what he had wanted.

'He can't be far,' he said. 'We should catch up with him in five minutes.'

She did not reply.

'Come on,' he continued. Then, 'Race you to him.'

Pat shook her head and guided her horse away, going diagonally across the valley in the opposite direction to Hendersons. John followed, close to her, waiting.

They trekked along for a mile or so without anything being said. The drizzle stopped, the clouds blustered open and lapping patches of blue showed; the colours lifted strongly and the land was swathed in high-tinted coverings. There were few streams; the hills were too settled in boned roundness to allow the dividing crack of water. Few trees, birds silent.

They arrived at a point at which John had never been. It seemed to belong nowhere. All the clues that distinguish a marked place were absent, and yet there was not that immense security which assures of a limitless similarity. An insecure remain, reminder of an old passing.

'This is where I like to ride,' said Pat.

They drew up. John scanned around him, quickly trying to

pick out what it was he could say to show that he understood. There was nothing. He wanted to touch her.

Carefully, almost heavily, she dismounted, Bonnie immediately trotted a few paces away from her and then stopped, bending its long neck to the grass. John slipped off his horse as quietly as he could. He lay down beside her.

As he delicately undid the buttons of her shirt, his hand trembled for fear that it would plunge right through her. His fingers were dry with cutting carefulness. She swung her body against his. He dared not look at her eyes; saw her face, cold; afraid to discover it, uncoil it. For both of them, everything was done with that painful first anxiety which fears both tragedy and farce. And John was afraid. Washing through him, the flowing smooth slide of her cheek, washing away all his uncertainty, all restriction; her legs were too white to bruise. Roots of desire sprung out of buried defeats of violence. A new root; that which could feel into him, not to destroy but to deliver. He buried himself in her. There would be no more cracking force. He spread open across her and his face touched on to the wet grass.

NINETEEN

'I'll tell him tonight then,' said Nelson.

'Just as you like,' Lizzie answered him.

'Or shall I tell him now?'

'Where is he now?'

Nelson looked through the small kitchen window. John was shifting two bullocks out of the yard. Nelson, with the eager satisfaction of a truant, grinned delightedly.

'Working,' he laughed. 'I'll give him that. He can work beside anybody when he has a mind to.'

'Tell him now,' said Lizzie, glad of the chance of a sudden pleasure.

'Why?'

'Go on.' She pushed his shoulders with flour-hands. 'Go and tell him.'

'No.' Nelson turned back from the window. John had passed through the gate and moved around the corner. He ought to have been out working himself. 'No,' he repeated. 'It'll be better of an evening.'

He began to go out:

'Do you think what I'm doing's right, Lizzie?' he asked.

'I think it's – just right.'

'He's not too young? You don't think it'll seem too easy come by?'

'That's for you to judge,' she replied, cautiously. Even now, it would be easy to check the offer.

'Yes,' said Nelson. 'I think it'll be all right.' He paused. 'Really give him something to work for.'

Lizzie nodded. It might. As long as Nelson gave without first demanding the returns and rewards of his gift.

He would go out and work and nurse the scene all day. By this one act, he would expect the instant assembly of a grand and loving family grouping. Tears would become it, even the mildest disquiet destroy it. He was going to offer John a half share in the farm. It was just, as he had explained already to Lizzie, and as he was set to retell; John would take on the farm after he was gone and out of his stock and capital would come the equal settlements on Avril and Shirley when needed – but never at a time when the farm could not afford it.

After he had gone. This phrase rubbed through Nelson's mind with particular pleasure. John would take on the farm. It was complete; or would be. For it needed completion. His satisfaction upon possession had had no areas into which it could spread, and the pride of doing what he had done, exactly as he had done it, but with a shifted ambition, had not lasted long. Because the ambition shifted from an objective to an object which, while related in aspect, was different in its demands. The one had to be gained, the other preserved; the one won, the other held; the one fought for, the other contemplated. And his aversion towards rest had been raised higher by the realisation that – apart from the continued pressure of steady improvements – there was no dramatic end to which he could be directed. This would be one. And from it – with John's notion and so his knowledge of responsibility established – he could aim for a further accumulation of land which could, anyway, most satisfactorily be worked by two independent units. Sometimes John questioned him to find out if he ever thought of anything other than extending his power and property; never. Never! Nelson would bellow. What the hell!

Yes this was to be an occasion when Sentiment would be felt. Not that he called it up cynically as cannon fodder for a private war; it approached him to his own astonishment, too distant from its early source to remind him of any gentle associations, but received, rather, as a deserved bonus and wondered at for its strength. For so long now his life had been bent along one tight line that all energy or sympathy which did not somehow come of that single pursuit seemed odd. To be entertained only as long as it did not interfere . . .

                            *   *   *

John had immediately thought of marriage, yet he could not even tell her what he felt. To name it would have been such a challenge that he dare not undertake it. He walked through his work muttering the words to himself, like an old man or a child, rubbing them across his tongue, ceaselessly pleased at their endless power and promise. 'I love her', 'I love her', 'I love her'.

And these days, he worked noticing everything. There was no locked slide from one break – whatever it was – to the next. He noticed his hands patting the flanks of the beasts, he noticed the perfectly fitted exactness of all his father's measures, he noticed the crop, the hedges, the fences, the stalls, the feed, the yard, the barn newly extended. To be on a farm, surrounded by the luxuriance which offered both beauty and reward, seemed the grandest state imaginable. He noticed his father's persistence; the dramatic lift from nothing to total and rich possession would be difficult to repeat, but the Galloways were being regarded well, Nelson could claim top prices for them, the farm was stocked beyond the normal limit, ripe for an expansion which would find full measure. He noticed this and was ashamed that he had let such progress pass him by without pleasure and a feeling of sharing in achievement. There was much to offer anyone; he need not be afraid of that. Other things settled calmly around him. Avril was engaged and John could now see that she would be happy with Tony and he was glad of it; and he could look at what Shirley was doing without being pushed to repressive savagery. He would even welcome it if the man she was going with gave her a child. Nelson would grow reconciled to it, get them a cottage nearby, the man would work on the farm. Shirley would be better away, she was a relic of a necessitous improvisation now no longer needed.

He was calm because he saw Pat every night. Sometimes he would rush down towards her house during a break in the day and she would be there and they would find somewhere hidden. He hoped that she would conceive and then it would be certain; yet this hope was weakness he knew. He wanted her to welcome him.

This was the battle and in this he was kept. His body rustled with incredible delight at its new purpose. Everything was

tranquil above to let the surge within him swirl its sharp-warm
marvels. Through the morning, through dinner, the afternoon
tea, he finished quickly, came in and made some large sandwiches – his mother was outside, collecting eggs – he stripped
to the waist, threw cold water over his face and chest.

'Where are you going?' Lizzie stood at the kitchen door, a
large basket of eggs on one arm, her skinny strength supporting
them easily.

'Out,' he gurgled. He had not told them; he wanted to be able
to say something definite.

'Not right away?'

'Yes.' He turned to her. He was lathered with soap. 'This
minute.'

'What about your supper?'

He took a towel and began to pummel himself with it.

'Had it.'

Lizzie saw the cheese and the half-loaf of bread on the
side-table.

'You need more than a sandwich.'

'No.' He threw the towel away and went to the airing cupboard
for a clean shirt. 'No,' he repeated, banging his stomach. 'Full
up inside.'

She came across to put the eggs on the table next to the sink,
looking out of the window to find Nelson.

'Go on then,' John said.

'Hm?'

The clean shirt was on, he was holding a newly-pressed pair
of trousers in one hand, the other unfastening the top of his
jeans.

'Leave a man alone, then.'

She went out.

'I hope she's worth it,' speaking from the other room.

'You can bet on that,' John replied. She did not know about
it.

When he came through to her, a comb dragging through his
hair, his feet kicking into shoes, she was standing by the fire,
which was still well-stacked even in such warm weather.

'Out of the way!' he shouted. The mirror was above the

mantelpiece. She jumped aside. John caught her and, lifting her up, swung her around.

'Put me down!'

'*And* again.'

'John!'

She bumped to a stop, but before she could use the moment to ask him to stay, he had squared himself in front of the small new mirror, raking his long hair.

'Make yourself useful, then,' he said. 'Get us my jacket.'

She did it. He took it out of her hands, pulled it on, opening his bright white shirt collar over the jacket collar.

'How do I look?'

He was blazing and triumphant.

'Very nice,' she replied. 'You just need a brush to those shoes.'

'Hell!' He rubbed the toe-caps against his trouser-legs. Then: 'That'll do, won't it?'

'It'll do no good.'

Catching her by the shoulders, he pulled her to him and planted a kiss loudly on her forehead.

'You're an old moaner!' he announced. 'That's what you are. Old Lizzie Joaning moaner.'

He went to the door.

'And don't sit up!' he warned her. 'Get yourself some lovely beauty sleep.'

Over the back way and into the field. Half-way down it he heard Nelson shouting to him. He turned. His father was leaning out of the window. John waved back at him and went on. Full spring rushed up at him from the lush stifle of cordoned late afternoon.

'She'll be late,' said Arthur. He was standing at the entrance to the drive. That was where he would meet Pat, both of them agreeing without mentioning it, that it would be better were John not to come to the house. Broad daylight; they walked over fields; one or two people saw them; still his parents did not know.

'Come in for a drink?'

John looked beyond him, afraid, for a second, that Arthur might be deceiving him, Pat hidden around a corner.

'Fine,' he answered.

They went towards the summerhouse.

'Will she know where I am?'

'Oh yes,' said Arthur. 'I told her you would be with me.' He smiled. 'She knew you would be safe and sound.'

The summerhouse was cold. John thought that Arthur had put yet more things into it. Over-crowded it.

'Whisky?'

'Yes. Please.'

Pouring the drinks, Arthur swung his shoulders to point at the chair in which John was supposed to sit. John stayed where he was, near the door. The glass was brought to him. They drank without saying a word.

'Black and White!' Arthur announced. 'It's supposed to be one of the best. I must say, I can't tell the difference. Can you?'

'They get weaker the more you have,' John replied.

'Yes.' Arthur laughed. 'And less expensive.'

John nodded.

'Did she say that she would be long?' he asked.

'No!' Arthur caught the glance which bounced right back from John's face. 'No,' he resumed steadily. 'She had to help with something. Shouldn't take more than five minutes.'

He turned around for the whisky bottle and advanced towards John.

'No, thanks.' He put his hand over the tumbler. Arthur had already begun to pour. Some of it splashed over John's fingers.

'Sorry.'

'That's all right.' He licked the back of his hand. 'Tastes good.'

'Yes. It would make a rather superb hand-lotion.'

He retreated.

'I haven't seen you about much lately,' John began.

'I've been catching up on the business side.'

'Tricky?'

'Pardon?'

'Does it give you much trouble?' John asked.

'Oh no. I like to take time, though. Pretend it's very complicated, you know?'

'I'm surprised you don't do more.'

'More of what?'

'Work. I mean, you could build this place up quite nicely.'

'We manage,' Arthur replied, coolly.

If he sat down himself, then perhaps John would sit.

'I think I'll go and see if she's waiting outside.'

'Right.' Arthur waved at him, vaguely.

Pat was standing beside the gate which led to the summer-house. When she saw John, she turned and went towards the road. He walked quickly to catch her up.

Arthur sat down and lifted the tumbler to his mouth. It was empty. For a while he sat, staring at the window; they did not pass by. Two weeks or two months; he could not tell. His skin prickled with a scrabbling sourness. He was a coward.

Outside, and he passed his mother working in the garden. She was on her knees planting some bulbs. Her garden always looked beautiful. It was almost dark and she would work until she could see nothing.

He lived like a fool. To keep three horses and a groom on such capital and investments as he had was so bloody idiotic as to be certifiable. Rotting gently, Rotten Gentry. He went for the car.

It was stupid to drive as quickly as he did along such narrow roads. Yet he knew it was no risk. He was a coward. He would have enjoyed crashing into someone, something. Bang. Smack. All gone.

They did not know him at the pub and as he looked so self-contained and elegantly desirable as a patron, no fuss was made when he knocked over the water jug after his eighth or ninth whisky. But they knew that he had smashed it deliberately.

John and Pat walked far beyond a point at which they would be out of sight of any evening strollers. When they reached a place, it was already dark and as they lay down, the seeping dew damped their clothes. He had not touched her, at first afraid, and then, as the walk lengthened, deliberately reserving his pleasure. To be naked together on the black grass. Once, then they talked. Again, longer – it must never end. An inexorable meeting, always away, outside, every day since that first time. Both their bodies were wet on the ground; tight together,

they swung and rolled away from the beacon-pile of clothes.
Everywhere. John's movement sharpened sweetly to a hunger
which constantly fed its need yet could always treat an end as
a pause and come back for more satisfaction. Pat bound herself
to him, glistening under him.

He moved from her, not only tired, but brimmed with a
contentment which could top itself for ever after. After a while,
he got up and went over to his jacket, took out a packet of
cigarettes.

'Bring me something to put on.'

He picked up her sweater.

'Better bring everything. It's cold.'

The whole pile lifted into his arms and he went over to her.
They dressed. Then he handed her a cigarette. When he lit the
match, her face flared whitely and the night thicketed around
her, entering the black hair which heaped on to her shoulders.
The two red tips burned at each other.

'We ought to be getting back,' he said.

He said it before she would. After they had been together,
she would want to go, straight away. He had to suggest it first.
Then, with a rush which held on to evenness for life, he said:

'Would you marry me?'

She was near him. He had spread out his jacket for her to sit
on. His shirt was wet.

The question fell into the dark.

There was no answer.

After they had been walking for about ten minutes, she began
to tell him about her father. His war record. She remembered
his battle descriptions perfectly. He had kept an expensive
collection of beautifully painted lead toy-soldiers which she had
brought to her own room and hidden in a cupboard after his
death. He used to play with them pretending that he was amusing
the children. He would never talk about his M.C. She gave John
a short history of his regiment, its battle honours, its heroes.
Arthur had joined his father's regiment. There was not really
'army' in the family; not on her father's side, anyway. He had
hoped to start a tradition.

Then, without changing to apology, she spoke of his gambling and drinking. Her words condemned him, soundly, almost savagely; her tone forbade any agreement in this judgement.

They were back at the gates leading to her house.

'You must come and see me when you say you'll come,' she said.

'Yes.'

'But you must.'

'I will.'

He would not ask her again for a few days. But he had spoken it. And the impulse which had shifted out his words warned him of the danger of forcing them. He had said it. He would be able to go on.

Pat walked around the corner and into the yard. The kitchen light was on. She hurried in.

Arthur was sitting on a bare, hard-backed chair. When she came in, he thrust out his legs in front of him, as if to trip her, from the other side of the room.

'Have a good – night?' he demanded.

She laughed.

'Come on, Patricia. You're a little too old to be the giggling schoolgirl.'

Feebly aimed, feebly shot. He was drunk. Pat took an orange from the large basket of fruit on the table, sat down on a chair similar to his, peeled the orange with indifferent concentration.

'I had a bloody awful night, I can tell you that, anyway.' He mumbled down to the top of his trousers. The shirt was bundled into a wad; carefully, using his fingers like new instruments, he pushed the loosened heap back under his belt.

'That's better,' she said.

'For what?'

'Whatever you want,' she replied.

'Huh.' Arthur thrust this through his mouth as contemptuously as his unsteady voice would allow. 'Huh!'

Pat broke the orange into two halves, kneading her thumbs into it at the top. Then she put one half on the table, picking the other, segment by segment.

'Would you like some?'

'Yes.'

She took the undisturbed part across to him. He chewed at it, messily.

'Aren't you going to get yourself a drink?' he asked.

'Do you want one?'

'Both. Both of us – should have one. One each.'

She went into the other room and came back with the whisky and two tumblers. Arthur was wiping his hands on his handkerchief; the large white handkerchief fled from his hands, fluttering away in every direction. She poured the drinks. Arthur guzzled his, deliberately slovenly. She poured more into his empty glass.

'You like it, don't you?' he barked.

Pat sipped the whisky. Arthur's face was scattering from each expression it collected.

'Pull yourself together.'

'But you *do* like it,' he went on, more quietly. 'That's it, isn't it? It's because you like it.'

She put the glass on the table, using the leverage of pressing it on to the surface to help herself stand up.

'I'm going to bed.'

Arthur's face swelled puffily, leering. Then he saw how Pat was looking at him. He said nothing.

She walked past him towards the door. His hand grabbed at her arm, slid on to her dress, gripped it.

'I'll leave, you know,' he said. 'I'll go.'

She stood, waiting for him. His hand was damp from the moist cotton of her dress. He took it away; the grip stayed, bunched in two thick old roses; a print. She knelt down beside him.

'Arthur.' He looked away.

'Please,' she went on. 'You know it could be all right. You know that you've been –'

'What have I been?' Turning, he pushed his face into hers, the smell of whisky breath bulging between them.

'Please, Arthur?'

He pushed himself out of his chair. The chair fell behind him. He had nowhere to go. Pat was still kneeling.

'Get up.'

She sank back on to her heels. Her hair came down the front of her dress and lay over her arms. Her face was white.

'Get up!' he shouted. 'Get up! Get up!'

She shook her head. Rushing over to her, he took her under the arms and tugged her to her feet. Then his hands dropped away from her, trembling.

'*I know* you like it!' he said, viciously.

He went out.

John had reached home and then decided against going in. He could not confine himself to a room or a house. Her father had been ill. She had told him that the Colonel had been expected to die at any time over the last two years, and had known it. There was nothing anyone could do! And a long guilt slid out of John's mind, easing out from the concealed fear which had fed it and covered it for so long that only now, when it pulled out from him, did he realise how much force it had had. There was nothing anyone could do. And as for the rest – his fights, his feelings towards his own father, his hatred of that sterile strength – that had left him the first time he had gone with Pat. Further and further away.

He stayed outside to realise his freedom properly. It bathed him. His body ran with it. It sent him in every direction – to nowhere with anger, everywhere to enjoy. He was in front of the farm, looking down at the black square of Pat's home. The moon was so bright that he could see its dense shape clearly; the trees around it were like shrubs protecting a stone. The strange light caught the field before him, swimming on its even wet surface, leaving untouched the dipped hollows, the pockets of hedge root. Beyond the Langleys there was no light but this; moonlight lapping empty fields for miles until it was stopped by the resting settlement of night.

He longed for action and yet his body was seeping with concluded pleasures. Just to stay and let himself be part of such an endless, powerless void, to share in that space by distilling its enormous mood. There was nothing in his past; he had been gathered together and then set high.

He believed that no one had ever been as lucky and as happy as he was at this moment. Pat had not answered his question – but then she must have been as surprised as he was himself that the question had been asked. He smiled to remember it;

asking it; just like that. Let it stand. At least she knew now.

That was enough. He trusted her to let him prove himself. To John, Pat seemed so pure, so profoundly intimate, that he could do no more than put his trust in her. If she had never said what he wanted her to say, if she pulled him to her with a resolution which occasionally made him pause to try to allow some play, some look, smile, to acknowledge it, if, even when they had finished, she would hurt him by rolling away like a cat, leaving him to carry alone any reflection from their act – then it did not matter. She took everything from him – but he was not afraid of her demand; this incited him even further. If she would never end, never speak, never show, then he would never leave, never waken. His question had been no more than a voiceless echo from a wall.

He was so free! – spreading into new sensations, able to move like a man who can defy anything, to dream without the lurch of a different reality, to let his mind leap to whatever small item, large idea, whisper, shout, it wanted to, with no tunnels, no routes. All led to her and in her he was silently massed; a king to his own mob.

It was late – or might be – he would go in. And this too – as he went around to the farmyard. This, too, he could build up and offer. It could be his and he would lay it across all the countryside for her.

They were waiting up for him. One on each side of the wispy little fire, miserably fed and refed, each time the hope that one log would last long enough.

'Would you like something to eat?' Lizzie asked him.

'He can have something to eat after he's said his piece!'

Nelson's retort smudged the hurt – already drawn up on her face and in her shoulders and hands like a total surrender – and she whimpered, thus pointing at once the clash which had led to the silence in which John had discovered them.

John sat down carefully, so that he could see his mother only in profile, his father full on. Nelson sat straight up in his chair, his braces half lost in the baggy rumple of his shirt, his right foot set on the fender as if ready to spring him to the ceiling, his expression fretting and sullen.

'Well?' Nelson continued. 'Where've you been then?'

John shook his head; those times were gone.

'We know.' Nelson looked across at Lizzie. She had told him. She had known about it. John leaned forward to see her face; she was looking into the fire; only the dead straggle of hair. 'You needn't make any daft excuses. You should have more bloody sense.'

'Why?'

'Well,' his right arm whirled a vortex of violent objections. 'More bloody damned commonsense! Commonsense! I suppose you think you're being smart, eh?'

'What's all this about?'

'You know,' said Nelson, furiously. Then, 'Why did you run off?'

'When?'

'Don't you give a bugger for this place, then? Eh? It's more important to go about with somebody you couldn't come near than stay with me. Oh! I know I'm not important. I'm just a common old farmer. I've known that for a long time.'

'Mam, would you tell me what's wrong with him?'

'And don't bring her into it! She has enough to do without worrying herself sick about all your daftness. Stupidity!' Nelson bellowed. 'Everybody's expected to work on this place except you. Eh? And what good'll that be? Is that how you would act? Carrying on. She can't sleep for worrying about you.'

'Is that right?' Lizzie was still looking away. 'Mam – is it right what he's saying?'

'He doesn't believe a word I'm saying,' Nelson went on, amazed. 'He thinks that we just make these things up to keep ourselves busy.' He whistled, and followed this by a short, spitting cackle, his head falling to rest on his hand. 'My boy. Eh? If I'd had opportunities like that,' he looked at Lizzie, shaking his head sadly, ignoring his son. 'What do you say? He thinks we just sit around here making things up. He thinks we have nothing better to do – folk like us.'

'WHAT THE HELL are you on about?'

'Don't you shout and swear at me, my lad!' Nelson jumped up, his arms beginning to pummel forwards as if looking for an opening. 'You'll have to be a damned sight better if you think you're gonna swear and shout at your own father in his own house!' Both of them could hear Lizzie sobbing. Nelson glared at John with total hatred. 'See what you've done now? Eh?'

Clumsily, he took the two steps over to his wife and looked down at her. Her head was bent right over, resting on her knees. Nelson stood above her, looking at her hair.

'I'm going to bed,' said John.

He lifted himself out of his chair quickly. He dared not stay.

'Ay. That's right. Run away to bed now that you've spoiled everything,' said Nelson, not turning towards him.

John paused. He did not know where to begin.

'What *do* you want?' he asked, as quietly as he could manage to.

Nelson waved him away.

'Oh go on,' he said. 'Get yourself to bed. Go on.' John waited; one more chance. 'You wouldn't understand if I spelt it out.' He hesitated; Lizzie had found a handkerchief from an apron pocket, and the large white square was dangling between her head and knees. 'I should never have considered it in the first place,' Nelson concluded.

John left them.

TWENTY

Shirley told him about it. Her mother had confessed about Pat only when Nelson's rage had grown so terrible that it needed some fixed point to stop it seething over the whole house.

'How did she know?'

'Everybody knows,' Shirley replied.

'What did he say when she told him?'

'He just looked,' Shirley smiled at him. 'Then he sat down to wait.'

Both his daughters had been ordered to bed. From what Shirley said, John could see that Avril had been very much on her father's side.

'What did Mam do?'

Shirley shook her head.

'She didn't know what to do,' she answered. 'Neither of us did.' She drew a deep breath. 'What's she like, then?' she asked casually.

John frowned at her.

'Didn't he say anything?'

'No.'

'Just sat down and waited?'

'Yes.'

'I thought he'd be pleased when I told him,' John said.

'She's nice, isn't she?'

'I thought that they would like her.'

Nelson refused to speak to him for about four days. It seemed to hurt him even to look at his son. At meal times, their diagonal disregard was so taut that the food was gobbled, wolfed, silently.

John saw Pat only twice during those days. Once, in the middle of the afternoon, the day after, when he called her as she came out of the gates on Bonnie. They had not said much to each other, she was in a hurry. The other time had been the following evening. They had walked only a short distance when she said that she wanted to go back. John had panicked, and she had promised to see him the night after next.

Tonight. Nelson was expecting a buyer to call – but John would not stay. His father would be displeased whatever he did – and John had neither the heart to continue a family argument in front of strangers, nor the desire to use such a disinterested third party as a bridge back to communication with Nelson; besides, there was no real question. He had to see Pat again.

Nelson still worked as he had always done; or rather, he resembled his previous self in all but the exact speed of each finishing movement. Seeing him move around the farm, with not a word, with every job timed and slotted into an indestructible pattern, the wrinkles on his face more like deep cuts from thin wire pulled hard into the flesh, his forearms swelling out from under his shirt-sleeves, John wondered at the power which had kept him going so hard in such a narrow area. Yet he knew that his father needed to have his son's confidence and purpose with him as an acknowledged possession. He would not dare offer it. His father walked like a man who has explored and wildly looted every inch of ground and by-road of the route he was taking and was only now beginning to have that unfixable heart-sickness which threatened doubt. No reconsideration of his achievements, no revision would satisfy him; there must be another addition.

At tea, John was so eager to see Pat again soon that he could hardly bear to sit still. He began to imitate his father's morose evasiveness; it was comical the way Nelson flung his eyes away whenever they threatened to light on his son for even a second. John acted in the same way with Shirley. Lizzie noticed and began to giggle, the sadness breaking away to a longing for relief. Nelson knew that they were laughing at him; he left, roughly, refraining from an outburst only when his glance touched on John. He was not going to be the first to give in – and he strode out of the kitchen as if to war, across the yard, grabbing a sickle, off to trim a hedge.

John rushed into his work. They had cut down a little on the milkers and now he did it by himself. Once Ben had collected them from the field, it was easy work. The cows trudged up the field through the deep grass, occasionally making use of the movement to joggle their bowels or shake out their intestines. So covered with laziness that even their stiffly raised tails stayed in the new position long after they had done their job. There was no hurrying them.

Into the long milking shed and he fitted the rubber teats on each fat nipple. The long brown tubes trailed across the cemented floor like surgeon's equipment, somehow mislaid. And still the cud rolled up into their mouths while the hot milk squirted into the bright cans.

Eventually it was finished. There were the cans to lay out and the beasts to be taken back to the field. He walked back quickly to the house.

The van was drawn up outside. Inside the door, his mother, pale, was pulling on a coat and trying to ram her hair under a scarf.

'Your father's hurt himself,' she said.

John went into the kitchen and saw his father bent double in his chair, a heap of white bandage around his hand, soaked crimson. His cap was off; there was blood smudged on his brow, blood on his clothes. Shirley stood to one side of him, afraid to say anything, afraid to leave. John, also, was too impressed by the pain which his father drew into himself to say anything.

'Ready.' Lizzie came into the kitchen.

With effort, as if his whole body were cut by one open wound, Nelson hoisted himself to his feet and went across to the door. His face was hard set, his normal toughness had been hammered, and then drained of all liquid.

'You'll see to Mr Lows,' he was the buyer, 'won't you?' Lizzie asked.

John nodded. With Shirley, he stood at the farmyard door while the small van pushed out through the gates. They stayed to hear it move down the track, turn on to the road, down the hill.

'They should go straight to the hospital,' said Shirley.

'Where are they going?'

'Dr Barwise. He won't be able to do much.'

They were still at the door. Ben was lying on a raised flagstone which used to serve as a stand for the urns. Otherwise the yard was empty, cut almost precisely in half by a shadow which stretched out from the stalls to their left.

'What did he do?'

'He was dyking,' Shirley began. 'He would never wear gloves. And those sickles are as sharp as razor-blades. The way he keeps them.'

'Yes?'

She spread out her hand and drew a line down the webbing between thumb and forefinger, almost to the wrist.

'It was hanging off.'

John stood tense against the lurch in his stomach. The sharp blade curving down through that leathered skin, stopping at the bone.

They went back into the kitchen. Shirley cleaned the sink and then began to rub the floor around her father's chair. Avril pottered in from work with Tony; they had begun to come to each other's house for supper once a week. She almost scolded Shirley in her persistence for details while the two men chatted.

Supper was laid – the meal John would have missed. It would be deserting something to go and see Pat.

Mr Lows arrived when they were half-way through the meal. Of course he was sorry to disturb them. No, he'd eaten. Just – maybe a cup of tea? Ah. Many thanks. And Mr Foster? Oh dear. Oh, what a shame. Very sorry. Should he go? No. John would – would he? Very kind. Very sorry. Another cup? Well – maybe just another half-cup. Well, if they could be out and looking? No rush. Right away? Good.

Mr Lows was on rather a special commission for a syndicate of rich Midland farmers who used him as a 'spotter', before either coming along for themselves or sending their farm managers. He wore a Harris tweed jacket, cavalry twill trousers, blunt brown shoes, still morning-slimy where the mud had not got at them, and a brown forester's hat which perched gamely on his brown, middle-aged face. His red Triumph Herald was parked near the door.

His chatter was not irritating, and, coming from such a town-for-country planned assortment of clothes, it was surprisingly informed. They went to the field in which the Galloways were grazing and he walked around each one with a detailed question-naire pattering before him. They were on that side of the farm furthest away from the Langleys, in a field which the previous owner of the farm had given up entirely; lying too low, boggy, full of large stones, some of them deep in grass, a few trees, unfenced on the side which could lead the cattle for miles into open country. John and his father had spent years on it, clearing, draining, re-sowing part, making good the fence. Now, it was perfect.

It was worse, not being able to see the Langleys' place. Had it been near him, he would have felt the soundness of his decision – the mere sight of it would have presented the comparison forcefully enough for him to have felt the virtue which his decision needed, to keep it steady. She would know that some-thing serious had prevented him from meeting her; bound to. He rehearsed his explanations to her but, as he did so, he seemed to be somehow proud of his father's accident. He shuddered.

'It *is* cold,' said Mr Lows. 'Shall we go – back?' The word was dropped in delicately; substitute anything more comfortable as desired. 'I think that I've seen everything.'

'Yes. Come back in.'

They went across to the gate. Mr Lows made no reference to Nelson's stock but, instead, began to tell John of the prices asked for a 'wonderful' collection of beasts he had seen earlier that afternoon.

Lizzie was back. It was not quite dark. John had the faint hope of depositing Mr Lows and racing down to Pat – there was still time. But his mother offered the buyer some whisky, obviously wanted John to stay and talk with him.

Nelson had been detained in hospital. He had lost a great deal of blood and had sixteen stitches put into his hand. He would probably be there for two days. The cut had gone through a tendon and the muscles.

'You can imagine what he had to say about *that*!' she said.

The danger lifted away. Mr Lows questioned Tony about his job and then found himself subjected to a lengthy interrogation in his turn. Avril looked on, approvingly; there was something remorseless about Tony's serious conversation which could not but win him admiration.

It was obvious that no business would be talked. Mr Lows never even made a single reference to the matter which had brought him where he was content, it seemed, to drink the whisky, sit by the fire, answer questions.

John went with his mother on her next trot to the kitchen. Yes. He could go if he wanted to. No. She did not mind at all. He hesitated. By raising the subject in the first place, the damage had been done, it did not matter whether he stayed or left.

It was dark but still the summer light held on to the ground, holding it until the morning. He walked along the track and down the road. The Langleys' house was totally without lights. He went through the gates and into the yard. There was no light, anywhere.

He looked over to the summerhouse. That, too, was black. Emptiness came out of the house, the gardens, the summerhouse; a proprietorial vacancy; he was a trespasser.

A weak headlight bobbed around the corner. John went over to it. It went out.

'Who is that?'

'Me,' John replied. It was Andrei.

He came closer to make sure that John corresponded in some way to his voice.

'Good evening,' he said.

'Hello.' Then, 'Do you know where they are?'

Andrei was wearing a flat cloth cap. The peak overhung his face with a shadow. Only his thin chin was clearly visible.

'Are they not in the house?' he asked.

'Doesn't look like it.'

Andrei looked around, his head sweeping slowly backwards and forwards across the huge black pile as if expecting some sudden flashed signal.

'No,' he said.

'Did they go out?'

Still Andrei scanned the house. Finally, his head came to a halt.

'Maybe,' he replied. 'Maybe that is what it is.'

'They didn't say they were going out? Did they?'

Andrei paused, looked at John, looked at the ground, bent behind him to lift the dynamo hub off his back wheel.

'Not to me,' he answered.

'Right,' said John. 'Sorry to have bothered you. Good-night.'

'Good-night.'

He watched John walk away.

'Maybe I should go and knock at the door,' he said, loudly.

'No thanks.'

'All right. Good-night.'

John waved and went on. He walked briskly until he was out on to the road. The emptiness around him was intolerable. He went across the road and looked at the house. Dark, black, empty, desolate. He would plunge into that shuttered density and find her. To have been without her for two days seemed a deprivation; he did not know what to do with himself if he could not have her. He wanted to shake away this hackled longing; not that he was ashamed of it, but it roused in him a lust which he was afraid of. It rose around him, like some odour from the ground. One second he wanted to laugh at it, stamp it away, move from the spot, the next, he luxuriated in its muffled ripeness, promising him sated excess. He would make her say that she loved him. But he did not want to make her do anything, she must realise her own need. Her bedroom was near, he could easily climb in. An entire night together. She was ill, she could not have conceived.

In that expanding night, his hunger flared up like fire. They would have a house together. Her shoulders were so purely white, flowing so roundly, beautifully, black hair heaped on them. He could not move from the spot: look at the house. It was terrible, the longing and the timidity, taking him from power to weakness.

Dragging his legs, pulling them under him as if they carried heavy weights, he went slowly up the hill, home.

Only Avril was there. The others had gone to bed. Efficiently, doing her duty so that no one could blame her, and somehow justifying the position from which she would speak she made and brought him tea and sandwiches.

'You'll be going to see him tomorrow,' she began.

'Hm? Yes.' He paused. 'What time?'

'Evening visiting tomorrow. Seven to eight.'

Eight. It would take no more than half-an-hour or so to drive back from the hospital at Carlisle; he could be with Pat by nine. Too late.

'He'll be expecting you to go,' she went on, firmly.

'I'll go.'

'See you do. Tony's going to take me. You take Mam. Shirley can stay and look after things.'

'Yes, boss.'

She tossed her head. Someone had to make these arrangements.

'And I can stay off in the morning if you want help.'

'We'll manage.' He looked round. 'Did our friend Lows push off then?'

'Yes.'

'Thought he would be part of the furniture by this time.'

'*I* liked him.'

'Huh.'

He chewed at the sandwiches and looked into the fire. Avril pecked at the lip of her cup, watching for the opportunity to say what she had stayed up to say. John gave her none. She had to attack it full on.

'John,' she started, hesitantly, 'are you sure you know what you're doing?'

He knew what she was talking about and immediately blushed with anger.

'Doesn't it look like it?'

Very carefully, Avril placed her cup and saucer on the table beside her. Then she gripped the chair underneath its seat, as if steadying herself for an earthquake. But it had to be spoken.

'There are some awful things said about her.'

John was still. She dare not utter one more word; dare hardly breathe; he would kill her for saying that.

He put his plate on to the fender; it trembled where it lay. Then he stood up, continuing the movement into a juddering, splayed yawn.

'Good-night,' he said.

He did not look at her.

TWENTY-ONE

She was not there when he went down at lunch-time. Working in the top field in the afternoon, he saw Arthur walking away along the Wall; he was too far away to hear John's shouts. After that, there was no more time before they set off for the hospital. Almost as an atonement for the fierce impulse of irritation which caused him the crudest fantasies while at the bare bedside of Nelson's illness, he dallied some minutes after the official leaving time – and, with one thing and another, they arrived home hopelessly late for him to do anything.

Nelson arrived back the next afternoon. His hand was thickly layered with neat bandage; he was quiet, even pleasant, and over a long tea while the details of arrival, doctors, nurses, bed-pans, injections, early tea, jokes, other patients, cleanliness, efficiency and pain were gone over with the bright aplomb of a schoolboy reporter – John grew afraid that he would not be able to get out yet again.

When at last he did leave, it was with neither exhilaration nor an energy demanding to be fed, but rather he popped out of the kitchen, uncomfortably leaving behind him the silenced quartet, grouped around his father, blank. He knew that something was bound to go wrong again.

First, as no arrangements had been made, he went towards the summerhouse where he thought to ask Arthur to take a message for him. He found it extremely difficult to bring himself to do this – but the stupidity of leaning against one of the pillars at the entrance would have been intolerable. Feeling increasingly discomposed, he went down the road, climbed into one of his

father's fields and approached the summerhouse by the back
route.

It was empty.

Standing on its steps, he could see through to the yard. No
one was about. He walked across towards the house, insulted
by the circumstances which forced such a hesitant, servile,
liaison.

Mrs Langley came to the door after Annie had gathered, from
his embarrassed, barely intelligible muttering, that it was all
something to do with someone in the family. Waiting on the
coarse all-weather mat, hearing the edges of an undertoned
debate, John was miserable.

'Yes?' said Mrs Langley.

John coughed. He had never once met her formally.

'I was wondering if Arthur was in.'

'I'm afraid not.'

It had not worked. It was twice as difficult to begin again:

'Pat?' he mumbled.

'Patricia?'

'Yes.'

He looked straight at her, his face blazing.

'She's out, too, I'm afraid.'

John steadied himself.

'Do you know when they'll be back, please?'

Mrs Langley was amused.

'Well, not exactly. But Arthur *did* say he might bring some
friends back for a drink. *Later.*'

'Thank you.'

'Can I give them any message?'

'No.'

'Can I say who called? No,' she added, kindly, 'I know who
you are. I'll tell them.'

'Thank you.'

'Arthur will be sorry to have missed you.'

He nodded. She smiled at him, again kindly. Awkwardly,
as if he were learning to move for the first time, he turned to
go.

'Good-night,' she said.

'Good-night,'

Throttled with shame, he went to the gates. He thought that he might be sick. He wanted to go quite away.

He waited for them to return.

When he heard the cars, he thought at first that it was part of his dream. There were lights sweeping across a large dark plain; occasionally, he saw the earth, all brushed with gorgeous colours, people laughing, dressed richly, ambling across bright green fields. The noise came from the laughter they made, the shouts. He woke up. The noise came from the cars.

He had been sleeping on the wide verge – just up from the Langleys. He remembered having sat down there to wait. The grass was wet.

The noise grew. He could see the headlights shooting out into the hedges, lifting into the sky, as the cars went along the short road which led from the village before turning down to the house. Their horns were crying wildly. There must have been about eight cars.

John found that he had turned to get over the hedge and out of the way. It was a shamed action. But the headlights fastened on to their short home stretch, and the motorcade aimed straight towards him, and he swung over and into the field.

All of them tried to slide and skid the right angle into the drive. Their horns locked with their brakes and the noise chased away the still-lying peace of the night, broke its shelled covering, and out of that tear came all the sounds which, until then, had been submerged.

In the farmyard, the doors banged, shouts, woken up, the hens chattered, something smashed on the ground, the horses stamped. John could see past the summerhouse, right into the milling lights. He stepped over the ditch and went through the hedge and past the summerhouse. He could not see her.

The cars, the lights, people scurrying around the yard, lacing the baldly lit dark with pastel summer dresses, flying ties, all this stayed still in front of him, like some outrageous display in a large fish-tank; he saw all that was happening and, mesmerised, he let himself be drawn up to it.

By the time he reached the outer ring of cars, the people from them had moved over to the house where they gathered at the door, unwilling to confine their loose freedom to a room before shaking all its enjoyment from themselves. John tacked and side-stepped around the sharp bumpers, noticing the slow assembly of interest in his progress, confining himself to thought of a single action. To talk to Pat.

She was staring at him from within the group. When he looked at her, she made no attempt to look away. By the time he cleared the cars, there was silence.

No one looked at him directly, but he found it impossible to leap their line. Then Arthur came out to him. The others began to talk; no one went in.

Arthur put a hand on John's shoulder and tried to swing him round, to take him almost roughly away from the public view. John resisted the pull and then, seeing that Pat was making no move towards him but looking at Arthur as if in him lay her explanation and so, perhaps, her reclaim, he turned, with Arthur's hand still gripping his shoulder. Arthur's face was almost idiotically unsettled. He stared at John, breathing whisky on to him.

'Glad you've come,' he said. 'Lovely to see you. Lovely.'

John waited.

'Your father?' Arthur's right eyebrow screwed up his brow. 'Your father all right?'

'Yes.'

'Good.' He nodded, pushing his hand deeper into John's shoulder. 'Good. Good, good.'

'I wanted to speak with Pat.'

'Yes.' Arthur looked at the ground, his head dropping forward as if it were unhinged from the neck. 'Yes,' he repeated.

He ought to push Arthur off and go and talk to her. Those people. They did not matter.

'Andrei told me you'd been down,' Arthur went on. Then, 'Andrew! Andrew! – he changed his name. Why don't we call him by it? And*rew*!'

'Look,' said John. 'Would you please ask Pat if I can have a word with her? Won't take a minute.'

Arthur peered behind him, as if expecting trouble. The group had quietened their voices. They knew that something was going wrong.

'Well,' he answered, eventually, 'you'd better ask her.'

'But I would prefer you to ask her.'

'Why?' This was said sharply.

John shrugged off the hand, and pushed away. Arthur seemed to stand erect, let drop his slurred manner, prepare.

'Please,' John continued, forcefully, 'please will you ask her if I can speak to her?'

'That's what you came for, isn't it?'

'Yes.'

'Yes, I've noticed.'

John almost snorted with irritation. It did not matter. No stupid arguments. Not now.

'In fact,' Arthur went on, slowly, 'you've been going around with her an awful lot. Every day.'

'Well?'

Suddenly, Arthur put his arm around John's neck, wanting to drag him into a fresh – start.

'Come in,' he whispered, 'have a drink, and then when all these people have cleared off – we'll talk about it. What about that, hm?'

He started back far more than he need have done when John slipped out of his confidential hug. Pat was talking to someone he did not know. They were on the outside of the ring. He went across and stood beside them. For a second, the man hesitated, allowing Pat the opportunity to turn away from him; she did not move, and he talked on, ignoring John, as she did.

'John!'

Arthur had gone into the middle of the cars.

'Could you come over here, please?' he shouted.

Still they ignored him.

He went to Arthur.

'You see,' Arthur began, with that composed assurance of the other's exact knowledge of what he was referring to which comes from having driven over the same points incessantly in solitude. 'I wouldn't have minded if you'd had a good time – as much as you liked.'

'Are you telling me to keep away from her?'

'If you like,' Arthur replied, coolly staring over John's head. 'Although you've arrived at a rather abrupt conclusion a little earlier than I might have done myself.'

'Sorry about that!' said John, viciously.

'Why did you do it?'

The attitude fell away.

'For Christ's sake!'

Arthur allowed the lightest flavour of a smile to scan his face.

'It's spoiled everything, you know.' He paused. 'You know that?'

'No. I didn't know that.'

'Come in for a drink, at least,' Arthur offered, again patently adjusting himself to a civilized action.

'I'm going to talk to Pat.'

'Please.' He hesitated. It was useless to touch him, and yet his arm had moved towards his shoulder once again.

John left him. As he came nearer to Pat, she began to push for the door. He turned; Arthur was waving her in. John went through the uncertain group and into the house. It was the first time he had been in the house.

There was a kitchen with some people from the cars sitting on the edges of the table. Pat was not there. He went through it and into a long hall. No one. The door at the end was open, he ran for it, his feet bumping softly on the thick carpet.

'Arthur?'

Mrs Langley was reading by a small table-lamp. She looked up and took off her spectacles.

'Sorry,' John said.

She smiled.

'If you see him – would you tell him I would like to speak with him for a moment?'

'Yes.'

'Thank you.'

She would not be downstairs. He walked towards the broad

staircase. Then he suddenly opened a door on his left and went into blackness. He could not find the light. Standing perfectly still, he held his breath.

In the corridor, at the far end, three people were watching him as he came out. She would be in her bedroom. He was at the bottom of the stairs.

He could shout for her. He could just stand there and shout until she was forced to come down to stop the noise.

Arthur bustled through the kitchen doorway.

'John!' He came close to him, glaring fiercely, determined to say what he had to say. 'You don't understand. What do you think *I* feel? You must realise that. My sister.'

John shook his head. He did not want to exchange one more word with him.

'You must consider *my* feelings. What *I* feel about her. You must realise that.'

He was leaning into him, almost pushing against him. John put a hand against his chest and thrust him away. Off-balance, Arthur staggered back.

'Want any help?' Duncan Collins looked at John while he asked Arthur the question. Hands lightly tipped in his pockets.

'No, please.' Arthur grinned at him, jerkily. 'Please.'

'Well,' Duncan went on, 'you just have to say if he starts to give you any trouble.'

'No. I'm perfectly all right, thank you.'

'I'll be just down there,' he flicked his head to indicate the door entrance, a few feet away. 'And if he decides to cut up rough – just tell me.'

'Go to hell!' said John, tightly.

Collins swung slowly around to Arthur.

'Are you absolutely *sure* I can't be of assistance?' he drawled.

'What do you think you could do, anyway?'

Collins shook his head, hugely. Then, talking this time directly to Arthur, he went on:

'I'm pretty good at the bar-room-brawl type of thing, you know.'

'No.' Arthur ushered him clumsily away. 'Please. Thank you. Everything's perfectly all right, perfectly all right . . .'

'And there's damn-all you could do about it if it wasn't!' John shouted.

Duncan stopped and cast out his most level stare. He allowed himself to be pushed further on by Arthur.

Arthur scurried back to John. The interruption had frightened him.

'Let's forget about all this. All this,' he said. 'I'm sorry. I am sorry. I'll call her for you. *Of course* you must talk to her if you want to. I'll call her for you.' No acknowledgement. He lifted his head back until his face was pouting right up the stairs. 'Pat! Pat! Come down for a minute, will you?'

Nervously, he smiled at John. They waited.

'Pat! Just a minute!'

The chatter in the kitchen had stopped. Duncan Collins and his two friends were looking at Arthur with concerned surprise. John was certain that Mrs Langley was standing behind him. He turned, sharply: the door to her room was closed.

'She can't have heard,' Arthur muttered. 'I'll go up and find her.'

He went up the stairs with over-long steps so that he rocked, unsteadily, lurched.

'Pat!'

John waited. The large front door was near him. He could be out through the garden and over the wall and away.

Standing, poised as if ready to heave himself down, Arthur looked at John from the small landing.

'I can't find her.'

'Wise girl,' Collins murmured.

'She must be down there somewhere,' Arthur continued, miserably. 'Pat?' More quietly. 'Pat?' A whisper.

Reaching for the door's lock as he took the first step towards it, John left.

Slowly, Arthur came down the broad stairs, and as he reached the bottom, the door against which he had staggered when John had pushed him, opened.

She stood waiting for him, no light coming from the room. Arthur stopped on the bottom stair.

'Why didn't you come when I shouted?'

Pat stepped out of the room and shut the door carefully behind her.

'Why did you want me to?' she asked.

TWENTY-TWO

'Come on then!'

He tried to shift on to his back but his body was so soft and uncollected. This was only the first time she had called.

Her hand was on his shoulder. He threw himself forward and glared at this mother.

'Get up,' she urged, impatiently. 'I can't shout at you all day.'

'Yes?'

'Get up.'

'What is it?'

'Your father's already out.'

'Now?'

'Do you realise what time it is?'

'No.'

'Eight o'clock.'

She pronounced it solemnly.

'That late?'

Lizzie nodded.

'Come on.' Then she added, kindly, 'You needed a good sleep.'

'Coming.' The words came feebly through weak lips.

She left him. He slipped back down into the bed. The light came in full through the curtains she had pulled open. It was a bright day. He could hear the throb of the tractor, a comfortable clatter from the yard. The sunlight came right on to his face. He went back to sleep.

'Tea?' He woke up, more firmly this time. His mother stood anxiously beside him holding a small tin tray. There were sandwiches and tea on it.

'Are you feeling all right?'

'Yes.' He sat up. 'Of course I'm all right. Why shouldn't I be?'

She nodded and put the tray on to the floor. Then she stood up, shyly straightening herself in front of him, worried.

'Christ!'

He shook his watch elaborately, then looked at her with enlarged astonishment.

'I'll be right down.'

'But you're sure you're not badly or anything?'

'No. Be down in a minute.'

Yet when she went out, and the automatic apology of action had been said and done, he felt no inclination to follow. It even seemed ridiculous that he should find such amazement in the fact of his having over-slept until eleven-thirty. And then even that passed away and he was lying in his bed, looking out of the window without seeing anything, calm. It would have been pleasant to have had a cigarette, but they were in his jacket and that was too far away to reach out to. It was not that it was too much effort to do anything; he was not anxious to change. That was all. The bedclothes were rather too heavy and the pillow was flattened, pressing against his neck. He could sleep again.

Nothing was said when, eventually, he went down to the kitchen to join them for the midday meal. It was not the reticence of tolerance or even of concern; perhaps his mother was bewildered and Shirley envious; but Nelson was suppressing a fury which had clearly pitched inside him throughout the morning. His bandaged thumb filled the table with anger.

After the afternoon's work, John ate and went immediately to his bedroom where he did not even bother to pick up a book to pretend to read. He lay on his side, his elbow resting on the bed, cheek cupped in his hand, legs drawn up towards his stomach. When it grew dark, he did not bother to put the light on.

His mother appeared again at his door, herself the patient to his unconcern.

'There's some supper downstairs.'

'Thanks. I don't think I'll bother.'

'You've got to eat.' The admonition was fragile.

'No. I'm all right, thanks.'

'But you can't just lie up here in the dark all the time.'

'I'm fine. Honestly.'

He was annoyed at the flare of irritation which licked up through him, suddenly shooting his body into violent, prickly antagonism.

'No tea?'

'No!'

He should have called her back – to apologise at least; that would be almost as good as an explanation. But she would be in the kitchen by now.

It was almost a week since he had been at the Langleys. All his mind had been concentrated on staying away. Simply that. Getting up the next morning he had wanted to run down to her immediately to forget that anything had happened; going through the morning's work, he had waited for the pauses, judging whether or not he would have time to run down to the Langleys again. Just to see her. To know that everything would remain some part of what it had been. He could have gone at lunch-time, but he volunteered to cut down the hour's break by half and go out with Shirley to clear some tools from a shed that Nelson planned to pull down. They finished early and he had to decide whether or not it was worth changing. He went into his bedroom and looked at himself for a few moments in his working clothes. Then he sat down on the small bedding-chest near the window and smoked two or three cigarettes. It was too early. He could not see Pat's house from his window and that made it easier to imagine that he would go down. Later.

He did not go, and the next morning he decided that he would never go. There was too much to explain, and after such explanation, there could be nothing but ruins to live in.

It was a decision which weighed nothing in balance – even the curt conclusion that examination would be useless and leave all things barren was no more than a quick daub almost irrelevantly applied – but he could go to the gate, along the track which led to the road, look down at the house; no further. The relief which, for the briefest of moments, accompanied his turn back to his own house was to be the small medal of reassurance which was to help him during the next few days. For he wanted to touch Pat, he wanted to talk to her; he saw Arthur apologising, he imagined all three of them laughing at what had happened.

But the notion of going there again came up against a barred unwillingness. He would think of it twenty times in an hour and each time he would reject it.

It became tiredness. That was the easiest name to give it. He preferred to be unoccupied.

Nelson was first sullen, then he got mad, then, in his anger, he tried to find out what was wrong. John could not be bothered to argue, to excuse or to talk. He walked away.

He announced that he was taking a week's holiday, immediately. It was after his collapse that Dickie drifted in like a stranger, on a summons to help, declared that it would be too much for him, and left. Shirley's boyfriend would use one of his two weeks off to replace John.

Lizzie packed his case for him. He was embarrassed about asking for a lift to the station and, finally, it was she who drove him there.

Still asking him if he was all right, she waited until the train pulled out of the small station and disappeared right into the tunnel. She watched the guard's van pulled into the blackness, arm half-raised as if ready for another final wave; and then she drove back, crying.

Eventually, Arthur went into the summerhouse. It was silly to avoid going in; he could build up so many taboos that he would never stir. Everything made him ashamed. He was ashamed of the half-used comfort of the unfilled rooms in the big house; the pictures, disregarded; the furniture and carpets limp with scarcely any look of lively habitation. He was ashamed of the straightforward talk of his mother which now seemed to come out of an unattainable simplicity and tranquillity. The farm suddenly seemed to have slunk back to the tumble-down inefficiency of his father's days – without even big spending to excuse it – and he was ashamed that, even so, its value rose because of the increase in land prices. Surrounded by the attendants of a time he understood but could not support, those who accepted him only because he represented their own younger memories – groom, lawyer, vicar, people to help and accommodate for this and that – he moved where he could make no contribution and lost even that confidence which the respect of others gave him, by a meandering inadequacy.

So he went to the summerhouse because there – he had told himself happily a hundred times – he was with the things he wanted. He was glad that it was dusty, its cleaning imposed a demand which assured him of a certain need. A small one, easily satisfied. Tidy, the windows opened, the gloomy summer's day neither inviting nor discouraging, there was nothing to do but adopt the pose; sit in the chair, take a book, light a cigarette, read.

He could concentrate, but the immersion in another's rounded creation only nagged his own fear of misery. It was to be kept out, this cold flame; it was to be raced from, ducked, stamped on, scorned; and it always came back. The knowledge that a feeble decision and its lazy execution had led him to an unassimilable complexity which he could neither resolve nor abandon.

He was ashamed of this self-indulgent collapse, as he had been many times before. But this time it was worse because it gave no benefit, offered no possibility other than its own growth. He tried to shake it off. He went out again with Craddock on a dig – but the whole affair seemed over-demandingly parochial; if you did not enjoy the life which could lead to exuberance over such a selfless hobby, then the work itself appeared as no more than pottering, time-wasting, boring. He rode. But again – as on the Wall with the Archaeological Society – he found no pleasure in a pastime which proclaimed satisfaction with the run of life which allowed it; and again, he was forced to see, even to pass, John's house, something which stung his shame to vicious self-contempt.

The only way to break it would be to destroy something around it. But what was there worth the effort? The decorations and furnishings in the summerhouse now seemed flaccid. No real pleasure or need had worked into their possession; they were pleasant hangings to hide him cosily.

And he read. With Oliver, he had once agreed that serious reading of good and enjoyable books was the activity most likely to civilize. But his seriousness seemed now to come from a desire to be civilized rather than a delight in reading, or to appear to be civilized – for he now believed that such scattering of knowledge as he had was a flat surface, within easy reach, on which he could display appreciation of talent to such advantage that he thought that he shared in it. He read to conceal his inactivity.

The first thing he had thought of was to throw it all up and go and join Oliver.

'I think that would be very sensible,' said his mother.

'Are you sure that you wouldn't mind being left alone?'

'I wouldn't be *quite* alone, darling. And I think you *should* try something else – at least for a year or two, before you finally settle down.'

'Yes.'

But would it clear away the jumbled meanness which seemed to be suffocating his conscience? Far more courageous to stay and see if he could do something to help John. For again, he would be accepting an appearance as truth; it would appear that helping Oliver would gradually disperse his shame. But to be charitable through such self-interested pity would not help any-one. It might. But then, so might any change of circumstances. And to change circumstances again in order to resolve a situation which had arisen from just such an unfelt, undemanding change would be useless.

Yet he could not go to see John. Not yet. The shame of his behaviour stung too rawly; it was not decent to go so soon. That 'decency' should be a reason in such a position as that in which he now felt himself to be placed, was ridiculous, even sinister; as if, driven to a personal unhappiness and bewilderment such as he had never before met, he was able to rely only on the words, and so the code of manners which – applied in such a way – directed friendship to the uninvolved areas of acquaintanceship. But it was neither decent to write to Oliver, nor was it decent to visit John. Not yet.

And Pat? They had hardly spoken to each other since that evening on which John had left them together.

TWENTY-THREE

Arthur saw John bundling along the side of the street, pretending, he thought, to be unaware of the indifferent bustle around him, running away from it, yet trying to be contingent upon it, restless. He stood behind the car and let him come towards the station.

He had arrived at the farm three days after John had gone off.

'Yes,' said Mrs Foster, 'he went away last Saturday morning. He's gone for a week.'

'Oh.'

'He'll be sorry to have missed you,' she added, reluctantly.

He thought that she was accusing him, and blushed.

'Where did he go?' he demanded, brusquely.

'I've just got a postcard this morning.' Although she must have known it by heart, she disappeared into the house and returned with it. 'Newcastle,' she read. 'Back on Saturday.'

He had heard about the accident through Shirley's boyfriend who, it seemed, had stalked half the length of a field in order to tell Andrei. Not much of an accident really. Nelson had begun to tackle jobs which obviously strained his hand. It had begun to bleed but he had ignored it. There was no time to see a doctor.

Lizzie had redressed it for him and it was then that he had noticed the raw little gaps in the skin where the stitches had burst. To be advised that it might be better at least to rest for an hour or two, was to be goaded. Andrei related with relish the scene which had been relayed to him; 'bloody John!' Andrei chanted, 'bloody John! bloody John! Worse than useless!'

That afternoon, Nelson had gone mad to discover the dirtiest and most strenuous work he could find for himself. He had collapsed the following morning – lain near the hedge in a field for over an hour before Shirley had discovered him. He was taken to the Cumberland Infirmary.

Arthur went up to the farm right away to see how he could help. John was not going to be back until the following day but . . . Lizzie tacitly assumed his wish to help in any way and this gave him so much certainty of his own acknowledged position on the close outer ring of the family, that for a moment he forgot what had passed between John and himself and considered it his duty to bring him back into their common fold.

On the road to Newcastle, the mission became an excuse and the excuse a cheapening of the mission. He drove slowly, attempting to give reality to the selflessness of his action by refraining from the indignity of bolting to what he wanted; but to take his time was to use the journey for his own ends just as selfishly. With, perhaps, a more unfortunate outcome possible; he would need as many hours in Newcastle as possible were he to find John.

At first, he drove around the streets, looking at the people on the pavements so earnestly that several of them stopped to return his stare while those cars that were behind him, assuming that parking-space was being sought, constantly lurched up beside him, attempting to pass. The centre of the town was not big; in an hour, he had driven over most of it, twice. He parked the car.

He did not know where to go. It made too much of an adventure if he went into the gallery or the museum. He did not like to hang around outside cinemas. It was silly – more correctly he felt that he appeared silly – bobbing into cafés and coffee bars, while to visit the places of interest with no interest other than hoping to catch sight of John, was miserable. The pubs were not yet open. When they did open, he found that embarrassment often prevented him from standing in the middle of a bar and surveying its clientele without the right of a drink; and so his progress was slow – and even when the amount of drink he had taken reinforced his boldness, it was still totally inadequate in a town which seemed to be supported throughout on its ground-floor by hotels, public-houses and bars. He was left trying to summon up a coincidence which refused to perform.

It was prosaic to arrive at the railway station at eight-thirty the next morning and wait for John's inevitable arrival – but the very ordinariness of the action excused his muddled feelings. Or emphasised them. For it could be called unnecessary. It would enable John to reach Carlisle in time for the afternoon visiting – but if he planned to catch an early enough train, he would do that anyway. And so, in his role as family helper, he watched the clock rigidly, hoping that John would be late and so justify the lift. After eleven-thirty, he felt himself to be in a position which was valid. And hypocritical.

John came straight towards him and the business was soon explained. While still enclosed in his self-concerned attribution of blame, he found himself out of the city and along the almost deserted road which was to run nearly parallel with the Wall right across the country.

He glanced at John occasionally and fleetingly. He sat bolt upright in his seat, one hand stiffly on his knee, the other holding the door handle as if ready to release it, staring straight and stiffly ahead of him.

To explain everything. To apologise. Certainly that, at least. To try to start again; stupid but courageous for once. Say, just say, simply, what had happened. How much their friendship had meant. Pat. She was no longer important – so negligible that he was incredulous before his own memory of her influence. At least tell him something. To establish a link, even to fabricate a false claim would be better than nothing. It would be evidence of effort.

John continued in independent silence.

Arthur reached back for the words; he heard his voice clearly and it sounded haughty.

'I suppose you wonder what the hell was going on the other night?'

John shook his head.

'You must have done.'

Silence.

'I can't understand,' Arthur went on, 'still can't quite understand what went wrong,' he laughed. 'I know I'd had far too much to drink. And everybody was behaving rather stupidly. I know that. But – I must apologise.'

'For what?'

'For the way I treated you.'

John turned to stare out of the side-window. Already Arthur was feeling the irritation of one who battles unjustly alone; yet this irritation was but another unjustifiable indulgence; he could not bear even the weight of a simple apology.

'I *am* sorry. And so is Pat.'

'Did she say that?'

'Yes.' Dryly. 'We both did.' Unsteadily.

A lie – obvious to both of them.

'In fact,' Arthur ploughed on, 'I felt so bad about the whole business that I couldn't face up to coming and telling you so. I ought to have been up the next morning – but I was so ashamed of myself that I couldn't face up to it. I really *am* sorry.'

The hand on the knee lifted for silence; conclusion; was still; and then dropped back into its original position.

'The thing was we got caught up in a party. Duncan Collins – you know him? – he's engaged – they had no official engagement party, just an informal affair with a few friends – not that we're *really* friends of his – although we *have* known them since we were children, I suppose,' he could not stop; the mundane inconsequentials strode out between them, impotent fighters on an empty battlefield, 'and, anyway, we were caught up in it – myself more than Pat really – I was feeling pretty miserable – and then, as I've said, we had too much to drink.' He paused. It was a bright Saturday afternoon – raising up even the scrubby grass which bordered that road. 'And so, the whole affair was a terrible cock-up.'

'What else did Pat say?'

'She said she was sorry,' Arthur replied, immediately, hesitantly. 'Oh yes, she said . . .'

'Did you tell her you were coming to pick me up this morning?'

'Hm – no, wait a minute. Yes, yes, I *did* mention it.'

'And she didn't want to come.'

'Well, I didn't exactly *ask* her whether or not she wanted to come alone, and . . .'

'Of course she didn't want to come! And even if she had, you wouldn't have let her come!'

'Why do you say that?' The quickness of the answer could not disguise its timidity.

'I don't know,' John replied. 'I don't know. Maybe you're just a snob. Maybe you thought I wasn't good enough for her. There might be something in that.'

'No!'

'What then?'

Arthur saw that John had turned to him with this question. It would be too dramatic to slam on the brakes and talk it all out. His duty was to take John to the hospital. But nothing else would do. He lifted his foot from the accelerator.

'It's all right,' said John, 'we've managed to talk so far while you've been driving. There's no need to stop now.'

Like a schoolboy, Arthur obeyed.

'I don't know what Pat's told you,' John went on, 'but I wasn't just – I was serious about it.'

'I could see that.' The remark came out with the confirming quietness of a sad observation.

'I was.' He paused. 'And I thought that Pat was,' he added very quietly.

What Arthur could do, he dare not do. To open up all that was so tightly closed. Snob. Not good enough. It was so mistaken – so completely, sadly, mistaken.

John was tight with misery. He could tell it in his voice, see it in his face and manner. He was pale and tight with misery. Explanations now could only impress it further.

It was better to leave him alone. It would be better for John if he were left with black and white. Already, Arthur knew that John sensed more; was just one snatch away from realising more. He had to stop.

Yes. Yes. It would be easier for himself if he stopped. He could go away. He could go away again. It would require less effort from him.

But that was not true. Not even the writhing of his own shame could convince him of that. He wanted to stay with John, to repeat those days together, to know friendship, to see something built by his own will grow into something admired by his mind, to enjoy – even on that thin-thatched foundation of a little learning – the company of a man whose difference from himself swept him into a brightened knowledge of passions outside his own cocooned and unimpinged bare loneliness, to be brought to consider what he had ignored in his inheritance and to be led to reconsider what he had overlooked in his life – all this – just to be with a man whose affection had only just begun to touch him – they had been stilted together, not long together, often cool together – but he had seen a possibility which was neither given, directed nor persuaded, but chosen. He was giving that up so that John would not suffer more. Maybe his suffering could be called little and pushed away, maybe he exaggerated its intensity and inflated the potentiality of his own effect on it. It did not matter. Nor did it matter that John was not anywhere near the bottom of any list which Oliver might have drawn up under the title of 'those who needed protection and help because of the penalty of their miseries'. He was young; he would have the farm. It did not matter. To inflict suffering on someone with whom you have known goodness is to maim the good in both of you.

'I don't know what to think,' said John, suddenly.

Arthur did not reply and, unanswered, John, too, became silent.

They reached Carlisle just before two-thirty. The car bounced on the cobbled streets. Arthur drove up the short road within the Infirmary gates. The others had already arrived.

John took his suitcase with him, into the Infirmary.

TWENTY-FOUR

He made more of it than he need have done, but the women and children in the narrow deserted street urged him to more extravagance by their good-natured laughing and shouting.

It was October. John had set off for Aldeby soon after seven with tractor and trailer to bring in the potato-pickers. They had the same gang every year, a family more than a gang, headed by Martha Tillard and staffed by five of her daughters and a few neighbours when occasion demanded. Nelson liked to get it over as quickly as possible and so he would always demand a force of ten. The children had to come along of course. The gang had to be picked up at eight and taken to the farm in a trailer which must be cushioned by half-a-dozen bales so that the journey was not too hard. While on the job, all breaks would be used for scavenging and Nelson had not to be too hard on demands for planks of wood, coal, beetroot, butter, eggs, even hens; half a sack of potatoes (they brought their own sacks) was to be part of the pay – complemented by twenty-five shillings cash delivered at five-thirty prompt; hot tea to be made and brought out at ten, twelve-thirty and three-thirty; speedy return home guaranteed; all attempts at privacy abandoned. For this, Nelson would receive a back-doubled day's work in all conditions and, provided that the children had been supplied with a large safe pen – again out of bales of straw – and provided that the tractor ripping open the furrows did not charge up and down the long field like a 'bloody motor-car', and always provided there were no arguments, fights or other dissensions, then he would have as efficient a gang as he could hope for.

This was their third morning. John loved the empty tractor ride to the town, hedged by autumn golds and yellow browns, with all the land around him fluttering steadily to sleep and the air spanking his face still brown from the summer. He saw the tails and flashes of animals amiably scurrying to fit themselves out still more for a plump hibernation; the birds flocking together even where they were not gathering for flight; and the great heaved swell of land which had worked yet another rich year's crop.

He had driven into the little town, past the church and the market hall, the closed shops – one or two people going to work – and round into the narrow street where Martha's daughters had cheered and laughed him down to Peters' sweet shop which was their meeting ground. Dickie was there, of course, always ready to come up and generally help to supervise and particularly expect twenty-five shillings plus a little more for being of the family.

It was he who had got John into his present difficulty, stepping importantly into the middle of the street like a plain clothes policeman, hand up, backside stiff, eyes watching that he was being watched, stripped of his disguise. The directions had been precise and by following them, to humour him, John found that the trailer had twisted around so tightly that it was almost parallel with the tractor, while any but the most delicate movement would send its back-end right through Peters' sweet-shop window.

'What the hell d'you think you're doing?' Dickie shouted.

It was impossible to move. He turned off the engine and jumped down to uncouple the trailer. Then he drove the tractor up the street and, with everyone's help, pushed the carriage up to join it. Dickie found himself bundled into the feet of the women instantly seated on the bales of straw, and his usual place, on the front edge of the trailer, feet on the shaft, rather like a flag-bearer – or mascot – depending – taken by the youngest of Martha's daughters. The only one unmarried. Noleen.

Noleen was after John. This information had been given to both of them within an hour of their arrival on the first morning, and while John had tried to ignore it, Noleen had accepted the statement of her role as an order and acted, since then, in strict accordance with it. She was seventeen with jeans washed-out blue and always a bright blouse which left its tight, belted confinement the second she bent over to begin work.

He drove them right on to the field. The children were settled, Shirley's boyfriend – now her fiancé – who had stayed on to be hired and lived in with them, was waiting with the tractor.

'Can't you go and finish your breakfast, sonny?' Martha suggested to him.

He would open the furrows, the women were supplied with shallow wire-baskets into which they dropped the potatoes and Nelson or Dickie drove up and down with another tractor and trailer – the one John had used – into which John hoisted the full baskets. To his relief, it was Dickie who was to do it this morning; Nelson was with his beasts.

Spread at their places down the field, the work began. John found that he hurried to empty the baskets in order to get down to Noleen.

'Here he comes! Make the best of your chance while you have it.'

'He's a rich man. Will be.'

'Isn't he lovely?'

'Ask him to take you to the dance, then.'

'Go on, mister, encourage her!'

She needed none. She almost burst with the attention paid to her and the attention her new woman's body demanded. Her hair was bundled into a pony-tail – but soon it flew out of the untidy knot and spread on to her shoulders.

'You needn't run away,' she said, as, slowly, he tipped her basket into the trailer, 'won't bite!'

'I've work to do.'

'All you farmers are alike. Can't you think of anything else?'

One leg went forward and her hips sagged with such an expression of provocation and impersonation that both of them laughed out loud; but the invitation was plain and open.

'Not while we're on the job,' he replied.

'But you must come off it sometimes.'

'Sometimes.'

'Well?'

He paused.

'We'll see.'

As if to help him out of a difficult situation, Dickie started up the tractor and was away.

'I'm not going to wait for much longer!' she shouted.

'You won't have to, love,' her sister, one up, answered her. 'He's just shy, that's all.'

John came to pick up her basket.

'Aren't you, sweetheart?' She opened her arms and mimed an enormous kiss.

'There's not much to be shy about with you lot around,' he said, grimly.

'Isn't he lovely?'

'Smashing!'

Nelson came into the field at the top. The women waved their fists at him and he grinned back at them. He enjoyed their being on the farm.

'See they make a decent job of it,' he warned Shirley's boyfriend as the tractor passed him. 'Don't let them miss anything.'

'You're a mean old bugger,' said Martha who, being first in the line, was quite near him. 'I bet you crawl over this place on your hands and knees after we've gone.'

'You do that when I'm not looking,' he replied, pointing at the sack, already a third full.

'There's nothing in there,' she answered, standing up straight, her long skirt still almost touching the ground, the cluster of rollers underneath her headscarf gleaming dangerously.

Nelson had only to tip the sack open to prove the lie.

'Look if you want,' she added.

One more day would do it.

'Back you go,' he said to the tractor-man.

'And not so bloody fast,' Martha warned him, 'or I'll be after you!'

He set off so slowly that the engine stalled.

Nelson went back to the barn to get on with some work of his own. John would manage it. He would never have *his* head for farming, but he could look after this job well enough.

Nelson liked to work on his own now. By straining the wound, he had hurt his hand badly, and the thumb was stiff, useless. Otherwise, he was all right.

'I look all right. I feel all right. What the hell do you keep on about it for?'

Lizzie was quelled.

The whole thing had closed over as if it had never been. Nelson was so centred on the farm that nothing but that which would lead to its benefit interested him for very long. The leap to get what he wanted, the slog to hold it, that had been the struggle. Now, properly middle-aged, with some grey hair and a hand half-useless, with a disinclination for heavier jobs – never for those which demanded great and obviously important effort – he was working at his new ambition and so the farm was left increasingly to John. But he had cut such a deep early groove for himself that he would run in it until he died.

There was the tool-shed to be given its annual overhaul and this he preferred to do alone. No one else would have thought it necessary; everything so neatly arranged, ordered exactly and cleaned after use daily, but Nelson was compelled to review the whole thing thoroughly every autumn. It was a job that John would have skipped.

With oil, rags, sharpening stone and leather, he sat down to it. There were many things that John would skip. He needed to be watched. But that man of Shirley's was reliable; they would live in after they were married – until he could find a cottage for them, anyway. It was good to keep the work in the family.

He wanted to be alone particularly because he had heard something which might lead him to expansion. Mrs Langley was going to sell. Her son had gone back into the army, and her daughter to London. The land would be just right; exactly the area he could manage without over-extending himself; exactly placed for convenience. And it was good land. But he did not want to be saddled with that damned big house. If he could make an offer for the land which was so worth considering that they would feel forced to sell the house off on its own; but he could not afford too much. It would be exactly what he wanted. The right offer.

Dinner; John spent only half of it in the house – the rest of the time policing the farm – talking with some of the women, keeping Noleen in sight.

Tea. He went to help his mother in the kitchen. For some reason – perhaps because of the approaching double marriage or, more probably, because of a sudden tiny surplus in Lizzie's budget (especially in the fortnight of upheaval while Nelson had been either in hospital or recovering in his bed) – the house had become less grim. There were new curtains and some new lino on the kitchen floor; a new tablecloth, new crockery; Tony had bought two prints for Avril for her birthday and John had framed them and they hung on the wall. The chairs had been re-covered; there were one or two little ornaments on the dresser.

'You're a good lad,' said Lizzie.

John was sawing a long loaf of bread into all-shaped thick slices.

'Come on, now,' he said. 'I'll do it for nothing. You needn't flatter.'

'How's everything going?'

'OK.'

'Dad all right?'

'Hardly seen him.'

'He'll be glad when it's over. He hates being diddled. And they're at it all the time.'

John grinned.

'Oh, it's all right. Just a few potatoes here and there. We can spare that. It's dirty work they do.'

'Hm.' Lizzie was unimpressed. 'It wouldn't be so bad if they asked.'

'Can I have some milk, missis?' It was Noleen, right inside the house, lounging against the entramce to the kitchen. 'It's not for *me*, I'm *asking*,' she went on, 'our Maureen wants some for her Jimmie.'

Lizzie went across to the larder.

'Haven't you got a fridge?' Noleen demanded.

'How much do you want?' She had a pint in her hand.

'That should do,' said Noleen, giggling at John. 'Thanks.'

Lizzie nodded, sharply, and turned back to the sink.

Noleen stayed where she was.

'How much do I owe you?' she asked.

'Oh!' Lizzie bit her lip. She had been overheard. 'It doesn't matter. It's nothing.'

'Thanks.' Noleen blew a kiss at John and flicked her head towards the farmyard. 'See you outside, then,' she whispered, loudly. And left.

'Cheek,' said Lizzie. Then, again, 'Cheek!' she laughed. 'But you can't help liking them, can you?'

'No.'

'No,' she repeated happily. 'There's no real harm in them. And they're cheerful enough.'

Lizzie herself was as cheerful as John had ever seen her. Nelson had not turned nasty after his stay in hospital, Shirley was to be married, and Pat had left. That news had brought her so much relief that she was prepared to wish for no more good luck for the rest of her life. She had been afraid of its effect on John – but he had not referred to it.

John felt his mother's cheerfulness thrusting into him. There she was, already an old woman in her looks, never had much, worked like a machine, nothing about her that women like, pulled out of her family by Nelson's desire and kept ever away from it by his pride – and she could still be thrilled to cheerfulness by finding that quality in a stranger. She was good in a way which made any misery of his own appear selfish.

He drove them home – now hardly able to get into the trailer with their sacks, and a broken spade, a piece of fence, a clothes-line, and, it seemed, twice as many children, each clutching a trophy, a tribute to their mothers.

He drove past the Langleys' house without looking at it. He had not seen them since Arthur had brought him to the hospital.

He had gone down – sick and bewildered by the pressure which seemed to force him there so much against his will – but the house was completely empty and Andrei had told him of their leaving. As soon as he knew that they were gone, he did not want to ask any questions.

He could not think of it without such pain that his mind had soon protected him from his memory by drawing it far away. Sometimes, he shuddered to think of what had happened; at other times, there would be only the bright threads, stroking his feelings with the days spent shooting with Arthur, the evenings in the summerhouse and Pat, Pat when she had been full and open to him; and then there was a twisted confusion of unexplained miseries; he did not know. Would never know. And already, it all slid towards a detached encapsulation, away from him. It was over.

'Light?'

Noleen had clambered across to the tractor and was now standing on the little ledge behind his seat. Her cigarette poked in his ear.

'Don't be daft,' he replied, 'you'll never get it going while we're on this.'

'Let's have a try, anyway, love. Come on.'

He felt in his jacket pocket for the matches and handed them to her. Already, it was nearly dark, and he kept his eyes firmly on the road.

He heard the scratching of first one match and then another.

'Slow down a bit, anyway!' she shouted.

He did as she asked.

'There.'

She bundled the matches in his pocket and, to steady herself, put her arm on his shoulder.

'That's right, Noleen!'

'He can't get away now!'

'"Hug me tight"!'

She bent down to his face.

'Want a puff?'

'No thanks.'

'Sure?'

'Yes.'

She stayed as she was. Her cheek almost touching his.

He would not take her out. She was too young.

'I'll say one thing for you farmers,' she said, eventually, 'you're a talkative bloody lot!'

For Want of a Nail
MELVYN BRAGG

FOR WANT OF A NAIL, a story of growing up in Cumberland, is Melvyn Bragg's first novel, written at the age of twenty-five and published in 1965. The reviews at the time correctly predicted his successful future as a writer.

'Moving and impressive . . . the impression is one of striking individuality – the sort of originality an author achieves when he has really meditated hard about his characters, loved them, watched them, and let them grow'
Sunday Telegraph

'A novel well worth returning to . . . a vivid and totally original imagination . . . tableau after tableau is spotlit into brilliant life'
The Scotsman

'A very good novel it is . . . sparkles with a keen awareness of both local landscape and character . . . We look forward to Melvyn Bragg's next book and hope it uses the background of Cumberland as his first book does'
Cumberland Evening News

'Fine, tense writing derived not from books but from passionate observation of particular landscapes and people'
Peter Vansittart in The Spectator

SCEPTRE

Without a City Wall
MELVYN BRAGG

Winner of the John Llewellyn Rhys Memorial Prize, 1968.

'It is gratifying to be able to record that a young Englishman writing in his native tongue in the second half of the twentieth century has written a novel, cast in a conventional form, that is as near to being a work of art as makes no difference. I became more and more deeply and enjoyably immersed in this simple and profoundly moving modern morality of Richard Godwin, aged twenty-four (who) quits a successful career in London in the 1960s and isolates himself in a remote Cumberland village'
The Times

'A very good novel, simply about a man and a woman; traditional in form – it has a beautiful arch-like structure – and Lawrencian in tone'
Daily Telegraph

'Undoubtedly, with this third novel Melvyn Bragg has become a writer of stature . . . Bragg has always been good at describing the bantering of youthful lovers. He excels himself here'
Financial Times

∫

SCEPTRE

The Maid of Buttermere
MELVYN BRAGG

'A triumph . . . I am overwhelmingly impressed'
Beryl Bainbridge

'An ingenious telling of a romantic tragedy'
Gore Vidal

'A detailed, eloquent and affecting panorama of truth and lies . . . His new novel thrusts him into the front rank'
David Hughes in The Mail on Sunday

'This the story of an imposter and bigamist, a self-styled Colonel Hope, who travels to the North, where eventually he marries "The Maid of Buttermere", a young woman whose natural beauty inspired the dreams and confirmed the theories of various early nineteenth century writers . . . It is a fine story . . . This is historical fiction with a human face'
Peter Ackroyd in The Times

'Very much enjoyed; a fine subject treated with great energy and imagination, and a gusto that Hazlitt would have admired'
Richard Holmes

'A vivid and erudite historical *tour de force* – romantic fiction for the thinking reader'
Penelope Lively

'Bragg achieves the most difficult feats, the telling of the changing perceptions and ideals of a radical age . . . He is also as powerful as ever in his description of nature'
Andrew Sinclair in The Sunday Times

'A skilled, ornate and convincing examination of a nineteenth century scandal in Bragg's own Cumbria'
Thomas Keneally

SCEPTRE

Josh Lawton
MELVYN BRAGG

'A pleasure to be remembered'
The Financial Times

'A portrait of innocence set in a rough, lovely
Cumbrian village. Melvyn Bragg's novel has the lilt
and inevitability of an old ballad. [He] skilfully portrays
the friendships and antagonisms in rural Cumberland,
a territory he has staked out as his own'
Paul Theroux in The Times

'The story unfolds with admirable simplicity . . .
beautifully told and even the most brutal and
inarticulate characters somehow manage to engage our
sympathies'
Auberon Waugh in The Spectator

'With this novel, Melvyn Bragg has established his
place in English letters to the extent that his Cumbria
is as potent a literary region as Hardy's Wessex,
Lawrence's Midlands and Housman's Shropshire'
New Statesman

'An effortless writer. He never strains for effect, simply
achieves it. The pleasure to be had from this book is
that of feeling, without having been exposed to any
lies or romantic evasions, that the world is perhaps a
better place than one had thought'
The Sunday Times

SCEPTRE

The Cumbrian Trilogy
MELVYN BRAGG

Melvyn Bragg's celebrated trilogy – THE HIRED MAN,
A PLACE IN ENGLAND and KINGDOM COME – traces
four generations of Tallentire history: from John in the
rural Cumbria of 1898 to Douglas in the competitive
and backbiting metropolis of the Seventies. From 'hired
man' to media man worlds have been bridged, but the
old ideals of success, freedom and happiness seem ever
elusive as each Tallentire must come to terms with
private uncertainty and pain.

'An uncommonly high talent. The people are "real"
enough to leave footprints right across the page'
The Guardian

'A novelist of power and imagination. It is one of
Bragg's gifts to create his own atmosphere and so
heighten feeling'
New Society

'Quite masterly'
The Daily Telegraph

∫

SCEPTRE